His Not-So-Sweet Marchioness

Lustful Lords, Book Four

SORCHA MOWBRAY

Published by Amour Press 2022, Second Edition

Copyright © 2021 by Sorcha Mowbray

ISBN Print: 978-1-955615-17-4

ISBN ePub: 978-1-955615-05-1

Cover design from Fiona Jayde Media

Chapter Images from Illustration 13209099 / Victorian Vines © Freeskyblue | Dreamstime.com

Chapter One

June 1862

Lord Flintshire's, cheek exploded in a flash of pain that quickly morphed into pleasure so intense it made his cock stiffen. He smiled at the man squared up across from him in a dark, slightly fishy, corner of London's wharf. The area was as rough and seedy as his five-foot ten-inch opponent whose shoulders seemed to span as wide as the man was tall. With his tattered clothing, tobacco-stained teeth, and the permanently swollen appearance of his ears, his challenger was a sight to behold.

Considering the man's rather ragged appearance, Matthew Derby, Marquess of Flintshire wasn't the least bit intimidated. In fact, just the opposite. "Come now, surely you can hit harder than that?"

The man's eyes widened in surprise. "That's a mighty smart mouth ye' have there. Perhaps I'll pop you in it next?" Flint's pulse spiked with anticipation. He wouldn't be kissing anyone later, but a split lip was a ten-fold gift—until it healed. All around him, the ring of voices acted like a shield, blocking out not only the late-night sounds of London. But the echoes of his dead brother's screams, the disappointed tones of his father's voice, and the throaty demands of his grandmother that he take a wife and continue the family line. Loudest of all was the shame that always accompanied his hunger for pain. All of them melded into a cacophony that trailed him wherever he went. One that he desperately sought to escape any way he could—even through violence.

He circled around to his left, leading with his non-dominant hand for now. Eventually, when his opponent had provided enough pain to satisfy the ugly hunger inside him, he would switch up to his right and end the fight. But for the next little while, he relished what was to come. It was too bad that he couldn't follow the evening's activity up with a rousing good fuck, but such was the life of a courting man.

Even a fiancée in name only wouldn't tolerate such poor form. And though Mrs. Rosalind Smith would only be engaged to him for a short while more, he felt bound to protect her. Damned if that same sense of honor wasn't what had driven him to act as her suitor to begin with when her sister's unwanted beau turned his sights on Ros. The whole situation was all confoundingly odd, considering he had never met her before that night.

Then he stumbled over a loose cobblestone, which jerked him out of his thoughts and back to the fight he was currently engaged in. That was when the hapless chap across from him dipped his right hand—a clear indication he was about to punch—and Flint reached in with a left jab, just catching the man's cheek. The hulk of a man stumbled back a step. While not as stout as his opponent, Flint was easily two inches taller and still roped with muscle. He trained with former bare-knuckle champion Jem Langston, the erstwhile leader of the Lustful Lords, Lord Stonemere. They trained together at the same boxing club. So, there could be no doubt that he kept himself in top physical form.

His opponent regrouped and leaned in with another solid punch to his left eye. The swelling set in quickly, limiting his vision, but not as quick as the man's follow-up body blows. After taking a combination of punches to his ribs and stomach, he decided it was time to make the switch.

The moment he shifted his stance, the stout man hesitated. "Here now, what's this?"

Flint offered up a bloody grin. "Just settling in."

Wary, but clearly still under the misapprehension that he had the upper hand, the man circled around a bit and then stepped in to drive a solid punch to Flint's gut. Except, with his shorter reach, the water hydrant of a man never made it. Instead, he stumbled backward in confusion after Flint's right fist connected with his face in a solid jab. Blood spewed from his opponent's bulbous nose spilling down his chin and onto his shirt. There was a decided nip in the air, making it too cool to be fighting shirtless.

Still on his feet and willing to continue, the man kept moving. Flint stepped in to land another punch, and the goon swung around, slipped in behind him, and landed a rabbit punch to his lower back right over a kidney. Pain lanced through Flint, sending another wave of ecstasy through his body. His cock was half-hard as his knees hit the ground.

Unable to take a moment to relish the feeling, he quickly popped back up to his feet and whipped around in time to catch the stout man with another solid jab to his already broken nose. The man bent over, screaming and clutching his face. At that point, his manager, more aptly his chum, stepped in to stop the fight. "That's it. The man's gotta be able to fight again."

Disappointment crowded out the pleasure and adrenaline coursing through Flint's veins. With a studied casualness he did not feel in the least, he dropped his hands and headed over to where the man holding the wagers stood. The money man growled, low and menacing. "This fight ain't over. Not until a body drops to the stones."

Flint considered the cobblestones beneath his feet and cast a glance back at his opponent. The man shook his head and walked away, clearly prepared to forfeit his money for the cessation of the fight. Flint looked back to the money man and shrugged. "Ain't my fault, the chap refuses to continue. I won, I suggest you pay up what you owe me."

It wasn't that he needed the blunt *per se*; it was the principle of the thing. Also, he used the money for a very specific purpose. With a fierce glare at the money man, he stepped closer. The man looked at him, perused his fine lawn shirt and the tailored trousers he wore. It was obvious, even in the dim lighting of a wharf-side alley, that the moneyman was considering stiffing him on his payout.

"Ah. Ah. Ah. I wouldn't do that if I were you." Flint shook his head.

"Do what?" the man demanded, though, with his thick cockney accent, it was all slammed together into more of a blur of syllables than words. The guy seemed to consider the mauling he'd just witnessed in addition to the fine clothing on Flint's back.

"Take my blunt and run. Appearances can be deceiving, none so much as mine." Where most men looking to intimidate another man would have crossed their arms at that point, Flint was not most men. He was a fighter, through and through. And he was all too aware of the fact that crossing his arms over his chest would only hobble his ability to react in the event the tosser decided to attack or—as he suspected—run.

Suddenly the man's shoulders slumped. "You're a nasty blighter despite all the spit and shine."

Flint grinned and held out his hand. "Just so."

The moneyman handed over Flint's winnings with a grimace.

"If you consider how the fight had turned, I was about to drop him to the stones at any rate. So, technically, you were going to lose whether he fought on or not." Flint tucked the wad of bills away and shrugged.

The moneyman merely grumbled about hoity-toity lords and their highfalutin ways as he melted into the shadows and disappeared. Most of the crowd had dispersed during their little exchange, so Flint grabbed his coat from the boy hovering nearby who held it. At the flip of a half-sovereign, the kid grinned, caught the metal disc, bit it, and then melted into the back-alley shadows.

The Market was unusually quiet when Flint strolled through the front door. In contrast, his body still hummed with the residual pleasure, pain, and adrenaline cocktail from his fight. Normally, he would have happily headed upstairs to work off his excess energy with one of the women who either frequented or worked at the notorious London brothel. But now, he had Ros to consider. He was many things, but one of them was not a cad.

Hoping to find Linc and Arthur having a drink, as opposed to other less suitable activities, he made his way up the grand staircase and down the hall to the blue room. His injuries were beginning to make themselves known. In fact, he was sure he had some bruised ribs, and his eye was quite swollen, which made the stairs a bit of a welcome challenge. Happily, he found his friends sans any female company. Pouring himself a whisky, he sat down with the duo.

Linc whistled as he looked him over. "Holy shite! You took a walloping tonight."

"I needed one." Flint snorted. "Besides, I think it probably looks worse than it really is."

"I don't know. You look pretty worse for wear." Both of Arthur's brows rose in punctuation. Then he took a great gulp of his drink and slammed the empty glass down. "Why do you do it, Flint?"

Linc grew quiet as Arthur's question lingered in the silence. Flint groaned internally. There was no good answer to that question—certainly none he wished to discuss—and though he knew what his friend was asking about, he decided to play stupid. "Do what?"

"Come on, chap, you know what I'm asking. Why do you fight?" Arthur stood up and sauntered over to the sideboard where the bottles of liquor were ranged. He poured himself another drink and then returned to the table.

Flint considered how best to answer that question. Stone and Cooper had never asked him why. They'd merely accepted that this was part of who he was. It was possible they simply understood what drove him a bit more than the others. As for Linc and Wolf, perhaps they never asked because the others hadn't? But Arthur was new to their group, and so clearly, curiosity had gotten the best of him.

"Why not?" Flint tossed out the flip response in hopes it would suffice. There were no words to fully explain why he fought. Why he needed the pain. Why it felt so damn good. So he'd long ago quit trying to find them.

Arthur sighed. "Bloody hell. If you don't want to talk about it, simply tell me to shut up. No need to be an arsehole about it."

"Then shut up." Flint tried not to glare, but between being denied the release of sexual pleasure after a good beating and the uncomfortable brush with an inner truth he'd long avoided, he wasn't feeling very chipper at the moment. His faux engagement to Ros had utterly disrupted his usual routine. He was fairly certain that any woman would take exception to her fiancé—even a decoy fiancé—having sex with another woman. But his current limitations were soon to be removed now that Lady Julia Wolfington, Ros' sister, was happily and safely married to one of his best friends. Ros simply had to break off with him at one of the upcoming balls. With his reputation already blackened of his own doing, the plan was for her to break off their association.

Now, he just had to keep his hands to himself long enough to allow her to do what needed to be done. Unfortunately, that small task was proving harder and harder to accomplish. Despite being more than aware of how inappropriate he was for a woman as sweet as Ros, something deep inside him wanted to possess her, to strip her naked, and show her all the ways he could pleasure a woman. After all, he was one of the notorious Lustful Lords.

Linc leaned over and slapped the back of Arthur's head. "Don't be a nosy nit. He doesn't hurt anyone who doesn't willingly sign up for it. Besides, watching Flint fight is a thing of beauty. The man is poetry in motion."

Flint rolled his eyes at his silver-tongued friend, who had a flare for the dramatic. A ruckus down the hall saved him from responding. The noise proved loud enough to draw the three of them out of their private retreat.

He was the first to the door and opened it, but Linc and Arthur were right beside him. Two doors down, a half-naked man stood in front of a cloaked woman. He leaned forward and then away before listing to the right. He was so obviously inebriated, it was laughable. But the woman was still clearly in distress, what with the way she was pressed against the wall.

With his cock hanging out of his trousers and no shirt to cover the gentle swell of his stomach, the drunken man lurched toward the woman. "Come on, luv. Come join us."

"I told you no. Now, take yourself back into your room this minute." The woman's voice carried down the hall and all but punched Flint in the face.

Ros? What the devil is she doing in The Market?

His gut twisted. Who the bloody hell was she here to see? Not him, since she was not aware he had planned to visit this evening. As far as she was concerned, he had plans with Linc and Arthur. And he had not indicated *where* those plans were to take place. But he would have thought that her assumptions on the matter would have leaned more toward White's than a house of ill repute.

With a growl, he stepped free of the doorway. He recognized the man as Lord Calhoun, a harmless drunk, really, but he did tend toward a bit of exhibitionism when the drink was on him. "My lord, I believe one of your companions is calling for you."

Surprised by his interference, Lord Calhoun looked at him in confusion for a moment, then turned and walked back into his room and shut the door. Whether the man retreated as a result of Flint's suggestion or Calhoun's recognition of him made little difference, though his penchant for violence was well known. Flint's goal had been achieved.

Ros turned to face him. "There you are. I've been looking for you for nearly a quarter of an hour!"

Chapter Two

R os's heart ached like a vise had it in a firm grip and was steadily being tightened. Damn the man for being in The Market when she had hoped that would not be the case. Anger carried her forward until she met Flint halfway. "What are you doing here?"

Flint stopped a few steps from her just within the shadows that fell between sconces lining the hall. "You should go home, Ros. This is no place for you to be."

She stopped in the shadows as well, the light of one sconce creating a gulf between them. "If you'd been where you alluded you would be, I wouldn't have had to hunt you down. Therefore, I wouldn't *be here* suffering the attentions of a Lord who is so deep in his cups that I feel lucky he was only half-naked."

"And why, precisely, did you have the overwhelming need to hunt me down?" He snorted.

She growled low in her throat. "Because I heard you were going to fight tonight. I needed to..." *Stop you? Make sure you weren't hurt?* None of those answers would please the man. And she had no desire to make herself—her heart—more vulnerable to him than was already the case. Their fraudulent engagement was due to end, but Ros had not been able to bring herself to end it. After the weeks she'd spent in Flint's company, she found herself on the precipice of losing her heart to the rough and tumble man. And after her disastrous first marriage—may her husband, Archie, rest in peace—she had sworn never to fall in love again. But here she was, teetering on the edge like a fool.

"You needed to what?" A gruffness edged into his voice

The gravelly quality sent chills cascading down her spine and between her legs. She found the edge of violence that he wore like a cloak utterly intoxicating. If she had thought for one moment that her emotional connection to him was not reciprocated, she might have given up on him long before now. But after weeks and weeks of listening to him, talking to him, and touching him in the most encouraging of ways with little but the most chaste kisses in response, she had reached her breaking point. She was done being sweet, gentle Rosalind. The sunny sister who always smoothed things over so nobody's feathers were ruffled. It was outside of enough.

It was time she took a page from her sister, Julia's book. Driven by a determination born of desperation, she pushed the hood and sides of her cloak back, exposing the deep sweep of her neckline. Then with lowered lashes, she stepped forward into the pool of light. Once more into the breach—only this time, her objective was the man she'd decided to claim.

As the light spilled over the deep green of her gown and lit up her face, Flint inhaled sharply. She knew he was not unaffected by her. He'd always found her beautiful and had minced no words in saying so. The spark of awareness between them was there every time they came near and grew sharper, more painful with every touch. Yet some unknown obstruction had held him back, had him doing nothing more than kissing her hand. It made a woman want to scream and stamp her foot!

"I needed to see you. To touch you." She reached up and laid a hand on his chest in the boldest manner she could muster. Little flutters of excitement skated through her as she made contact with fine linen stretched over hard—*oh my, so hard!*—pectoral muscles. Her hand trembled ever so slightly.

Something heated and wanton flashed through his gaze, something that promised carnal delights if she dared. She had been confident, determined when she'd charged into The Market brandishing the guest coin she'd found in her sister's former room. Suddenly, when faced with the living, breathing embodiment of all her fantasies, she faltered.

Doubt crept in to undermine her earlier confidence as the silence stretched.

"Did you?" One single dark eyebrow lifted as he reached up to where her hand lay on his chest and covered it.

Her stomach plummeted from where it normally sat to somewhere closer to her knees. "Yes, well." She darted her tongue out and moistened her dry lips as she let her gaze dip to their hands only to roam back up to his shadowed face. "I can see you are whole."

"Can you? Perhaps a closer inspection is in order to allay your fears?" His lips twitched. Then one corner lifted up, followed by the other.

Ros blinked. *Is he smiling?* Her breath caught at the sight. But then a dollop of blood pearled up and dribbled down his lip. "Flint! You're bleeding!"

With a swift tug of her hand, she was free of his warm grip. Leveraging an economy of motion that was more muscle memory than a conscious decision on her part, she grabbed the man's shoulders and tugged him forward into the light. Considering his bulk, she knew he'd allowed her to move him. She certainly did not have the strength to manage a man of his size and weight. But all was forgotten as the light splashed over his face revealing the damage he'd suffered. Her breath caught in her chest as she reached shaking fingers up to his split lip.

Stoically, he stood there and let her explore. Next, she inspected his swollen eye, and then finally, she took in the bruise on his cheek that had begun to form.

"What room were you using?" She demanded, though her voice came out low and husky. Worry had tightened up her throat until she'd had to force the words out.

"We're down here." Linc waved at her.

Ros looked past Flint's shoulder and blinked in surprise. Somehow she'd missed the fact they had a small audience. But, she was past caring about that. Flint had injuries that needed tending. She grabbed his hand and marched him down the hall into the room Linc and Arthur were leaning out of. As she dragged her patient into the room, all thoughts of seduction were forgotten with the need to render care. She quickly scanned and assessed the space before she dragged him over to a chair at the table and pointed. "Sit."

Then she turned and looked at Linc. "I need fresh water, bandages, and if they have some salve, it would not come amiss."

The blond jokester saluted her smartly and marched out of the room.

Eyeing Arthur, she nodded at the alcohol-laden sideboard. "Pour me two fingers of brandy or whisky in a glass."

He moved immediately. She turned to look at Flint's face in the brighter lights of the room and bit her lip to hold back the gasp that sought to escape. His dark hair and fair skin shined in the glare of the lights, highlighting the mottled mess of purple, blue, and red that was the rest of his face. Looking him over further, she spotted his raw knuckles, and then she noticed him breathing very shallowly. With a sharp eye, she stood straighter and looked down at him, using her height as an advantage. "What other injuries do you have?"

He darted a worried glance up at her. "Nothing to worry over."

"Tell me right now, or I shall discover them for myself. I can't imagine you will enjoy being poked and prodded." She set her hands on her hips and glared at him.

It was hard to tell with all the bruising, but high on his right cheek, she swore she saw a patch of dusky pink appear where there had been none before.

He drew in a deep breath.

Having tended to soldiers in pain on more than one occasion over her few years of marriage to a military man, she noticed two things immediately. First, the indrawn breath was deliberate. And considering how slow and deep he breathed with what she suspected were damaged ribs of some sort, she was shocked. The second thing she noticed was the way his eyes closed, and his mouth opened ever so slightly as if he welcomed a lover's kiss. If she was not mistaken, that was pleasure sweeping across his face.

Her own breath caught in her chest when she imagined that same look of pleasure as he slid inside her for the first time. Shaking her head, she tried to refocus on the present and pushed what she hoped would be the future to the side. Clearly, her desire for this man was making her barmy.

Arthur distracted her when he set the glass of whisky she'd requested on the table near to hand. Flint reached for it, but she swiped the amber liquid before he could wrap his hands around it. "That is mine."

And then she tossed the contents down her throat.

Handing the glass back to Arthur, she said, "A refill, if you please."

"Mrs. Sm—"

She waved a hand at him. "The next one is for medicinal purposes." She turned her focus back on her patient. "And I do not mean for you to imbibe. I'm sure you've had quite enough to numb the pain already."

Flint looked at her balefully and mumbled, "Now, why would I want to do that?"

"What was that?" She demanded, not at all certain she'd heard him correctly. She couldn't have, could she? *Who wants to feel the pain?*

The door of the room opened again, and Linc appeared, followed by a small troop of servants. Between the three footmen following him, they appeared to have everything she had requested, including a jar of salve. Determined to get to work, she motioned for them to set everything on the table. The three did as directed and then quickly departed. By that point, another glass of whisky had appeared as well.

"My lords, thank you for your kind assistance. Perhaps you could give us some privacy while I see to his injuries?" She looked first at Linc, then Arthur, and finally, she dragged her gaze to the door of the room in clear invitation.

With a smirk and a nod, Linc nudged Arthur, who'd stood there in surprise. In short order, the pair hustled out the door. She heard Arthur ask, "Did she just toss us from our room?"

Linc laughed. "Indeed, she did. But I saw a fine specimen downstairs. I think we should grow better acquainted with."

The door closed on whatever Arthur was going to say, leaving her alone with a battered Flint. Her stomach did a little twirl before settling back down where it belonged. After all, the man was injured. Whatever she had hoped would occur when she'd left for The Market that evening was certainly off the agenda now. Stowing her disappointment alongside all the other many disappointments in her life, she focused on the task at hand.

The man's eye was swollen, so she started there by dipping the rag in cool water and pressing it gently to the affected area. Flint didn't wince. Instead, he drew a small sharp inhale through his nose as his eyes closed. Silence enveloped them as she held the rag for a few moments. Then, there was only the sound of her dipping the rag again and wringing out the excess water. She repeated this over and over for what felt like an eternity.

She had so many questions for him. So many things she wished to ask him about why he fought and how this had all started. But, in truth, the thing she most wanted to know was, why wasn't he a better fighter if he did this so often? His injuries suggested that his opponent had meted out a fair amount of abuse. It all left her to wonder if Flint had even won the fight.

Having learned of his violent reputation and with the way everyone appeared to avoid him, she'd assumed he was very good at fighting. Now, she was not so confident about that. Mostly because it would be logical to assume that a man of his intelligence would have found ways to improve his skills and hone his strategies to accomplish his goals. And yet, that did not seem to be the case with Flint. Perhaps her experience around military men shaded her judgment, made her a harsher critic. But, based on all the evidence, it would be ridiculous for Flint to continue to fight, considering he was being beaten so badly.

Next, she gave his bruised cheekbone the same treatment as his eye, though there was significantly less swelling there. As she cleaned his face and the small cut in the center of his bruise, she chewed on her lower lip to keep from scolding him.

Flint remained stoically silent as she tended to him, which frustrated her further. "Your lip is split."

Not that she believed him to be unaware of the state of his lip—it must hurt every time he spoke, not to mention her earlier declaration that he was bleeding—but the silence had become a leaden weight in the room. He merely grunted in response.

She rinsed her cloth and turned to tend his lip. For such a hard man, one who seemed carved from marble at times, he had amazingly soft, kissable lips. She'd felt them against the skin of her hand and even her cheek once. But she wondered what it would be like to feel them against her own lips. Wanted to know how they would feel wrapped around the hard pebble of her nipple. Gooseflesh rippled over her arms as a wave of desire rolled through her.

Flint's nostrils flared as though in reaction to the need pummeling her, but she brushed it off. It was more likely in reaction to the pain of her dabbing at his injured lip. She had thought at one time that he might desire her, but now? No, he grew more distant each day, which was why she had thought to stand and fight for what she wanted.

His face looked marginally better, though only time would remedy his wounds. Taking a fresh rag, she dabbed it in the whisky before blotting it against the cut below his eye and his split lip. Finally, she applied the salve to his cheek and lip and then eyed him with a determined look. She would brook no resistance on his part. "Where else are you injured?"

He cleared his throat. "You have done enough."

"That is not an answer to my question. If you force me, I shall follow through on my earlier threat to poke and prod your body until I discover where else you might be injured. Do not test me, my lord." And oh, how she wished to get her hands on him, even if only to suss out his injuries. Though kissing him all over to make it better would be no hardship. When had she become such a sex-obsessed harpy?

He sighed. "You'll not let this go, will you?"

"Not in the least." She smelled victory in the air and yet somehow managed to stifle the unruly grin that threatened at such a prospect.

He grunted again. And if she were not mistaken, his lips may have twitched in mirth. "My knuckles are cut a bit."

She tsked and berated herself for not thinking of such an obvious place to look. She quickly addressed his hands going through the now-familiar ritual of water, whisky, and then salve. "Where else?"

"My ribs are likely bruised." He drew another surprisingly deep breath.

Her heart skipped a beat. "Are you able to lift your shirt?"

He reached down and untucked the hem and then lifted it on his left side. The flesh she could see was mottled red with some dark blotches appearing. They would be fully black and blue by the next day, she suspected.

"Off with your shirt."

His gaze locked with hers for a long, tense moment. Then he grunted once more and made to lift the garment. He hesitated as he pulled at the fabric. She quickly saw his difficulty and aided him in slipping it over his head. As the broad expanse of his chest came into view, she bit her lower lip and suppressed the groan that sought to escape. A mere puff of air slipped past her lips, and yet it drew Flint's attention. Dark blue eyes filled with pain found her lips and froze as if waiting for her to speak. Or perhaps breathe.

Lips once again dry as the Saharan Desert, she darted her tongue out to slide over them. The darkness seemed to swallow his eyes as the blue ring shrank to almost nothing. Need pulsed through her body in response.

He let his gaze drop to the floor as his hands settled in his lap. "Best get on with it."

She marked the subtle shift he'd made and quickly realized why he'd moved. Her cheeks heated—most likely turning pink—when she realized the man was attempting to hide his erection. Hope warred with her modesty. Could he be as aware of her as she was of him? She certainly hoped so because, based on his reaction, she had every intention of pursuing her desire for him at the next opportunity.

With that decided, she bent over and nudged his left arm up. "You're ribs are bruised, as you expected."

He snorted.

She poked around his rib cage, starting near the back and working her way gently forward. He winced, but she felt no loose sections of bones floating about. "If you've cracked them, it would be the same direction. So, bed rest for a few days and then gentle movement. No lifting of heavy things, and certainly, no fighting."

Her fingers tingled where they'd touched his skin. Where they still touched his skin because she had yet to remove her hands from his person. With her cheeks growing hotter by the minute, she snatched her hands away from him and spun around so that she gave him her back.

Behind her, she heard him groaning as he replaced his shirt, and then a small sigh that sounded like pleasure. Sneaking a peek over her shoulder, she caught him in an unguarded moment. His head was tipped back, and a small, clearly indulgent smile tipped the corners of his lips. She'd call them pillowy, but he was much too masculine for such a description.

"Why do you stare?" Flint's tone was full of curiosity.

Abashed at being caught, she busied herself cleaning up the mess she'd made. "You are a handsome man, but I am sure you are aware of this."

"Am I? Most women are too scared to come close enough to express such sentiments. Most simply see a hard man. A violent man." His tone was deceptively casual. She had not missed the loneliness hidden beneath.

She turned to face him. It was best she laid her cards on the table, so to speak. "I am not most women."

"So it would seem." He let his brows drift upwards.

She stopped fussing and looked him square in the face. "I came here tonight to seduce you. I intended to tempt you beyond all reason with my body and my willingness in bed. In light of your injuries, I have put those plans aside for the moment. But, you should know I have *every* intention of following through at the earliest opportunity."

He frowned. "Why?"

Confused by his reaction, she struggled for an answer. "I find you attractive. Why shouldn't I pursue that?"

He shrugged one shoulder. "As I said, most women are scared of me."

"This conversation is growing repetitive. I am not most women."

Chapter Three

F lint growled. He was well aware she was nothing like the women he'd encountered, both in The Market and outside of it. She alone drew him like a lodestone, despite all his best intentions. The moment he'd walked into Julia and Ros's home, he'd been taken by her beauty. With her red hair that was a softer, lighter version of her sister's flame-red tresses and her sparkling green eyes, she was lovely beyond compare. Though there was more that shone through and captured his attention, such as her inherent sweetness. Her vulnerability. Her quiet strength.

"The man who'd agreed to act as your suitor has taken ill," Wolf said.

Ros's smile faded. "Oh, why that's terrible news. I do hope he will be alright."

A whirlwind of desire and the instinct to protect such a delicate woman drew Flint forward, his gaze locked on her. "It's just a cold, he should be fine in a few days."

She looked up and seemed to hesitate before she spoke. "Th-that's good."

Julia's nose wrinkled as she stared hard at her sister, Ros. "Well, I suppose we shall have to close ranks around Ros then during the ball. I had hoped having an obvious suitor would stave off Wallthorpe."

"I'll act as her suitor." He made the offer as he stepped closer to Ros. The urge to touch her grew stronger every moment he was near.

Ros turned a fetching shade of pink.

Wolf looked as worried as Julia about this change in plans. "Are you sure Flint? It can't be just for tonight. This issue may drag on for a bit."

Flint stole another look at the beauty who was his to safeguard and then nodded. "I'll not let anything happen to such a lovely lady."

Julia's alarm was clear enough in her voice that it caused Flint to stop where he was and refocus on the room at large as she spoke. "Wolf, perhaps you should introduce your friend before we make any changes to the plan?"

"Apologies, Lady Wallthorpe, Mrs. Smith, may I present Lord Flintshire?"

He bowed over each of their hands, though he lingered much longer—uncaringly so—over Ros's. He could have stayed there, bent over her hand and at her service forever.

"My Lord." Ros's breathless reply snaked down his spine with an unfamiliar tingle.

"As I said, I'd be happy to offer my protection if Mrs. Smith requires it." Flint repeated the offer once more, he hoped his words did not reveal a strong emotion one way or another. Yet his gaze continued to drift to where Ros stood.

"Flint, are you even listening to a word I have said?" Ros cut into his momentary lapse.

Unbelievably, he felt heat drift across his cheeks. Oh, he'd heard the important bits. She wanted to seduce him, and she'd planned on doing so that night. His cock surged in his trousers once more, eager for any and all attention the fair Rosalind might be willing to pay him.

Rising to his feet was an experience full of the pleasure-pain dichotomy he'd come to embrace. Pain seared his side as his ribs objected, quickly followed by the rush of satisfaction that he often found in the experience. But there was a new source of bliss mixed in like a punch to the gut. One that was wholly unexpected and carried a force he could not credit. It was his desire for Ros.

She watched him, concern creasing her brow as he took a step closing the distance between them. The intensity of what he felt for this woman, of his need to protect her, to care for her, shook him to his very core. He had thought such instincts had been beaten out of him over his years of fighting. He knew his lifestyle and his predilections in the bedroom made him a terrible choice for a husband. But despite the swirl of conflicting thoughts and desires, there was one need that overwhelmed them all—the need to taste her, to touch her, to bring her all the gratification he could muster from his vast experience. So, despite his aching ribs and throbbing lip, he pulled her into his body. Her breath hitched in the most delightful way as he cupped the delicate curve of her cheek and slid his roughened thumb over her silky flesh. "I heard you."

And then he captured her lips before another word could escape. A delicate shiver rippled through her body as he cradled her in his arms and invaded her mouth. He pushed past lips, teeth, and tongue to discover the heated depths of her. He traced the arching roof of her mouth and then dropped down to twine his tongue around her own. The sensuous slide of each of them exploring the other had his cock straining hard to escape his trousers. Yet, he wasn't sure he was willing to risk her safety to pleasure himself in such a manner. What if she became pregnant because of him?

But then the sweetness of her burst through his thoughts, scattering them like mist. All he could focus on was how good she felt in his arms. After an eternity of kissing that was still not enough, he withdrew to trail kisses down the column of her neck. The pale skin beckoned him as he swept down the length of it and over her collar bone. She shivered again as he allowed the edge of fabric at her neckline to be his guide. When he reached the hollow between her breasts, he could not help himself; his tongue darted out to taste and explore. He wanted to strip her bare and have his fill of her, and he would in time. He had no intention of rushing things when this might be his only opportunity to secret away enough memories to last him a lifetime. Because he knew after this, no other woman would compare for him. No other would be as perfectly suited to him as fair Rosalind. And yet, he knew she would never be his. Could never be his.

Reaching behind her, he worked the laces of her gown free while he worked his way up the other side of her chest. Finally, the bodice gaped forward, exposing her corset and undergarments. With trembling hands, he pulled the top part of her gown free and moved on to the next obstacle, her skirts. There, he quickly released the ties for her skirt, underskirts, and crinolines, letting the whole pile sink into a billowing heap at her feet.

The vision she presented had his lungs seizing as he found her wearing nothing but her corset, under-blouse, garters, and hose. She was the picture of seduction with her red-blonde hair piled in jaunty curls and her rouged lips smiling in welcome. All she needed was a staff, a green field, and a flock of sheep, and she would have made a picture-perfect shepherdess. Alas, he would have to suffice as her flock for the moment.

Unable to physically lift her with his injuries, he helped her step free of the piles of fabric. She hesitated and bit her lip. Her big green eyes looked up at him, filled with worry. "Are you sure you are in any shape to engage in such activity?"

He glanced down at his cock with a wry grin. "I can't think of a better shape to be in to *engage in such activity.*"

"Do not jest. I do not wish to cause you pain. Your ribs may yet be broken, and your face and hands are a mess." Worry tinged her voice.

Perhaps she was having second thoughts? Yet the thought of her causing him a little pain as she rode him had him growing harder if that were even possible. He struggled for a moment and then wrestled the words free from his lips. "If you've changed your mind about wanting to seduce me, then we shall stop immediately. I've no intention of forcing an unwilling woman to my bed."

Pink flared delicately across her cheekbones as she shook her head. "My desire for you has not changed; I am merely concerned for your health."

He pulled her into his arms. "Do not worry; I have survived far worse injuries than this smattering of bruises."

Desire wove itself around the throb of his lip and the ache of his ribs as he pulled her into his arms. She trembled still, or perhaps it was again, he wasn't sure any longer as his lips slowly lowered to press against hers. The soft pillow of her kiss was akin to sinking into an ethereal cloud. And then he probed past lips and teeth to once more find the warm haven of her mouth.

With a moan that rocked him to his core, she snaked her hands up around his neck and hung on to him as though she might never let go. He set his hands free to roam over her lush curves and, ultimately, to find the laces of her corset. As fetching as she looked, the garment needed to be gone with all due haste.

He continued the sensual slide of their tongues as they kissed, all need of breath set aside for the greater desire to taste and touch each other. Breathing had become secondary.

Finding the knot of her laces, he worked them free as he continued to feast on her. All the while, she pressed against him as though she wished to crawl inside him and stay, and he couldn't say the notion was unappealing. Something about this woman made his cock hard and his heart light. He wanted more. He wanted all of her.

Her stays came loose, and he pulled them free of her body quickly, followed by her chemise. With her gloriously naked, he needed to pull away so he could see and appreciate the full beauty of the fair Rosalind. Breaking their kiss, he stepped back and inhaled sharply, ignoring the spike of pain in his side. She was everything he'd imagined and more. Soft curves, lush yet compact. High, pert breasts that begged to be attended to. To be sucked.

He sat on the edge of the bed and let one corner of his lips tip up. "Help me with my shirt *again*."

Ros bit her lip as though she considered stopping things, but they'd gone too far to stop now. He knew it. She knew it. But, he gave her a moment to reach such a conclusion on her own. Then with a nod, she stepped over to him and, just as before, grabbed the hem of his shirt and guided it over his head and off his arms. He decided it might be the last time he bothered with a shirt for a few days.

Then she was hovering over him, her breasts at the perfect height for his earlier intentions. "Come here."

Placing his hands on her lush hips, he guided her between his legs to stand where he wanted her. The tips of her breasts beaded, hardened in anticipation, and made him dizzy with need. He leaned forward and captured one point, gently rolling it over his tongue as he savored the elongated nub.

Breasts came in all shapes and sizes, and among men, there were many philosophies on what constituted perfection. Some focused on whether a breast could fill a champagne glass; others found an overflowing handful just right. And still, others focused on the size of the areolas, preferring larger or smaller. But for him, it always came down to the nipples. He liked a set of nipples that were about the size of a woman's little finger at the tip and just long enough to latch on to with his lips or teeth. He'd heard one soldier refer to them as bullet sized. And Ros had the loveliest set he'd ever been privileged to see.

"Mmmm..." he reveled in the firmness of the nub. The feel of it rolling over his tongue and the way her breathing shifted from soft and even to breathy and choppy. Then he switched to her other breast and repeated his attentions. Her fingers threaded through his hair until her hands cupped his skull in a demanding grip that prodded him for more.

The tip of his cock leaked pre-come, dampening his skin and his underclothes. He'd never felt such a strong desire for a woman as he did for Ros, and he'd fervently hoped that having tasted her, his need would ebb as it had always done in the past. Though, if he was honest with himself, he had his doubts that such a pattern would hold true. Releasing her breast, he eased her back from the edge of the bed. "You are an enchantress with your deceptively lush curves packed into what feels like such a delicate package."

"Come, Flint, we've no need for pretty words. I have every intention of laying with you." Her cheeks remained flushed as she stood there proudly, almost challengingly.

He rose up and placed a finger under her chin. The pulse at her throat fluttered wildly under his scrutiny. "A beautiful woman should always be treated to pretty words whether she chooses to lay with a man or not." Something fierce and protective jolted through him at the notion she had been given short shrift when it came to compliments.

A shadow flitted through her verdant green eyes. Had he not been watching her so intently, he no doubt would have missed the darkness as it was replaced by a look of pure desire. With her glittering gaze locked on him, she stood there waiting for his direction. Something warm wrapped around his heart as he rose from the bed and traded places with her. "Lie back, Ros."

She bit her bottom lip, yet easily complied with his direction. Once she was settled, he placed a hand on each knee and pressed her legs open wide. Her breath hitched, making his cock throb with need, but he refused to rush through this first time with her. He was determined to savor every moment, engrave every image on his brain since he doubted he would have another opportunity to be with her again. He *shouldn't* be with her again inasmuch as he knew he couldn't offer her more than a fleeting intimacy that could not last.

Pushing aside the unwelcome truth, he focused on the moment, which meant concentrating on bringing her to a shattering, toe-curling orgasm. Kneeling, he wedged his shoulders between her legs and leaned in. The lightly sweet scent of her desire drew him in, made his mouth water with the need to lick her quim. But her hands had fisted the coverlet as her body stiffened. *Had her husband never tasted her?* He couldn't imagine having such a woman in his bed and not doing so. And with that, he leaned in and put action to thoughts.

The soft pink folds of her pussy were slick with the evidence of her need for him, a heady reality that pushed the bounds of his limited self-control. He slipped his tongue along her slit, savoring the burst of salty sweetness.

A soft gasp of surprise escaped her as he drove deeper, seeking out her entrance. She wiggled her hips a bit, either in encouragement or an escape attempt. He wasn't sure which, and he didn't care as he looped his arms under her thighs and used his hands to pin her to the bed. Then he dragged his tongue over her pussy from her entry, across her sensitive tissue, and around her swollen clit.

Slowly she gave in to the pleasure he delivered as he swept across her soaked folds over and over again. More and more. And then the sweetness of her climax exploded on his tongue as his name burst from her lips. With her hips flexing up to meet each lingering pass of his tongue, she shuddered beneath him. Desire pummeled his body as violently as the stocky brute had earlier that night. He could have spent hours worshipping between her thighs, but he knew he'd never last.

He eased up onto his elbows, absorbing the waves of pleasure-pain that shot through him, stealing his breath with each shift. After standing, he shed the last of his clothes before making his way around to settle on the bed with his back propped against the headboard. As his ability to breathe returned, he crooked his finger at a dazed Ros. "I suspect you are quite the horsewoman. Come and ride me."

Chapter Four

Ros rolled over onto her belly as her pulse still pounded through her useless limbs. Archie had licked between her legs—once. But, comparing the two experiences was akin to suggesting that riding a pony on a lead was the equivalent to galloping across a field on the back of a full-blooded stallion. Her husband had never attempted to repeat the intimate act after his dismal failure to bring her any pleasure, let alone to orgasm. From there on, he'd kept to more staid territory in the bedroom.

Not Flint. With a gleam in his dark blue eyes, he leaned against the headboard and watched. When he wasn't beaten up, his deep sapphire eyes and dark hair stole her breath. She let her gaze linger over his muscle packed body as he patiently waited for her. Need bubbled up from deep within her once more as she found the ability to sit up and answer his summons.

"I was a horse-mad child. My father caught me sleeping in the mews with my pony on more than one occasion." She smiled and crept across the mattress to where he sat.

Flint grinned, a breath-taking display. "I can imagine your mother's horror at that discovery."

She huffed a laugh. "Oh, no. She never learned the truth. My father worked very hard to keep my love of horseflesh from her. It would have, no doubt, been an insult to her delicate sensibilities. But enough about my childhood. I believe you were questioning my seat."

"Not questioning. Merely requesting a demonstration."

Ros knelt beside him on the mattress and stared at his swollen reddish-purple cock. She couldn't cease imagining what it would be like to wrap her lips around the rigid flesh and swallow him. Her cunny throbbed with excitement and desire as she leaned over and took hold of his shaft. Darting her tongue out, she swirled around the mushroom-shaped head.

Flint groaned, and she could feel the sound vibrating through him as his salty taste teased her. Needing more, she opened her mouth wide and took the whole of his tip in her mouth. His cock twitched in her grasp as he mumbled some incoherent words above her.

Eager for more, she pushed down further on his length until he tapped the back of her throat.

"Bloody hell," his low murmur encouraged her to keep going.

Determined to take as much as she could, she retreated a bit and then returned to take more. She pushed down until he popped into her upper throat. The burn caught her off guard, but not as much as having him pull her off his shaft with a barked, "No more!"

Still a little dazed from her orgasm and the new pulsing need that already thrummed through her limbs, she didn't understand what had happened. "Oh! Was I doing it wrong?"

A strangled noise erupted from Flint. "Anymore right, and I would have spilled down that pretty little throat of yours."

"Would that be an issue?" Confusion had her brows creasing as she tried to follow the man's objection.

He shook his head. "Only if you wanted to actually have me sink deep inside you. A man does not recover so easily as a woman."

"I see. My husband and I only came together once a night. I did not realize that was because he could not do it again." Her cheeks heated.

Flint sighed. "Oh, we can do it more than once a night, something I shall prove to you later. But we do require some recovery time between bouts of intimacy, and I am in desperate need of having you sink down on my cock."

She bit her lip, need warring with her reserved upbringing. "I want that, as well. Another time, I shall endeavor to pleasure you thoroughly with my mouth." Impossibly, her cheeks grew hotter still. "I was enjoying it, and I have read that men do appreciate that form of gratification."

"We do. But not now. Come and mount me, fair Rosalind. I have need of you." He held out his hand as though he was a knight of old aiding a damsel.

With a nod of agreement, she swung up and over him so that her thighs stretched across his lap, and her calves lay parallel to his thighs. Hovering over his erect shaft, she reached down to take ahold of him and press his head to her opening. But he removed her hand with an unexpected gentleness.

"Let me." Then he aligned his tip to her opening and placed a hand on her hip to guide her down. "Ease over me, nice and slow. I fear I might shoot off before I can fully fill your sweet pussy."

She clenched at his dirty words, shocked at how they affected her. He groaned again as she continued to slide down over him. Her channel stretched wide to accommodate him until the stretching morphed into a light burning. She was no virgin, but it had been years since she'd lain with a man, not to mention Archie had not been so well endowed as Flint. Once she fully sank down on him, she thought she might explode, she felt so full.

Needing to touch him, she reached up and placed her hands on his chest and then rose to slide up his length. The fullness receded until just the tip remained inside her, then she reversed course. As she sank back down, bliss coursed through her veins. The intensity of it all overwhelmed her and made her feel as though she verged on flying apart.

Deep within her body, or perhaps it was her soul, something was pulled taut. Having him inside her, his flesh beneath her fingertips, and his masculine scent surrounding her, was like nothing she had expected. A sense of fullness, the heat of a man, the strength of him, and even the pleasure he could bring were all things she had considered. But the closeness, the soul-stirring intimacy, something bordering on...love? No, she hadn't anticipated that.

Digging her nails into his chest, she moved to lift up again, but Flint groaned and grabbed her hands. Wasting no time, he pulled them behind her back and gripped both wrists with one hand. "I'm afraid I can't have you touching me right now. I won't last."

His words surprised her, but with the way he had her arms pulled behind her back, her breasts were thrust up and forward. He grinned wickedly as he leaned forward and captured one hard tip in his mouth. As he sucked and pulled on the distended nub, she felt every tug first in her breast and then in her pussy. The bliss made her light-headed, but also in need of more. As he continued to lave her breasts, she began to ride him. Up and down, she slid on his shaft, relishing the stretch and burn of his intrusion. With each downward plunge, the ecstasy swelled until it coalesced into the beginning of another orgasm. Desperate for the coming onslaught, she rode him harder, stopping to grind her clit into his pelvic bone as he continued to suck on one of her nipples.

And then as she was about to tip over the edge, he slapped her ass and let go of her pebbled tip. "Come for me."

When he latched back on to her other nipple, she exploded around his cock. "Yes! Flint," her cry rang out and mingled with his own cries of pleasure as he joined her.

The climax that slammed into her shattered her consciousness into a million little pieces. It was as if her soul had been pulled free from its moorings. Floating somewhere above their physical embodiment, crest after crest of satisfaction swamped her. And even as she returned to herself, the waves of pleasure continued to roll through her leaving her spent.

Together they rode out the waning burst of pleasure as he pumped his hips up to meet her lackadaisical downward slides. Out of breath, her head spinning from the intensity of her release, and her legs now truly turned to jelly, she collapsed forward against his chest.

He held her wrists still as they both sat there recovering, their breaths heavy and sweetly timed. Eventually, he released her hands, opting to wrap his arms around her waist. She would have happily remained where she was forever but knew he must be in pain with her weight pressed against him. Rising up to her knees, caused him to slip from her body, and she suddenly felt inexplicably bereft. It was not a feeling she could reconcile, so she chose to staunchly ignore it for the moment. Instead, she focused on necessary activities.

"Here, let me get a rag." She eased from the bed and fetched two of the unused rags from the table to clean them both up. She returned, handing one to him and using the other to wipe between her legs.

Flint unexpectedly swore viciously using a litany of words she was unfamiliar with. He pinched the bridge of his nose as his brow furrowed.

"I should have worn a French Letter to protect you." He looked almost confused by his lack of care.

She smiled and patted his shoulder, ignoring the swooping feeling in her stomach. "You need not be concerned. I inserted a sponge before coming here tonight. I certainly had no intention of trapping you by becoming pregnant."

He paled, blinked once, and then shook his head. "Do you always think of everything?"

She smiled, but she could feel the tremulousness of it. "No, not always."

She had not considered that lying with him would cause her burgeoning feelings to take deeper root. How could she have understood? She'd never felt anything remotely as strong for her dead husband. And certainly, nothing that rivaled the physical intimacy that they had confoundingly shared. Did he feel the connection pulsing between them as though it were a real, carnal thing?

As she stared at Flint, the man seemed as shaken as she felt. For a moment, she feared saying the wrong thing and sending him fleeing. Luckily, he saved her from having to think of something else to say.

"We should dress, and I should see you safely home." He moved to the edge of the bed with a wince.

She tutted at him. "I should dress and see myself home. A night's rest in bed would serve you well, even one housed in a brothel."

He grinned. "Wouldn't you worry for my virtue? Some other strange woman might wander in here and molest me in my weakened state."

She let one brow lift as she stood naked before him. "Are you suggesting I took advantage of you, my lord?"

He barked out a laugh that instantly morphed into a groan of pain. To her consternation, his cock twitched and lengthened anew.

Her confusion returned. Was he reacting to the pain or to her nudity? Unsure, she turned around and went in search of their clothes. Upon retrieving them, she dropped his on the bed. "I suggest you wait a few moments so I can assist you."

He looked down at his newly erect cock. "I believe you could best help me if you remained nude."

Her face heated as she took in the obvious evidence of his renewed vigor. "I see you were not playing me false. I wasn't sure the first round was a good idea, I'm certain a second one would be disastrous for your injuries."

He reached over and snagged her wrist, using it to tug her across his lap and into his arms. "The only thing that would be disastrous for my injuries would be if you made me chase you down. Though I'm game if you wish for the thrill of the hunt."

Her heart thundered in her chest. If she was intimate with him again, she feared she would be doomed. This man possessed the ability to own her body and soul, but that was not something she could afford—not yet at any rate. But she did not wish to leave him in such a state. Remembering the pleasure of taking him in her mouth, she decided she might be able to survive that.

But before she could offer up the alternative, he captured her lips and staked his claim. Their tongues dueled as he kissed her long and deep. Her fingers tunneled into his slightly too long hair as he pinned her against his thighs. Needing to breathe, she gently pulled back from their kiss. "I'll not risk hurting you further, but I suppose I might be able to offer you some assistance."

Desire flared in his deep blue gaze, making her legs wobble once more as she stood up. The weakness was of little import since she immediately sank to her knees before him.

His sharply indrawn breath was all the encouragement she required. Leaning forward, she captured his erection in her hand and aimed it toward her lips. Flicking her tongue across the head had him moaning, and when she sank down over the tip, engulfing him with her mouth, his hands tunneled into her hair. As she worked up and down his length, he groaned and muttered encouragement. She continued to work his cock, taking him as deeply as she could manage and then swallowing to take more. Soon, she had his shaft worked down her throat until his balls smacked against her chin. Quickly, she reversed direction, allowing herself to take a breath.

"Bloody hell, Ros." The gravelly tone of Flint's voice told her just how much he was enjoying her ministrations.

So she repeated the action over and over again. Her pussy grew wetter and wetter as she worked his cock. And then he yanked her up, threw her on the bed, and with a yelp of pain thrust into her body. She wanted to stop him. Knew she should tell him *no*, but her body cried out *yes* with each plunge of his shaft. As she worked her hips, meeting him stroke for stroke, she relished the pleasure of having him inside her once more. Pleasure coiled tight within her, a spring ready to release.

"Fuck, you feel so good wrapped around me," he grunted. "So tight and wet for me. *Just me.*"

She wrapped her legs around his hips and drummed her heels against his arse. "Yes. Just you."

And then the coil sprang free within. Her peak swelled until it swamped her with bliss.

"Don't stop!" She demanded as she came apart.

Flint followed just behind her, coming on a harsh shout of release. He continued to pump his shaft in and out of her as they both slowly returned to earth. Finally, he slowed and then came to a halt.

Ros looked up at him, saw the lines of pleasure still etching his face, and she felt the first crack in her walls emerge just as she feared. This man could easily claim the power to wound her if she did not protect herself better, especially since she wasn't sure he returned her feelings.

Chapter Five

Two days later, Ros sat nervously across the tea service from Flint. A light sheen of perspiration dampened her brow as she sipped her cooling tea. Her stomach knotted up, making it hard to swallow. Through sheer force of will, she pushed her nerves down with the tea. "Flint, it has been lovely spending so much time with you of late. I truly want to thank you for all you have done for Julia and me."

Flint smiled. "I was hap- uh, was glad to be of assistance. I am sure you are looking forward to returning to your old habits rather than having to entertain me quite so much."

"Oh, I can't say I'm looking forward to a return to normal, so to speak. I've quite come to enjoy our time together. I had forgotten that men can be engaging, even pleasant to be around." Her cheeks heated as her teacup rattled in its saucer. Images from their one night together flashed through her mind's eye. Setting the pair down lest she drop them, she clasped her hands in her lap.

Flint looked up at her, his dark blue eyes growing darker with something unspoken. "I, too, have enjoyed our time. I am pleased to know that I have perhaps reminded you of some aspect of your life that you had forgotten. Though I am sure we shall have plenty of opportunities to visit in the future since your sister and Wolf are so happily wed."

Ros licked her lips.

His brow creased, as though he'd grown concerned. "Are you perhaps a bit nervous about our pending split? I'm certain it will not reflect badly on you in the least if you are perhaps..." he cleared his throat. "If you are considering looking for a husband."

She wanted the floor to open and swallow her whole in that moment. Was she a fool? Did he not feel the same way? "I was thinking that perhaps we didn't need to end this just yet."

Flint set his own cup and saucer down with a distinct clatter as he stared at her in confusion for a moment.

Ros watched as the purpose of her words sank in, and his confusion morphed into shock. "But Ros, that has always been the plan. This was never intended to be real...to be forever."

Her chest felt heavy as she watched his reaction. "I am well aware of what this was meant to be; however, I had also not anticipated this attraction between us. This...this pull. Surely, I am not the only one of us that feels it? The only one that felt it the night we were together at The Market?"

So many emotions crossed his face that she couldn't help but wonder how others saw him as closed off and stoic. She saw worry and fear, caring, and then to her despair, she saw horror quickly followed by resolve.

"I'm not the kind of man that you want, that you deserve. You are a wonderful woman, and you deserve a man who is able to love you and treat you with the gentleness you deserve. I am not that man. I shall never be that man. Do not do this to yourself or to me." His words were kind but direct, his tone, implacable.

Anger and frustration bubbled to the fore as she realized that he did, in fact, feel the pull between them, but was denying it. "You did not answer my question. You have danced around it, but you have not answered it. And I should warn you, do not dare to tell me what I want for myself. I have been on my own long enough to know my own mind."

He shook his head and stood. "I'm sorry, Ros. I shall see you as planned for the Halpern's ball."

With that, he left her sitting alone amongst the remnants of their tea. Fear spiked through her at the thought of losing him. She couldn't say she loved him, but she was increasingly aware that she cared for him quite deeply and that not having him in her life was not an acceptable option. If she broke with him, she was certain she would not see him again for a very long time if ever. But could she convince him to give them a chance? Or would he fight her on this?

Flint stood in the front parlor of Ros's home and waited for her to join him. It had been a week since their encounter at The Market and three days since she attempted to alter their planned break. They had spoken of many things, but not one of them had been about their night together. After their second joining, he'd collapsed on the bed, pulled her into his arms, and held on to her the rest of the night as she slept. He'd refused to sleep knowing it was the one and only time he'd have to hold her.

The door of the room opened, and she swept in, a vision in a deep rich purple gown that showed far more of her cleavage than he was comfortable with. Other than the gown she wore to The Market, it was the most daring gown he'd ever seen her wear. She was stunning.

The bloody woman was making their inevitable parting as difficult as possible for him.

Never the gentleman, unless he chose to be, he bowed to her. A streak of pain ripped around his ribs as he straightened, followed by the most pleasurable tingles. He smiled, causing his lip to join in the pleasure-pain symphony. "Good evening, Ros. You look ravishing."

She smiled, her cheeks tinging pink. "Thank you, Flint. And good evening to you." She hesitated and then stepped closer. "You look quite handsome, despite the remnants of the abuse you suffered. Are you ready for tonight?"

Something had her green eyes dancing as she placed her palms against his chest and leaned into him. He resisted the urge to groan and instead took her by the shoulders and helped her take a step backward. "Thank you, and yes, I am quite prepared for the evening ahead."

Her brow creased. "I don't suppose you've changed your mind about our looming break?"

He sighed. He hadn't realized how attached she'd grown to him until earlier in the week when she suggested they abort their planned split. There was no possible way he could marry her. She deserved a good man, a normal man, not one such as himself. Not a man who spent his free time trolling London's wharves and back alleys for fights. Not a man who needed pain to feel pleasure. He would never do as a husband for any woman, let alone one so sweet as Ros.

"Not in the least. I've told you this was never intended to be a true engagement." He cringed inside as something in the vicinity of where his heart was purported to be twisted.

Her brow smoothed, and a look of calm certainty appeared. "Very well then, we should be on our way."

The worry and doubt that had been hounding him all week eased at her seeming acceptance of their fate. Perhaps the evening would go smoother than he'd thought?

Two hours later, Flint stood with his longtime friends and their wives in the Halpern's ballroom. Lords Stonemere, Brougham, and Wolfington were once half of the Lustful Lords. Over the last couple of years, things had changed dramatically as one by one they'd married, thus, giving up their hedonistic lifestyles. All that remained of their once merry group were himself and Lord Lincolnshire. Of course, they had added Lord Dunmere to their ranks, so at least there were three of them to pal around.

"Are you ready for your big moment?" Wolf grinned.

Flint's stomach knotted as he considered what was to come. He hated being the center of attention. "As I'll ever be. At least, Ros finally agreed to go through with it." He looked around for Ros and failed to see her. She'd been swept onto the dance floor by one eager young swain after another. Normally she hid her dance card, preventing anyone from claiming a dance. But tonight, she had eagerly provided it each time she'd been asked.

Wolf's smile slipped as he darted a glance at his wife as she chatted with Ladies Stonemere and Brougham. "What in the world do you mean? Was Ros refusing to break with you?"

Flint continued to search the crowd for her, a kernel of worry not allowing him to rest easy until he spotted her once more. "She suggested we not break up multiple times this past week. I reminded her how unsuitable I am each time, but she persisted with the silly notion until this very night."

His friend groaned beside him. "And she said she would go through with the public break with you? Tonight?"

"Yes. I reminded her our betrothal was never intended to be a real commitment, and she said, 'Very well then,' and suggested we leave." Flint turned his gaze on Wolf. "Why?"

"If she did not agree directly to the break, then you may find yourself still engaged to her at the end of this soiree. Ros is a stickler about lying. If she didn't give you a definitive answer, she may have other intentions."

The pained look on Wolf's face had Flint's doubt resurfacing with a vengeance. If she didn't initiate the break-up, he could be in trouble. She might be stubborn enough to refuse to throw him over, no matter how abominably he treated her.

The song ended, and the musicians took a short break, which led to Ros being returned to his side. Her dance partner bowed and departed quickly, leaving the two of them in semi-privacy as everyone around them was already engaged in conversation. Taking the opportunity, he leaned close. "Are you ready for our little vignette?"

She darted a quick glance his way and then whispered a reply. "I should think you would be wiser than to discuss such business so openly."

"And I would have been, had I not been given some reason to doubt the sincerity of your earlier agreement." He wanted to growl in frustration but repressed the urge by attempting to smile. The motion felt so awkward that he was sure he must have appeared ready to attack and not as though he were enjoying himself.

She looked up at him and blinked. "I don't know what you mean."

"Of course, you do," Flint insisted. "You gave me a sufficiently vague response to my assertion that this evening needed to unfold as planned."

Just then, the musicians returned to their seats and indicated they were about to resume playing. Frustration slapped at Flint as he spotted the mischief dancing in her eyes.

"Did I?" The innocence she exuded was directly at odds with his sudden certainty that she had no intention of following through with their break.

A throat cleared, interrupting their little tête-à-tête.

His grandmother stood there peering at the pair of them. "Flintshire, despite your refusal to abide by any of the proprieties, I hope that once you've wed this gel, you will produce the long-absent heir." Her throaty tones had long ago morphed into something that sounded more like rusty cogs grinding together.

Flint sighed. "Mrs. Smith, you remember my grandmother, the Dowager Duchess of Shropshire?"

"Of course, my lady, it is a pleasure to see you again." Ros curtsied and dipped her head.

The old shrew merely lifted her brows and snorted, "I'm sure." Then she turned back to Flint. "A grandchild, my boy. Before I die, if you please."

And then she trudged off without even a by your leave. Flint found himself wanting to growl but was interrupted as yet one more unwelcome interruption occurred.

"Lord Flintshire, Mrs. Smith." Lord Cunningham bowed to each of them. "I believe I have the next dance."

Ros made a great show of looking at her card, and then she bestowed a brilliant smile on the charlatan that had come to collect her. "Indeed, you do, my lord."

Flint resisted the urge to growl at the man. He detested Lord Cunningham, whom he had long ago discovered to be a cruel man behind closed doors. He'd been banned from The Market by Madame Du Pompadour for mistreatment of her girls, and rumor had it that he was a harsh man to work for. His servants always looked fearful of any possible misstep. With his frustration level already high from their too brief conversation, it was all he could do to keep himself in check as he watched Ros prance away—*When did she start walking in such a fashion?*— on Cunningham's arm. His hands fisted at his side as he clenched his thighs to keep his feet firmly planted where they were. While he could cause a scene, it would not ensure Ros's cooperation. Which meant he'd simply appear to be an utter buffoon at best and a complete cad at worst. With an agitated sigh, he settled in to see just how his supposedly guileless fiancée would proceed.

Ros feared she might cast up her accounts at any moment as her stomach churned uncontrollably. Lord Cunningham flung a smile in her direction as he led her onto the crowded dance floor. With his blonde hair and blue-gray eyes, he was by all accounts a handsome man. But there was something about his patrician features that left her cold and uninspired. When she considered how a fleeting smile from Flint heated her blood, there was no comparison. The opening strains of the quadrille sounded, prompting the dancers to move about in the familiar patterns. The intricate steps forced her to focus on moving with the others around her as they wove around the formation until she returned to her partner.

"You are a most beautiful woman," he said as she circled around him.

Heat danced across her cheeks. "Thank you, my lord."

As she moved through the dance, she reminded herself that she needed to find a way to circumvent Flint's need to protect her—even from himself. She'd hoped their night together at The Market would do the trick. Instead, it seemed only to have reinforced his intention for them to break up as planned—and that simply would not do.

Resolving to not make her dance partner aware of her erstwhile focus, she came back around to Lord Cunningham and forced her most winsome smile his way. Her cheeks hurt, and her face felt as though it might crack like overfired china at any moment, but he seemed not to notice.

"I understand that my felicitations are due on the marriage of Lord Wolfington and your sister."

"Thank you, my lord. They are quite happy." *Now*. She, of course, left the last part off. After all, she was grateful they had resolved their issues, but there had been a short while where she had not believed they would do so. That they managed to find happiness gave her hope for her own happy outcome.

The dance parted them once more, and she spent the rest of the dance smiling and nodding at whatever comment Lord Cunningham imparted when they neared each other.

When they finally were able to leave the floor, she wanted little more than to be returned to Flint's side so she could resume the siege she'd waged on his defenses. However, it seemed Lord Cunningham had other plans. He led her around the crowd of people making their way from the dance floor and out onto the terrace overlooking the rear gardens. It was a lovely view, though the June evening air was a touch cool for her without her wrap.

A chill crept over her as he led her toward the balustrade. "My lord, I fear there is a decided nip in the air."

A mottled pink stole into Lord Cunnigham's cheeks as he swept his coat off and draped it around her shoulders. "My apologies. I should have realized you were not as well fortified against the cool evening as I."

Dread knotted her stomach as the warmth from his coat seeped into the cooled flesh of her shoulders and arms. She had done nothing to invite such familiarity with this man. "Truly, I should return to my escort. He will have noticed my absence."

Lifting her hands to the lapels of his evening coat, she was about to push it off when he reached up and halted her movement. "Please, I merely ask a moment of your time."

With the knots in her belly only growing more snarled by the second, she glanced over her right shoulder at the safety of the ballroom and tried to tamp down the urge to flee. The man was a peer of the realm, and there was no reason to suspect him of nefarious intentions. He had been politeness itself so far. Silence stretched out between them as she tried to decide what to do.

"There you are." The familiar rumble of Flint's voice sliced through the hushed atmosphere. "I wondered where you'd gotten to when the next set began, and you had not returned."

She turned slightly to her left to see a raised brow paired with stern disapproval written plainly on his face. "My apologies, my lord. Lord Cunningham wished to speak with me for a moment."

She glanced over at the fair-haired man who was decidedly shorter in stature than Flint, and who now looked ill at ease. "It was nothing of consequence."

Flint stared at her, then shifted his gaze to Lord Cunningham. The silence grew heavy and tense with unspoken threats. Finally, Flint broke the standoff when his adversary's gaze dipped submissively. "It would seem you have mislaid your coat, my lord."

His face turning a rather rancid shade of red, the blonde man retrieved his coat from her and then scuttled away. Annoyed at Flint's quiet aggression, she wheeled around and stepped into his immediate space. "That was unnecessary."

Flint continued to remain implacable. "Was it? Last I knew, no man led a lady onto a balcony without some inappropriate intent."

Annoyance reared its head. "First, this is a terrace, not a balcony. Second, there are plenty of people milling about to sufficiently guard my virtue. " She stepped closer to keep her last thought private. "And finally, my virtue was well and truly compromised years ago—by my husband." Straightening up to her full height, she stared at him in frustration. "As I seem to be destined to be a free woman, I have every right to indulge my interests wherever they may lie."

She stepped around the hulking man and made to storm off, but was efficiently thwarted when he grabbed her by the arm and drew her into him so that his stomach pressed into her back as his arm caged her against him. "First, I don't give a bloody damn if this is a dais in the Queen's throne room. Second, the people milling here came for their own private encounters. They certainly would not take note of yours. And finally, until you have officially broken with me, we are still engaged. I shall not be made a cuckold in such a public fashion."

She couldn't see his face, but the anger fairly simmered off him in waves. It was both frightening and intoxicating, a heady sensation that could easily become an addiction, not unlike the man himself. Turning to face him despite the steel band of his arm surrounding her, she pressed into him, seeking his warmth and the masculine smell of his cologne.

"I would not betray you in such a fashion." Her voice cracked as emotion overwhelmed her.

With a low growl, he leaned down and snared her lips with his as he dragged her into the shadows of the terrace. Their tongues twined and dueled, a sensual dance that had her heart skipping beats as her knees turned to aspic. How was she supposed to let this man go? To release him for some other woman to claim one day? With her heart lodged in her throat, she tore free from his kiss and took an unsteady step back. Nearly choking on the need to demand an explanation from him, she turned and flew from the darkened patio and back into the safety of the ballroom. The true threat to her person lay in Flint, not in a lord who merely showed a little interest in courting her.

Chapter Six

It had been three days since the Halpern's ball, and he remained as unsettled by what had occurred as he'd been that night. When he'd spotted Cunningham leading Ros off the dance floor and toward the terrace, his protective instincts had been stirred. At least, that's what he tried to tell himself.

Looking back, there was no denying he had been driven by possessiveness and jealousy. And when he'd stepped onto the terrace to find her swathed in the lout's evening coat? He'd wanted to rip the garment from her shoulders and stomp upon it. While dueling was no longer acceptable behavior, throwing a glove at the man had crossed his mind. Despite the bubbling rage inside, he managed to leash his beast and use words to send the blighter off in short order. Of course, when Ros had turned to him, her eyes flashing annoyance, he'd lost his head and kissed her thoroughly. He'd silently laid claim to her even if he knew it was the last thing he should have done.

A woman like her deserved far better than a man like him. He was far too rough for such a sweet woman, and though he'd hidden his darker needs, she'd certainly matched him well in every other aspect in the bedroom. That had been quite a surprise, an unwelcome one if he was truthful. The more he found to admire about the woman, the harder it was becoming for him to do what he knew he must.

Hence his lingering consternation. Though he knew he needed to convince her to end their connection, he could not bring himself to approach her about it once again. Reverting to form, he'd embraced his urge to excise his excess emotions through violence. And that is why he found himself haunting the London docks in search of a fight. His blood pulsed beneath his skin with the need to feel the bite of pain that included a much-desired rush of pleasure. Intently ignoring the persistent itching and tightness of his skin, he went in search of a familiar face.

Normally, he scheduled his bouts in advance, making prowling about the underbelly of London wholly unnecessary. He embraced his violent side, but he didn't have a death wish. Rounding the corner out of a dockside alley, the smell of rotting fish smacked him in the face. With his eyes watering, he pressed on, determination carrying him along the eerie boardwalk. Unfortunately, the wharf appeared relatively quiet. A few intoxicated men stumbled along, ignoring the soft beckoning of the prostitutes lurking in the doorways of the taverns that dotted the docks. But there was a subdued quality to the scene that was at odds with the usual hustle and bustle.

Finally, Flint found the sign he'd been seeking—the Fisherman's Noose.

When he slipped inside the salt-weathered building, all merry-making paused as the smattering of drunken dockworkers and the tavern wenches entertaining them all turned to note who'd entered. Keeping his battered hat tipped low, casting a shadow over his face, and his old cloak wrapped tight to hide his evening finery, he shuffled up to the bar and ordered a tankard of ale. As he settled on a stool, the low hum of revelry returned. With a careful turn of his head, he scanned the shadows for his usual contact to arrange a bout. The man was nowhere to be seen, but he recognized a competing fight coordinator, though they styled themselves fight chancellors. Spying the man, he rose and stalked across the tavern.

With a slightly drooping face and eyes dulled by drink, the man sneered. "Go away. I haven't got a farthing to spare."

"I'm not here for money." Flint contained his snort of derision. "I'm in search of a fight."

The weathered man stopped and peered closer at him. "I know you. You're one of Chancellor Waters' fighters."

"I've been known to fight in his circle. But I'm looking for a match tonight, and he's nowhere to be found."

The man eyed him, speculation a living breathing thing. Flint knew approaching him would be a risk, perhaps more so than he'd anticipated.

"Boy!" The chancellor grabbed a stick that had been propped against his bench and jammed it over the high back and into the shadows.

A young boy, sleepy-eyed and scrawny as a rail, appeared, wiping the crust from his eyes. "Aye?"

The man leaned over and whispered something to the boy, who then turned and darted out of the tavern and into the night. "I'll know shortly if there's a match to be had. It's a quiet night what with the weather being so nice. Everyone's taken off to the countryside."

Flint blinked in surprise.

The chancellor cackled loudly. After a few moments, he managed to contain his mirth. "Ha! The look on your high-falutin face." He took a swig of whatever was in his tankard and set the mug back down. "Bah. Abbess Jones is having some big shindig down on the other side of the docks. Any man what got paid today took his bloody coin down there to spend in cock alley."

"So, there are no fights to be had." Flint made to rise, but a gnarled hand whipped out and latched onto his wrist.

"I've not said such. Though the fight may not be wharf-side."

Flint settled back in his seat. "I am able to go where the action is."

The man nodded. "Then we wait for the boy to return. He'll bring word one way or the other."

And so, an hour later, Flint found himself in Seven Dials well after dark.

The hack he'd rented stopped before the ramshackle building where the fights were to take place that night. As he leaned out the window to confirm he was in the right place, the stench of rotting food, other waste that lingered in the air, and the general smell of the unwashed masses that lived in the gutters of London co-mingled to create a stomach-turning miasma. Quite incredibly, it was worse than the smell of the wharf. Ignoring the punch of nausea, he exited the cab and searched the shadows of the building for the entrance. He spotted the listing door and stepped forward to enter when a man materialized from the shadows and blocked his forward progress. Adorned in clothing that aspired to be well cut, the man approached with a confidence that caught Flint's attention. As the pair squared off, the hairs on the back of his neck rose in warning.

A quick glance over his shoulder proved the cab he'd arrived in was well down the street and out of reach.

"Hold on there, governor," the poorly dressed man said as he swaggered forward a few steps.

Flint narrowed his gaze. "Out of my way." His voice came out as a low growl.

The other man grinned and shook his head. "I don't think so, my lord. I was sent to deliver a message to you."

Widening his stance, Flint stared impassively at the unknown man, even as fear lanced through him. For the first time in a long time, he realized he had a reason to know fear.

He never should have trusted Chancellor Gates.

"Mr. Bodwell wants you to throw your next fight."

Flint had always expected this day would come. In truth, he was surprised the thugs who ran the underbelly of London had allowed a lord to win as long as he had, though this turn of events couldn't have come at a worse time. "I'm afraid that won't be possible."

The unkempt man just shook his head. "If you know what's good for you, you'll do as you're told."

Flint shifted his weight and was about to swing on the overdressed back-alley goon when two large sets of hands grabbed his arms while another arm wrapped around his throat from behind. The ringleader smiled.

Flint jerked his arm, trying to break free of one of the assailants holding him. Unable to do so, he was rendered powerless to defend himself when the leader slammed his fist into Flint's gut. Thinking him defeated as he doubled over, the foolish thugs released his arms and throat. Bent in half, he breathed through his nose as the pain morphed into a deep intense pleasure. Energy and purpose flooded his body and focused his mind.

In an unexpected surge, Flint swung upwards with his right and caught the ringleader under the chin. As he crumpled to the ground unconscious, the others grunted in surprise before they quickly retreated. Frustrated by the poor showing of the assailants sent to accost him, he stepped over the unconscious body and opened the door, only to find an empty building. With a curse fresh on his lips, he turned and stomped down the street.

As he walked through Seven Dials, he had far too much time to consider the ramifications of this unexpected threat to himself. It occurred to him that anyone who was associated with him could become a target—his friends, his family, and more importantly, Ros. Under the circumstances, his proximity to Ros was now a detriment, and the only way he could truly protect her was by not being near her. He had to make her see reason about their split. Whatever it was that he felt for her was of no consequence when her safety was in jeopardy.

By the time he emerged in an area of London where he could hail a cab, his mind was made up. He would have to force her to break with him.

Ros sat in her front parlor and sipped her tea. The knot in her chest hadn't loosened since the Halpern's ball. The night had not gone at all as planned. Well, not entirely as planned. Though Flint was still insisting on her breaking with him, he had kissed her out on the terrace. No, that was no mere kiss. That was pure unbridled possession.

She'd loved every moment of it.

And honestly, with the way the passion between them caught fire, how could he possibly still want to part ways? It boggled her mind to learn Flint was such a contrary sort. In the beginning, he'd been such an agreeable beau. So courteous and attentive that she'd almost immediately found herself falling for him. But lately, he'd shown her a side she was less than pleased with. The question was, what would it take to convince him they were better together than apart?

She refused to give up so easily, refused to be a doormat for a man ever again.

She'd do as she pleased, and it pleased her to have him.

The front door knocker sounded, and a few moments later, the very subject of her thoughts stood in her front parlor. He looked pale and drawn.

"What has happened?" She managed to set her teacup down without spilling as she lurched to her feet.

Flint's blue eyes darkened. Was he in pain? Distress? *Oh, God! Has something happened to Julia?*

He wrapped his hands around her upper arms and held her at a distance from him. "Nothing has happened."

But for some reason, she couldn't shake the feeling that there was a *yet* dangling on the end of that statement. "Then, what is wrong? You are clearly upset."

He nodded and stepped away from her. "I am. I am upset that you have not yet broken with me."

Ros took a step backward and then another before sinking down into the seat she'd previously occupied. Taking a deep breath, she prepared herself for the coming onslaught. "I see."

"Bloody hell, woman!" Flint spun around, giving her his back as he thrust a hand through his hair. "I don't think you do."

She drew a breath and attempted to steady her racing heart. "Perhaps you're correct. I don't see any reason we should not be together. We have grown fond of each other these past weeks." She paused. "More than fond even. There is a chemistry between us that I have never experienced with another man. Why should I be forced to give that up?"

"Would you believe me if I told you it was one-sided?" He shot her a baleful glare.

Impervious to his affectation, she pursed her lips in annoyance. "I would not."

He huffed and let the glare slip from his craggy features. "I thought as much."

"Then why would you ask? Why are you so insistent that we part ways?" Frustration boiled up from deep within her. Were all men so typical? Did they all hide things from the women in their lives? If they were going to work, he must learn to trust her.

"I am not the right man for you. I shall never be able to be the husband you need, to make you happy." His head hung between his shoulders as if in defeat.

"Perhaps you should let me be the judge of that. I may be a woman, but I am intelligent enough to discern who and what is best for me." She sat upright with her hands clasped tightly in her lap as she fought the urge to go to him and cradle him in her arms. He looked so lost, so distraught, that it broke her heart.

With a grunt and a shake of his head, he looked up at her once more. "Please. Don't do this. Don't force my hand in this. Simply let me go as we had agreed."

Perhaps she was being selfish, but for the first time in her life, she was taking something for herself alone. She wanted Flint, and she would have him. "I'm afraid I can't do that. I care for you. Very deeply."

It was as if her words were a dagger that she had shoved into his chest right where his heart resided. Tears welled in her eyes as she took in his stricken countenance. Then he stumbled back a step and turned even paler than when he'd walked into her home. "I'm sorry, Ros."

With a pained groan, he turned and fled from her parlor.

Needing to watch him go, she rose and moved to the window. As the front door slammed behind him, she jumped. Her heart skipped a beat. Her lungs constricted as she tried to breathe, but nothing moved. Her chest seized, surrendering to the pain that laid siege to her body. Then the first tear slipped free. She'd said she cared for him, and he had...*apologized*. Her heart broke as she watched him running away, but from what she wasn't sure. From her? Or, from something else?

Chapter Seven

R os was dressed and ready to go by the time Julia and Wolf arrived. She stood near the window, watching for Flint as they entered.

"Good evening, Ros. You look lovely." Julia swept into the room, bringing a much-needed fresh breath of happiness with her.

Ros had hoped she would hear such words from Flint, but since he'd not yet appeared, that was rather difficult. "Hello, and thank you." She smiled as best she could. "That green looks stunning on you."

"Thank you. I had to have it when I spotted it at Madame Le Fluer's." Julia twirled like a girl in her first ball gown. All the while, Wolf looked on with doting adoration.

Ros fought back the tears that had been slowly surfacing as the minute hand moved relentlessly forward.

"Has Flint not arrived yet?" Wolf looked concerned as Julia took in the otherwise empty parlor.

Ros managed a watery smile. "I'm afraid not."

Julia looked worriedly at her and then back to her husband. "Well, I'm sure he'll be here any moment."

A mean little voice in her head countered Julia's positive words. *He's not coming. He doesn't want you.* "No doubt."

A knock came at the door, and Ros whipped around to peer outside, but she couldn't see who was standing on her doorstep. Johnson appeared a few moments later and presented a note. Plucking the correspondence from the salver, she recognized the masculine hand. With trembling fingers, she opened the note.

Ros,

*My deepest apologies, but I am running late. Please go on without
me, and I shall find you at the Culpepper's ball shortly.*
    Yours,
    Flint

It was then she noticed a particularly strange odor coming
from the page. Warily, she lifted the sheet closer and sniffed.
The page held traces of whisky and perfume. Her gut twisted, but she refused to let on that there was an issue. Tucking
the note away, she turned to Wolf and Julia. "I'm afraid Flint
has been detained. We should press on, and he will catch up
with us later."

Julia shot her another concerned glance but accepted her
statement. "Very well, we should be off. The Culpepper's ball
is going to be an absolute crush!"

With a pit in her stomach, Ros followed her escorts out. It
seemed Flint was going to stand her up for the evening. She
highly doubted he would bother to drag himself away from
whatever flowery smelling entertainment currently held his
attention.

An hour later, they had made their way inside the ball
only to find themselves practically shoulder to shoulder with
everyone in society. Wolf spotted a clearing in the crowd up
on a raised area overlooking the ballroom. They made their
way across the crowd and up the four steps to the sliver of
space. They were quite far from the action of the ballroom
floor, but it gave them both a lovely view of the event and a
bit of breathing room. They had missed the first dance, but
considering the only partner she wished to dance with wasn't
likely to be coming, she wasn't particularly concerned.

For the next few hours, Ros watched as Julia and Wolf
danced while fending off inquiry after inquiry on Flint's
whereabouts. Wolf and Julia returned from another dance,
and Ros couldn't help but notice her sister's probing stare.

"Wolf, dearest, could you go and fetch some punch for
myself and Ros? I'm feeling rather parched." Julia smiled at
her husband.

Ros tried to ignore the unspoken dialog, but she'd always
been observant. She steeled herself for the coming conversation.

"All right, Ros, spill. What has occurred between you and Flint?" Julia had morphed from sweet wife to bullying older sister in the blink of an eye.

Stifling an inappropriate curse, Ros tried for a blank face. "I don't know what you mean?"

"Oh, enough with such nonsense. I know you far too well, Ros. You were never a deft hand at dissembling. What is going on with Flint? Where is he?" Julia crossed her arms beneath her breasts and waited.

Ros considered her options and decided it was pointless to try and hide what was happening. "I don't actually know where he is."

Julia's gaze narrowed as she drew a breath to speak.

"Truthfully, I have no idea where he is tonight. But that note he sent stunk of whisky and perfume. I imagine that whatever is detaining him is of a relatively pleasurable nature." Pain shot through her chest.

"Oh, no!" Julia leaned over and pulled her sister in for a hug, despite their competing skirts.

Ros pulled back quickly. "Please, not here. I do not wish to have a cry right here and now. It is horrible enough standing here sans beau."

Julia growled a little. "You're right, of course. No need to make a scene now. But I promise you when I get that man in private, I shall trounce him soundly."

Ros tried to smile. Having been on the receiving end of one of her sister's tirades, she knew Flint had quite the storm coming his way. But it failed to make her feel any better.

Wolf returned a few minutes later, bearing the warm lemonade often found at these affairs. He tilted one side of his lips up. "They were fresh out of punch."

Julia took the tiny glass and sipped the tart drink and her face puckered. With that indicator, Ros decided to skip the beverage.

"I think I shall go home. This is silly to remain here and ruin the evening for the two of you as well."

Julia latched on to her arm. "Absolutely not. You need to dig out your dance card, fill the remainder of it with eligible bachelors, and dance the night away. Flint can go rot."

Wolf grunted and let one brow lift in query, but his wife waved him off. "I'll explain later."

Ros shook her head. "I think I'd rather go home."

"Go home?" A booming, masculine voice slurred through their conversation. "But I've just arrived!"

Flint stood on the second step up to their little platform weaving back and forth. Ros couldn't contain the little cry of dismay that escaped.

"Where have you been?" Julia hissed the question at him.

Ros had little doubt about where he'd been. From where she stood, she could smell the all too familiar stink of alcohol and perfume. "Don't be ridiculous, Julia. He's been at The Market."

"Always knew you were a flash one, Ros." Flint listed forward and then reversed course, only to find the banister before he tipped too far backward.

Ros pinched the bridge of her nose and drew a deep breath. This was too much to bear, but bear it, she would. At least, until they escaped their prospective audience. If they hurried, they might escape without too much notice. "Wolf, if you will fetch the carriage and bring it around the rear by the garden, Julia and I should be able to steer his drunkenness out the back way and avoid any further embarrassment."

Wolf nodded and moved past his friend. He stopped for a moment and said something to Flint that caused the intoxicated man to straighten up for a moment. Then as Wolf departed, Flint seemed to return to swaying. Whatever Wolf said, it's effects were short-lived.

"Very well. Julia, we'll need to make this look as natural as possible. I'll take his arm; you walk on his other side and do the same. Between us, we should be able to keep him steady." Ros stepped down and got him turned around with his arm tucked safely in her arm. They stepped down two steps and waited for Julia to join them. Then, the three of them went for a stroll.

By the time they'd gotten Flint down into the garden, a man materialized from the shadows. "It looks like you ladies could use a hand."

Julia gasped and stopped, but Ros had no time for anyone. "Not at all. We are getting along just fine if you'll move aside."

Ros made to move past the dark-haired, black-clad man, but Julia was a bit slower, throwing them all off balance.

"Whoa." The stranger said as he stepped in to assist. The next Ros knew, Flint had been hoisted over the man's impressive shoulder, and they were moving quickly toward the rear gate of the garden.

"Excuse me—not to sound ungrateful—but who are you?" Ros was worried about the unknown man being aware of how intoxicated Flint was.

"A friend of sorts," the stranger said and continued on.

Off-balance, and not a little concerned that the man had waltzed in and taken charge, Ros practically ran to catch up with him. But Julia grabbed her arm and pulled until Ros fell back, and her sister could lean in to whisper, "That's Mr. Lucifer!"

Ros wanted to groan. *Bloody hell!* What was the man doing in the Culpepper's gardens, and why was he helping them? What did he want from Flint? So many questions popped up that she was practically dazed as she followed the man through the rear gate. Then he deposited Flint in the carriage that Wolf had miraculously arrived with.

"Lucifer?" Wolf looked as shocked as she felt as he got a glimpse of who was aiding them.

"Don't look so shocked, Wolfington. The ladies were clearly struggling with their burden." Lucifer tipped his hat at them.

He was a handsome devil...and it was the devil part that worried her.

Wolf's face hardened. "I don't know what you are playing at—"

"I'm not playing at anything. Merely attending to a small bit of business. Now, if you'll excuse me, I am late for my appointment." Then with a gallant bow, the infamous Mr. Lucifer disappeared back through the rear garden gate.

With a confused shake of her head, Ros climbed into the carriage followed by Julia and then Wolf. The three of them rode in silence for a few moments.

Wolf looked at Flint, worry drawing his brows together. "Did he hit him?"

"Of course not." Julia chided her husband. "Mr. Lucifer appeared at a most auspicious moment. Flint was fading fast.

If he hadn't been there to assist us, I imagine Flint would have wound up flat on his back in the Culpepper's garden until you came to find us."

Wolf grunted, clearly unconvinced of Mr. Lucifer's good Samaritan role. Ros was of a similar mindset. The man was in that garden for no good purpose. She hoped it wasn't in relation to Flint. Not terribly long-ago Lucifer had pumped Julia for information about Flint. In the aftermath of Wolf and Julia's wedding and their ultimate happiness, they had all forgotten about that interrogation and what it might mean for Flint. Had he? Could that be why he was seeking to distance himself from her?

The carriage came to a stop.

"I had the driver take you home first, Ros. Julia, may I ask that you stay with your sister until I am able to come back to fetch you?" Wolf reached out to caress his wife's cheek.

"Of course." Julia cast a glance at Ros that did not bode well for the next little while. "My sister and I have much to discuss, I think."

"Excellent. Don't be too hard on her. I am certain much of the blame for whatever this is lies squarely on Flint's shoulders." Wolf grinned. "The male of our species tends to be a bit foolish when it comes to the women we love."

"Too true, but the females can be equally stubborn and hard-headed." Julia leaned forward and kissed her husband on the lips. "Hurry back to me."

"Always."

And with that, Julia and Ros exited the vehicle.

Julia preceded her into the house and turned as soon as they were in the front salon. "I want to know the full story, this instant."

Ros sighed and found a seat. "There isn't much to tell. Flint wishes for me to end our engagement, and I am refusing to do so. Or I was." She glanced down at her hands and felt her tears returning.

"Why does he wish to break?" Julia looked as confused as Ros felt about the whole thing.

"That is the problem. He keeps telling me that he isn't the man for me. That he can't be the husband I need. It's ridiculous tripe, but he'll not listen. Not even when I told him that I care for him." Her voice cracked on the last admission.

Then Julia was by her side on the settee and crooning to her. "Oh, my poor Ros."

They sat there and rocked for a while as she let the pain of Flint's rejection out. Until tonight she hadn't realized how desperate he was to escape her. And suddenly, she couldn't help but wonder what was so wrong with her that he refused to marry her. That he didn't want her.

But she knew deep down it wasn't her, not really. There was something wrong with him. Something that was preventing him from loving her. In the end, she didn't want a man if she had to force him to be with her. And that was what she faced.

As her tears lessened, she asked her sister, "Do you know what it could be that is keeping him from me?"

Julia shook her head. "No, I have no idea. But, if he is willing to go to such lengths to push you away, then perhaps you should consider letting him go."

Ros sighed. "I know. Just as I refuse to have my choices taken from me, I cannot take them from him. No matter how much it hurts."

Then her tears returned, and she contemplated his friendship with her brother-in-law. How would she ever face Flint again? Would the rest of her life be filled with awkward gatherings where they all pretended none of this occurred?

Chapter Eight

F lint rolled over, his hands flying to his head. He was quite certain that if he didn't hold it, the thing would split in two, spilling its contents all over his bed. The reoccurring spike of pain did not pair well with his desert-dry mouth and the roiling nausea in his belly. He groaned.

"I imagine you aren't feeling up to snuff." The sardonic tone of Wolf's words drove him to attempt to crack one lid open. A bright light seared his eye, which caused him to wince and retreat back behind his closed eyelids.

"My God, have you no soul? Do something about that blinding morning sun," he ground out from between gritted teeth as he hid under the covers.

"Morning? Ha!" His friend's laughter was not welcome. "You missed that joy by nearly ten hours. It is late afternoon and pushing toward evening."

He groaned again. "What do you want, Wolf?"

His friend's boots slapped the ground with a sound that felt as though a hammer had struck the spike currently lodged in his skull.

"What I want is to make sure you are well, and then to find out what the bloody hell you were thinking showing up to the Culpepper's ball so pissed that you could barely stand and stinking of another woman's perfume?"

Flint didn't particularly feel like explaining things to Wolf, but it seemed he may not have a choice. His friend looked well and truly furious, not that Flint could blame him. He cracked his lids open. "Well, that was me trying to make it easier for Ros to break with me. She seemed reluctant last we spoke."

"You bloody fool." Wolf shook his head.

Sprawling on his back, he let one arm flop over his closed eyes. "I can't be what she needs, the man she needs. It's simply not safe for her to be with me."

"Bollocks. You are a good man. You may have a taste for a bit more violence than the rest of us, but at your core, you are not a bad person." Wolf cursed softly. "Though I don't imagine it matters much."

A piece of paper smacked against his chest, causing Flint to shift his arm and look down. "What is that?"

"A missive from your betrothed."

Flint eyed the sealed note with both finality and trepidation. He needed her to break off their engagement. It had been his entire goal the night before. But he also dreaded the moment Ros would no longer be part of his life. She had brought a light, a radiance into his world that he had never thought to experience.

Sitting up, he carefully arranged the pillows behind him. Then he broke the seal on the note.

Dear Flint,

As you know, I have no desire to end our association. However, the events of last night have made it more than clear that you do not feel the same. I am saddened that I pushed you to such an extreme display in order to make your wishes clear. I certainly would not wish to be forced to do something against my will, as it seems I am forcing you. Please accept my sincere apologies for being so difficult, but I felt it was important to fight for what I wanted. Now I see that perhaps I fought too hard. I shall release you from your commitment to me, and wish you the best in your future endeavors.

Sincerely,

Mrs. Rosalind Smith

His heart hurt. The pain of it far outstripping the pain in his head. The tightness in his chest felt as though a vice squeezed his torso. For a moment, he wished he was alone to absorb this blow, though, on second thought, perhaps it was best Wolf was here. With no ability to indulge in self-pity, he closed the note and let his lids slide closed once more.

"What did she say?"

Surely Wolf was aware of the contents of the note. It shouldn't have been a mystery after his actions the night before. "As expected, she has severed our connection."

"Well, I suppose that makes you happy." Wolf sounded as though he couldn't care one way or another.

It should have pleased him immensely, but it didn't. "It was the outcome I sought," Flint said mildly. "It doesn't particularly matter how it makes me feel."

"In that case, press on, good man. I shall not pester you further." Wolf patted him on the arm, and then he heard his friend depart.

Alone, he attempted to focus his thoughts elsewhere. After all, he still needed to figure out who was behind his beating earlier, though he had his suspicions. The problem was his suspicion did not make a great deal of sense. He would think with Cunningham's wealth and status that garnering Ros's attention would be sufficient retribution for their past quarrels. But, when he considered the whole of who he knew and who might wish ill upon him, his former nemesis was the only name he could call forth. To his knowledge, he had not offended or upset anyone else.

Unsure where to start with his investigation, still dealing with the aftermath of his over-indulgence, and wishing to not think about Ros, he rolled over and sought oblivion in sleep. Because remaining awake offered only searing agony that carried no zing of pleasure with it.

Flint sat in his darkened study, his servants all dismissed for the night. It had been days since his break with Ros, and though he had sobered up, he felt no better about what he had done. He'd barely roused himself from bed for the evening ahead. His shirt was untucked, hanging long over his trousers. He eyed the decanter of whiskey that sat on the tray off to the side and considered the wisdom of having a drink. His guest would arrive at any moment, and he knew he needed to have his wits about him for what would come next. Of course, one drink would merely take the edge off.

He poured a single finger of amber liquid and tossed it back. The burning sensation warmed him inside, disintegrating the frustration and shame at what he was about to do. It wouldn't last, he knew both would return in short order, but for a moment, there was nothing. No pain. No misery over Ros. No self-reproach over what he needed.

A loud knock echoed down the main entry hall.

Setting his glass down, he padded down the cold tile hall and to his front door. It was after midnight, so most of London was either asleep or well engaged in their own night-time pursuits. He opened the door and found his expected guest waiting, covered head to toe in a black hooded cloak. Without a word, he swung the door wider and let them enter. After closing the door, he turned and walked back down the hall, passing his study and up the stairs. He led them into his bedroom where he finally stopped and faced them.

"Thank you for coming to me, Mistress Lash."

She pushed the hood of her cloak back and then slipped the garment from her shoulders. "You are lucky my usual client canceled this evening, and that I know and trust you, my lord."

Flint nodded. "I know my request was unusual for your customers, but having visited you in the dungeon before, I preferred not to do so again." A mask alone was not enough to hide his mortification at what he needed from this woman.

"Well, let's get on with this, shall we? Where would you like this done?" She glanced around the room as though seeking out some indicator of where he indulged his needs normally.

He walked over to his four-poster bed and pulled his shirt over his head. Then he spread his arms, grabbing a rope that hung from each corner of the huge bed. "I believe this should give you enough room to wield your whip."

"It will do." Then she set her bag down and pulled out a coiled whip. It was a long braided piece of leather that, in the right hands, could bring great pleasure. In the wrong hands, it could wreak havoc, tearing the flesh from a man's bones. "Assume the position, if you please."

There was nothing more to say at that point. All the details of what he wanted, what he needed had been sorted out earlier. He slipped his wrists through the loops of the rope and grabbed the length that led up to where the rope was tied to the bed. The first lick kissed his back, barely a caress. She worked him slowly, warming his back up and preparing him for the firmer, more pleasurable strikes that were to come.

He stood stiffly to start, and then as his blood began to pump through his veins, his cock took notice of what was happening. Pleasure zinged through him as the first hard strike landed on his shoulder. He shuddered from the pulse of satisfaction that followed. For the next hour, she worked him hard, landing the whip up and down his back. His cock grew impossibly hard, and then he faded out into the place where everything receded. This was what he sought, this place where there was no pain, no shame, no loss, no failure to measure up. He could just exist and feel good. It was as if he floated for a time, free of everything.

At some point, he felt his arms slide free of the ropes that he held, and then he tipped forward onto his bed. His legs dangled off the bottom, but a soft blanket wrapped around him. The slide of the fabric over his welted back sent more jolts of bliss through his body. He shuddered.

"My lord, may I get you anything else?" Mistress Lash whispered the question near his ear.

"No, you may leave. Just knock on the door to the adjoining room as you depart."

He swore he felt her brush a lock of hair from his face, but she was gone by the time he managed to open his eyes. He sighed and enjoyed the last few moments of contentment for a little bit. His valet would be along any moment to salve his back and ensure he recovered without incident. He would be sore for a few days, and then the need would begin to build again. Unfortunately, the fighting only ever worked for so long to stave off what he really needed. Eventually, he always caved to the need for pain, the right pain. And tonight, it offered the added benefit of escape from his despair.

He sighed as the sound of a door closing indicated his valet was near. For now, he wanted to focus on the mellow feeling that left him weak as a newborn kitten. Later, he could wrestle with his demons.

A week passed, and while his back had recovered from his visit with Mistress Lash, his torment had grown worse. He was lethargic, irritable, and generally poor company. Linc and Arthur were making no bones about it.

"Do stop your moping, Flint. You knowingly forced the lady's hand." Linc slumped in a chair next to him in his library.

Art shook his head. "It really wasn't very sporting of you."

"It was necessary. She refused to break off the faux engagement, and it was past time she did. She left me no choice." Flint swirled his whisky and stared into the cold, charred fireplace. It seemed a kindred spirit at the moment.

Linc sighed. "But why? You've not indicated what necessitated ending things when you clearly care about Ros."

At that moment, Gordon entered the room, bearing a salver and a note. Grateful for the interruption, Flint took the correspondence, read it, and then stood. "I'm afraid I need to go. It seems Chancellor Waters has an engagement for me."

"Still fighting?" Arthur asked as he stood.

"It's a distraction, and a profitable one, at that." He shrugged. He wouldn't tell them the real reason he was still fighting. That he'd tried having Mistress Lash visit him, but the succor he found did not last. In the past—when the need grew too great to mute with fighting, and he could gain an appointment with her—a visit could leave him with a contentment that lasted many weeks before he required pain again. Though inevitably, after being whipped, he felt worse for having indulged his deviant needs. The fight against his dark nature was a constant battle. At least, when he fought down on the docks, something good came of the effort.

An hour later, he found himself once again engulfed in the familiar. Around him, the hustle and bustle of the wharf swirled as surely as the smell of fish, the tang of salt, and the ribald curses of the laborers who worked far harder than anyone of his class could understand. There had been a short period of his life when he would come to the docks to work shoulder to shoulder with these men, relishing the pain that came with the daily abuse of his body. All too soon, the effectiveness of such harsh treatment subsided. Though by then, he'd discovered the bare-knuckle fight circuit that coexisted with the laborers, the prostitutes, and the tavern owners.

Approaching Chancellor Waters, Flint nodded. "Who am I fighting?"

Waters grinned. "He's a virgin to our circles, but he comes highly recommended by a colleague."

Grunting in acknowledgment, Flint glanced around the alley where a growing crowd milled about. No one in the group stood out as this possible newcomer. This both eased and irritated him, since not one of the current men lingering about looked physically able to offer the punishment he required. Flint was left to assume that his opponent was yet to arrive. But that didn't mean the man who would eventually come and fight could meet his needs either. To his credit, Waters was aware of Flint's preference for pain. It was one of the things that made him such a lucrative fighter. His bouts were not typically short, they offered a great deal of entertainment whether the spectators were winning or losing their bets, and in the end, he always came through so the house could consistently lay odds on him winning.

Then the crowd parted, and two men strode through. One stood nearly a head taller than Flint, but he was lanky. The other was of a similar height to Flint and just as muscled. If he was his opponent, there was hope of a decent fight and some much welcome pain.

"Waters?" The lanky one looked at both Flint and the man next to him.

The fight manager stepped forward. "Which of you is Andrews?"

"He is." Lanky pointed to the man next to him.

Flint felt the tight knot of doubt release in his chest. Relief was within his grasp.

"You ready to fight?" Waters looked the man up and down.

Flint noted the ragged appearance of the man's clothing as well as the once fine quality. But having long ago learned to not ask too many questions, he pushed the odd detail aside.

"Sure. It's what I'm here for," his opponent said and slipped his coat off.

Flint followed suit, eager for the bout to begin.

As the crowd noticed the men disrobing, they spread out and circled around, creating a ring of sorts to contain the coming brawl. The rush of blood through his veins sounded loud in his ears as he took a few warm-up swings and loosened up a bit. The other man was going through his own pre-fight movements, and then Waters called them to the center of the ring.

"There's only two rules. No weapons, and you fight until someone hits the stones." Waters nodded and then stepped out of the way.

Flint circled around the man Waters had called Andrews. The other man watched him warily, each of them sizing the other up. As usual, Flint started out leading as though he were a lefty. It gave him some time to assess Andrews' skills and allowed him to take a bit of a beating...which was the point of the whole exercise.

The other man stepped in and swung. His left jab connected with Flint's jaw, though he could easily have swatted it away. The right hook that quickly followed came up short as Flint danced backward. It wouldn't do to make the audience think this was in the bag for the new bloke.

Andrews cursed and pulled his arm back in quickly. Flint used that window of opportunity to push forward and land a right jab to his opponent's left eye. He took the blow like a seasoned fighter, shaking it off quickly as he squared back up.

Certain that the fight would not be a short one, Flint settled in. They continued to exchange blows as they moved around the space. A quarter of an hour later, Flint was growing tired, and the audience restless. When a sneaky right hook slipped under his guard and landed in his ribs, he decided it was time to switch up. As soon as he switched his stance, Andrews' eyes widened, and then, the man offered a bloody grin. "Ah, I see you've been holding back."

Flint sort of shrugged—without dropping his fists—and smiled as well. "Just wanted to be sure the crowd got their money's worth."

"Generous of you." The man seemed a bit confused by Flint's reasoning since most fighters sought to end fights as quickly as possible.

Refusing to waste energy on further chitchat, Flint merely grunted in response. Then the pair set to engaging more fully in the battle.

While normally, Flint's fights ended fairly rapidly after he made his stance switch, this one did not follow that pattern. Instead, Andrews grew more aggressive in his assault on Flint's guard. After a bit, they fell into a steady rhythm of exchanging punches. With each new strike to his face and body, the pleasure-pain coursed through Flint, carrying away any worries he may have brought with him into the ring. All that remained were himself and his opponent—his odd partner in pleasure.

The man continued to slam his fists into Flint until he decided he was nearing a point of exhaustion that might allow him to sleep without needing to visit The Market after the fight. With that in mind, he unleashed a powerful jab and then a right uppercut that sent his opponent straight to the ground. The man lay there dazed and unable to muster the wherewithal to stand back up. The man's lanky friend stepped in and called an end to the fight.

Waters smiled broadly and handed over a nominal fee to the loser while he counted out the substantial fee he owed Flint. After handing over the money, Waters nodded. "Always a pleasure doing business with you."

Bloodied and in exquisite pain, Flint nodded and grinned in utter satisfaction before he departed.

A bare quarter of an hour later, and he was home. The euphoria of a well doled out beating already waned as he cleaned himself up. Ignoring his useless erection, he poured himself a whisky. Sitting in his room in his trousers and shirtsleeves, he considered his options. Normally, he would go to The Market to play since he was no longer an engaged man. But he found the idea a lackluster solution, even in the face of his fading high. His face and ribs ached like the devil, but there was no rush of pleasure any longer. Even his cockstand had begun to flag. It was a disturbing turn of events.

Settling back in his chair, he pondered what it all could mean. For more than half his life, he'd associated pain with pleasure. He could not have one without the other. What had changed?

Unbidden, a face framed in a red-gold halo with piercing green eyes came to mind. He imagined her much as she'd been their night at The Market when she'd tsk'd and prodded him into allowing her to treat his injuries. Her touch had been firm and no-nonsense, but every brush had shot the most intense bolts of pleasure through his body.

As he imagined her hands upon him once more, his cock rose again. Opening his trousers, he gave in to his body's need and reached down to stroke his length. Wrapping his hand around his shaft, he jerked on it roughly as he drew upon the pitifully few memories he had of taking Ros. With each rough pull, he conjured the feel of her lips around his cock, the clasp of her pussy when he slid deep inside her, the glaze of pleasure in her eyes as she came for him.

His balls tightened as he roughly ran his hand up and over the head of his cock using his own precum to lubricate his rough movements. With a moan, he dropped his glass and gripped the arm of the chair, his hips bucking up in desire.

Finally, he came on a shout of her name as he shot his load onto his shirt and higher onto his exposed chest. As his heartbeat slowed and the blood didn't pulse so loudly, he glanced about the room and took in his lonely existence. Was this all he had to look forward to for the rest of his life?

Chapter Nine

July 1862

Jules sailed into the sanctity of Ros' bedroom in a cloud of bright green silk. "Get up, Ros! No sulking."

Miffed at her sister's intrusion, Ros rolled her eyes. "Nobody is sulking. I'm considering all that has occurred of late, but I would not engage in behavior so childish as sulking."

Jules looked at her and let one flame-colored brow lift accusingly.

"Do cease with your well-intentioned assault. It is unnecessary and unwanted." Ros huffed and rose from her chaise lounge where she'd been resting.

"Excellent!" Jules clapped her hands together in obvious delight. "Then, do get dressed, or we shall be late."

Ros wanted to groan. "Late for what, precisely?"

Her sister grinned. "For tea with our new friends."

Tea? With our friends? "I'm not sure I am following you."

"Oh, don't be obtuse, Ros. We're due to have tea with Ladies Stonemere, Brougham, Carlisle, and Heartfield." Jules pursed her lips. "You forgot, didn't you?"

"Forget? No. What I did was assume that having dropped Flint, I would be *persona non grata* amongst his friend's wives." Ros frowned as her stomach flip-flopped in her belly in a singularly unpleasant fashion. "Even were I not, I don't think I could face them. I'm rather embarrassed at having tried to bully the man into staying engaged to me. What kind of woman does that? I'm simply mortified."

She knew better than to follow her heart, after all, doing just that had gotten her caught up with Archie, who had quickly fallen in love with her only to fall out of love just as swiftly. The unfortunate reality was that by the time he'd figured out he didn't love her, they were already married, and she was living with him near the front lines fulfilling her duties as a good military wife should. Pushing aside her maudlin thoughts, she focused on the problem at hand: tea with the wives of her now ex-fiancé's friends.

"Oh, Ros, I know you harbored a tender for him. But it really is for the best that you part ways."

Jules' blithe reply set Ros's teeth on edge. Were they so unlikely a pairing? Was it so unbelievable that a man such as Lord Flintshire would find her appealing? "I know it was initially the plan, but you never thought there might be more of a connection between us?"

Jules seemed to finally understand what was bothering Ros. "Dearest, do you really care for him?"

"I do…or I did until he showed up at the Culpepper's ball drunk and reeking of another woman. And it was all my fault because I had refused to release him when he asked." Ros ignored the pang in her heart that said she did, in fact, still care for him, that they belonged together. Clearly, her heart was no sound judge of things. Particularly, men.

"I disagree that it was your fault. You fought for what you wanted. How could anyone blame you for that? If he did not share your tender emotions, he should have simply said as much."

"He did tell me in no uncertain terms that he wanted to break with me, Julia. I refused to listen. Besides, I am not sure his feelings are what is at issue. Not once did he deny caring for me." Ros tried to make her sister understand.

"Irrespective of his reasons for wanting to break, going to such theatrics as he did was ridiculous. And if you come to tea with me, I am sure the ladies will agree."

Ros doubted that would be the case, but she also knew that her sister would bully her into going, regardless of her protestations. "I suppose I shall find out. Come help me pick out a dress to wear to face my newest enemies."

"Pshaw! You will see. These ladies are nothing if not loyal to their men but also to their friends." Jules seemed terribly confident about what would happen. Ros, couldn't help but hope her sister was not wrong. It had been nice having female friends, if only for a short time.

An hour later, Ros was sitting in a lovely blue and cream salon in Lady Stonemere's home. Arrayed around her were a bevy of beautiful ladies who all looked rather reserved except for a beaming Theo. "I am so pleased you decided to join us, Mrs. Smith."

Ros blinked. "Yes, well, my sister insisted you all wouldn't mind my joining you despite recent events."

"Recent events? What has occurred?" Theo asked.

"Oh,...um..." Nonplussed, Ros glanced at the other women and saw that most of them looked curious, perhaps even friendly, but not one of them seemed to register awareness that she had ended things with Flint.

Jules spoke up. "Why, Ros finally cut Flint loose. Though she only did so when he forced her hand with that horrid display at the Culpepper's ball."

Theo sighed. "I swear, not one of my husband's friends is capable of wooing a woman without assistance from us. What did that dense man do?"

Ros sat staring at the women now, her mouth hanging open in shock that they had no idea what had occurred and yet still appeared to welcome her into their circle. Closing her mouth, she pulled herself together. "Well, he showed up at the ball drunk and stinking of rather expensive and flowery perfume."

"Unbelievable!" Theo threw her hands up in clear exasperation. "Why on earth would he do such a thing?"

Ros felt her face heating up. "I believe it was my fault."

"Nonsense," Theo declared. "I assure you that not one of the Lustful Lords has ever done the expected thing, nor the appropriate thing when faced with a challenge by a woman they are fond of."

Lady Carlisle laughed, her blond curls bouncing slightly. "I dare say the ladies that win the Lords' hearts generally must be of a stalwart constitution to survive the shenanigans those men cause. Winning my Carlisle was practically a sedate trot through the park when compared to Theo, Emily's, and your sister's experiences."

Lady Heartfield nodded. "Lizzy is right. Not one of them has had a conventional courtship. Though, I suppose that makes winning the prize all that much sweeter. It certainly did for me."

"Yes, well enough about us." Theo turned back toward Ros, expectation etched across her face. "I want to hear what has transpired. I always knew Flint would make a muck of things when he finally fell in love."

Theo seemed to relish the prospect of the tale to come, which made Ros more nervous than she'd been mere moments ago. "Well, I wouldn't say that he is in love. In fact, he has made it quite clear that he wished nothing more than to break off our arrangement as originally planned. I, however, had other ideas. But the stubborn man refused to consider that we might be well suited. So he disgraced himself in such a public fashion as to force my hand into breaking with him."

Emily and Theo tipped their heads together and spoke in excited tones. Then their hostess looked at her and grinned. "Oh, Flint is most assuredly in love with you, which is *why* he behaved so abominably. This is fantastic!"

"It is?" Ros's head spun as she tried to follow the whirl of conversation among the ladies. They jumped around, taking turns offering their opinions on why his display indicated his feelings for her. But truly, Ros didn't see how it changed anything, even if they were correct. Finally, she had to stop the women. "But I have broken with him. And I am determined to move on since I am clearly not what he desires."

"I think you would be foolish to let him go if you truly care for him," Emily said and then leaned across Theo to place a hand on Ros's knee. "Lizzy truly is correct. It takes a stalwart heart to win one of the Lustful Lords and possibly an open mind when it comes to finding pleasure with them."

"Could that be it?" Jules finally spoke again. "Does he have some need in the bedroom that he is unwilling to seek from Ros?"

Heaven help her, Ros wished she could hide behind the drapes!

"Well, I suppose there might be something," Theo allowed as the door to the salon opened, and a maid wheeled in a tea cart laden with pots of tea, sandwiches, and all manner of cakes.

Embarrassed by the intimate turn of the conversation, yet deeply curious as to what Flint might be unwilling to share with her, she waited on tenterhooks. As the maid poured tea for each of the ladies, plated treats, and otherwise fussed over their group, Ros did her best to remain a composed version of herself.

At last, alone once more, Jules turned to Theo. "I shall expire from curiosity if you do not share. What could Flint be hiding?"

Ros was grateful her sister pressed the question, allowing her to remain silent.

"My husband has mentioned that Flint has a rather increased capacity for pain." Theo took a sip of her tea.

Ros looked at her sister and then back at Theo, utterly confused. "I'm afraid I don't understand."

Marie cleared her throat. "What Theo is trying to say is that Flint finds the bite of pain erotic. It stimulates his arousal."

Ros blinked and whispered, "But we've had sex..." Then thoughts crowded in, flashes of their night together. Flint's black eye, split lip, and injured ribs. His groans of pain. Heat seared her cheeks as realization careened into her. *We had sex while he'd been injured.* At the time, she'd taken it as evidence of his interest in her, but then he'd stated time and again that he desired her to end their connection.

Humiliation blazed through her, torching her feelings and searing her emotions. Sitting there, it felt as if someone had ripped out her heart and cauterized the wound. He'd tried to tell her, but she was so certain of how she felt, of how she believed he felt.

A hand patted hers, drawing her attention back to the group.

"Oh, do not despair." Theo smiled brightly. "If pain is what he needs, Mistress Lash is certainly able to teach you how to service his needs. She has a deft hand with the whip. I've heard that she has a waiting list of men who wish to be her clients."

Ros fought the urge to cast up her accounts then and there at the notion she had forced Flint to be intimate with her and rose from her seat. "This has been most informative. Thank you, ladies," she squeezed the words past the constriction in her throat as despair nearly overwhelmed her. *What have I done?* Pivoting on her toes, she fled the room on a chorus of *Ohs*. Walking as quickly as her skirts would permit, she found the front door and departed the house. Unfortunately, it was an unseasonably cool afternoon, and despite that, she dismissed the afterthought of her cloak as she hustled down the busy residential street. She'd been walking for a while when a carriage clattered to a stop just ahead of her.

"Ros, come along. Your home is too far for you to walk," Julia called out.

Ignoring her sister, she continued to stride briskly down the walkway. The light breeze defied the summer sun and cooled her heated cheeks. *How could I have been so foolish? So blind?*

Suddenly, her sister appeared before her, causing her to pull up short.

Julia grabbed her shoulders and gently shook her. "Cease this at once!"

Ros looked at her sister's face, the crease between her brows, the worry slipping through her green gaze. Pain, loss, and an insidious feeling of vulnerability tangled in her chest. A sob caught on the gnarled mess as she fell into her sister's arms and let loose the swirl of emotions.

Somehow, Julia guided her into the carriage and got her settled on the seat. For the rest of the ride home, Ros lay in Julia's lap and cried. Because she was certain all was lost.

By the time they'd entered her home, Ros had calmed herself. She turned to her sister and offered a tepid smile. "Thank you for seeing me home."

"Ros, I'm sure it cannot be so terrible. Perhaps, if you meet this Mistress Lash, she can better explain what Flint needs."

She shook her head. "No, I've made enough of a spectacle of myself. I see now that Lord Flintshire was merely being a gentleman in coming to my aid. I've obviously misconstrued fondness for something deeper."

Julia sucked in a breath. "I was wrong earlier. I erred in trying to help you past a painful moment by suggesting what you felt was not real. Undoubtedly, I was against it to start, but I came to see how much you two care about each other. You cannot give up on him."

"I appreciate your support—however belated—but I refuse to force a man who does not care for me into marriage." She'd made the mistake of ignoring the signs once; she refused to make the same mistake a second time.

Chapter Ten

I nexplicably, a week after tea with the ladies, Ros found herself trailing behind her sister and her new husband, the Viscount Wolfington, at a dinner party hosted by the inestimable Lady Doughton. A pillar of the London social circle, an invitation to one of her intimate soirees was a much sought after prize. Despite that, Ros had tried begging off. At least three times.

Nevertheless, Julia had strong-armed her into joining them with a relentlessness that only a concerned big sister could possess. First, she'd claimed to be busy. Her sister had gone behind her back and confirmed with Johnson that her calendar was, in fact, quite open. Next, she'd tried to convince her sister that she didn't have an appropriate gown. Julia all but laughed at her before she dragged Ros upstairs and quickly sorted out a dress to wear. Finally, the morning of the dinner, Ros had sent a note around to Julia indicating she had come down with a headache. By noon, Ros was being dosed with a tisane of healing herbs that Julia assured her would banish the pain and leave her feeling refreshed enough to join them for a night out.

Ros knew when she was beaten.

As the party—a small gathering of only twenty or so guests—wandered through Lady Doughton's adjoined salons, Ros spotted Lord Cunningham. He had been politeness itself at the Halpern's ball, if somewhat disturbed by Flint's overly aggressive nature. Although not surprised to find him among Lady Doughton's set, Ros had hoped to stay far away from anyone connected to Lord Flintshire that evening. Curious as to who she would be paired with at dinner, she slipped away from the pre-dinner conversation and maneuvered into the dining room where servants scurried about making final preparations.

Walking along the long table, she searched for her name card. Finding it tucked neatly between Lord Wolfington's and Lord Cunnigham's, she silently cursed to herself. Of course, she knew she'd not be seated next to her sister; most hostesses were rather hardnosed about the male-female disbursement. How else could they potentially take credit for any matches that may have resulted from one of their dinners?

With a desperation to avoid anything Flint related, she snatched up her name card and sidled down the table looking for a more suitable dinner partner. At least, one more suited to her needs.

She had just found the perfect spot at the far end set between two notoriously bookish lords when someone cleared their throat. Whirling about with a gasp of surprise, Ros found herself face to face with Lord Cunningham.

"My lord! You startled me." She breathed as she clutched her name card to her chest, nearly crushing it in her dismay.

"Mrs. Smith. It is lovely to run into you once more." He bowed gallantly.

"Thank you, my lord." She curtsied. "It is a pleasant surprise to see you again, as well."

Ignoring the heat simmering high on her cheeks, she glanced about in search of a convenient exit.

Lord Cunningham looked at her hand, clutched to her chest, and smiled. "What have you found there?"

"What?" She looked down at the slightly bent card that had her name elegantly scrawled across it. "Why, it is my name card."

Her heart pounded in her chest. It was the height of bad manners to shuffle the seating around at someone's dinner party. After all, most hostesses spent a great deal of time and thought in laying out who would sit next to whom at dinner. Would Lord Cunningham call her out? "I- I- found it here on the floor and was searching for where it belonged."

The surprise on his face appeared genuine enough. "How odd. Well, let me see if I might assist you in locating its rightful place."

"How kind of you, my lord." Ros could barely meet the man's gaze as he offered her his arm. They strolled down the length of the table, merely a few steps. However, to her, it felt like the longest distance she'd ever traveled. Perhaps this is what prisoners experienced when walking to their execution? *Dear God, what have I come to? Gallows humor?*

"I must say, you are looking fetching in that soft green gown. The color makes your eyes sparkle like emeralds." His words both charmed her and made her feel wretched.

How could she find even the smallest pleasure in any man's attentions when she still mourned the loss of Flint? Was her heart so treacherous? "That is kind of you, my lord."

"Not kind at all, merely the truth." He stopped. "Ah-ha! I have found the empty spot, and lucky man that I am, it appears I shall have the gift of your gracious company at dinner."

"So it does." She gently set the card back where she'd found it. "If you will excuse me, my lord. I'm certain my sister will have marked my absence." Ros turned and walked calmly from the dining room, doing her best to hide her dismay. Her foray into the dining room had not gone as planned, and now, there was no escaping the attentions of Lord Cunningham. Of course, the vengeful side of her—and despite her best efforts, there was a vengeful side—hoped that Flint would learn of her dinner companion and find himself knotted up in a fit of jealousy. Perhaps then, he would relent on his refusal to consider her for his wife. She sighed at the errant thought. It was bad form, and she knew it, but she was finding it difficult to let Flint go gracefully. Was love truly so blind?

"There you are," Julia's brow unfurled. "I was beginning to think I would need to send out a search party for you."

Ros smiled. "I ran into Lord Cunningham, and he detained me for a few moments as he said hello."

"Oh, is he here?" Wolf looked around the room.

"He is. And while I know he and Flint are not particularly friendly, he was nothing less than a gentleman while we spoke." Ros eyed her sister's husband, trying to gauge his response. Perhaps he would be the one to carry the tale back to Flint? Trying hard not to relish the prospect, she could not pass up the opportunity to see if that was true. "In fact, he implied that I would see him at dinner. I wonder if he might be my partner?"

Wolf offered little to no response, though, Julia cringed.

"That man is a bit too full of himself to make an adequate dinner partner. I imagine he will spend the entire meal regaling you with tales of his supposed exploits."

Ros considered. "Well, he was perfectly polite and a passable conversationalist when I danced with him at the Halpern's ball. I would expect nothing less again this evening."

Julia snorted. "That man is far too conceited to be either of those things. If he was, then he wants something."

Ros wanted to swat her sister but refrained from such uncouth behavior. "We shall see."

An hour later, everyone went in for dinner, and Ros took her seat beside Lord Cunningham. Wolf took his seat on Ros's other side while her sister sat across the table from them.

With a forced smile, she turned to Lord Cunningham, "Have you been enjoying yourself this evening?"

"Indeed." He offered what Ros assumed was meant to be a charming grin, but with the sharp glint in his blue-gray eyes appeared more predatory. "Between the lovely company I found earlier and again here, how could I not enjoy myself?"

Julia coughed—not so delicately—from across the table as Wolf stared at them utterly nonplussed.

Ros felt her cheeks once again warm from the attention paid her, even as a pit formed in her stomach. Cunningham's attention felt wrong. She supposed she was simply not over Flint, yet gamely tried to respond. "You are too kind, my lord."

"Never say it. I speak nothing but the truth. You are a lovely woman, and I find myself fortunate to be your dinner partner." His gaze drifted from her face, down the column of her throat, and lingered on her breasts.

Whereas she would have found such a look from Flint to be arousing, she couldn't deny that the shiver snaking down her spine was one of distaste. But, she reasoned, if Wolf carried the tale of his attentions back to Flint, perhaps the man would be moved to see reason with regard to their entanglement.

Feeling childish at using such a tactic, she nonetheless found herself encouraging Cunningham. With an awkward titter that grated on her own ears, she flirted with him. "I must admit I had worried about whom I would be paired with for the evening meal. I was pleased to discover a familiar face."

From the corner of her eye, she caught Julia rolling her eyes as Wolf choked on his wine. A moment later, the first course, a lovely cream of asparagus soup, was served.

By the time the fish course, merely the third course in what was to be a long procession of food, was placed before them, Ros was full of regret and guilt. She felt like an awful person for encouraging Lord Cunningham when she was still thinking of Flint. Determined to push the ornery man from her mind—and heart—she focused all her attention on her dinner partner.

By the time they reached the ice course, a welcomed palate refresher of sorbet that came mid-meal as the sixth course, she found herself genuinely liking Lord Cunningham.

"So, when my governess found me, I was knee-deep in mud, and my younger brother was splattered head to toe from my efforts." Cunningham grinned.

It was difficult to remember that she had earlier been so suspicious of the man. In truth, she was certain she had not given him a fair shake, having had her perception tainted by Flint's acerbic comments and her own sister's sour observations. Determined to reserve judgment until she had gotten to know him better, she encouraged his sharing. "I do love hearing such stories. It reminds me of my own childhood."

The stories of her, Jules, and Wolf's adventures were legion, though perhaps not appropriate for her current audience.

"You must have been a model child. I cannot imagine you traipsing about the countryside or knee-deep in mud."

She cast a conspiratorial glance at her dinner partner. "Oh, it was not I who was often knee-deep in mud. I was simply the lookout for Julia and Wolf."

Clearly surprised by her revelation, Lord Cunningham slid his gaze across the table to her beautifully coiffed sister. "I see. I had no idea someone so refined as Lady Wolfington would participate in such hijinks."

Ros sighed. "Indeed, she not only participated, but she often instigated. I was never so brave as she."

"Impossible," he declared. "You married an officer and followed him into battle. Do not minimize your courageousness, Mrs. Smith."

Resisting the urge to preen a bit, after all, she was quite accustomed to being overlooked in favor of her sister, she waived his comment off. "Doing one's duty as a wife is not courage but simple necessity."

Although, she had never had that feeling of invisibility when Flint was about. The man had a keen eye that seemed to always find her no matter who else might be in the room.

But he no longer wished to spend time with her.

Flint had made that painfully clear, she reminded herself once again.

Lord Cunningham shook his head. "I disagree entirely. But, I shall defer to the lady for the moment. Perhaps another time, I might be able to persuade you to see my perspective?"

Julia and Wolf each fell silent, as though they had been listening in on her conversation with her dinner partner. And yet, she highly doubted that was the case. Nevertheless, her stomach knotted as she forced herself to smile. "Perhaps you might."

She cast a glance over her shoulder at her sister and brother-in-law and saw that they were deep in their respective conversations once more. Obviously, it had been her imagination that they were listening. But it was easier to focus on that question than address her own distress at the notion of spending time with a man other than the one she...*absolutely not*. Flint was gone from her life. It was the way he wanted it.

Cunningham—quite oblivious to her inner struggle—grinned cheekily. "Perhaps a drive through the park would sway your thinking?"

The sorbet seemed to swirl in her stomach along with the fish course that had come before. Her head spun a bit, and for a moment, she was certain everything would re-emerge. Then, with a strength of will she had only discovered after following her husband to the front lines, she took hold of herself. She clamped down on the wayward desire to be sick, put a stranglehold on her errant emotions, and marshaled her face to go along with it all. "A drive would be lovely."

"Excellent." Cunningham beamed. "I shall pick you up tomorrow afternoon. We shall drive Rotten Row, and I shall persuade you of your courage."

Ros nodded, no longer able to speak for fear of what might slip past her lips. With an unsteady hand, she picked up her wine and took a sip. Then another. After her third overly large sip, she set the glass down and stolidly ignored the sympathy she saw in her sister's eyes. Lord Cunningham was right. She was courageous. She had to be, or she'd be home curled up with a pot of tea, a spot of whisky, and a book to help her forget. Because she absolutely, without a doubt, did not love Lord Flintshire. She simply couldn't.

Chapter Eleven

F lint sipped the whisky in his glass and stared at the amber liquid. It had been weeks since Ros had done as he asked and broken with him. Ignoring the dull ache in his chest, he focused on the alcohol and his upcoming fight. The who was of no consequence, but the why was...everything. Every fight helped him keep his deviance at bay. How he spent his winnings also helped ease his conscience, not that he would not—

A sharp knock broke into his thoughts before the door of his study opened. Wolf walked in and promptly settled on a couch across the room. "Hello there, Flint."

Feeling surly, he chose to grunt an acknowledgment of his friend.

"Ah, I see you are reverting to form." Wolf sighed. "Well, that's probably for the best, considering the news I bear."

Flint let his bulk rest against the woodwork of his library. "What news might that be?"

"That, my friend, would be the news that Lord Cunningham is taking Mrs. Smith out for a drive tomorrow afternoon."

Wolf sat with his arms stretched out along the back of the settee, appearing for all the world as if his news was not intended to disturb him. Flint knew his friend was making a point, was goading him. "Is he?"

He ignored the rush of anger that thrummed through him. The need to storm out of his house to find Ros and demand she stop encouraging Cunningham. Instead, he absorbed the pulse of anger and stored it for later. Saved it for when he could release the buildup, excise his demons once again. Instead of acting, he swirled his whisky in his glass.

Wolf tipped his head to one side. "Indeed, she seemed quite pleased by his attentions."

Flint's fist curled as he fought to temper the rage that threatened to break loose. "She is better off with someone society is able to accept, someone who will not bring chaos—*and danger*—into her life."

Wolf let one brow lift. "Do you really believe that?"

"I do." Flint pushed off the wall and set his glass down. "Now, I believe I am expected elsewhere."

With clipped steps, he left his friend sitting in the library as he headed out for his late evening appointment.

The next afternoon as Flint swung up into the saddle, he groaned. His ribs ached, but overall his opponent had inflicted little damage. For once, Flint had been more focused on hitting than being hit. By the time he'd finished pummeling the other man, he'd resolved that he would keep an eye on Ros and Cunningham. He knew the man couldn't be trusted, and certainly not with someone so precious as Ros.

Which was why he was currently sitting in a saddle when he should have been doing literally anything else.

He made his way to Ros's home and waited for Cunningham to appear. Standing down the lane in the shadows of an oak tree, he glanced at his watch as a rather ostentatious landau pulled up to the curb. With its gold gilt trim and surplus of cherubs, it was a wonder passersby weren't blinded by the sight. Flint rolled his eyes. At least, he was courteous enough to be prompt.

In short order, Ros appeared dressed in a fetching concoction of rose and white. He was not close enough to see, but it was not hard to imagine how the color would make her cheeks glow and her red-gold hair vibrant as though lit from within. *By God, I've become fanciful.* He shook his head and started off after the pair. If he was lucky enough, he might be able to catch a bit of their conversation. Failing in that, he would at least be able to ensure that Cunningham comported himself as a gentleman should.

They clopped along through the city streets until Hyde Park came into view. Once on the busy path, he was able to move a bit closer to the vehicle.

Cunningham's voice carried on the light afternoon breeze. "About our conversation...last night...you must...acts of daring..."

Flint growled low and angry. It sounded as though they had already become intimate—friends. Could she have so quickly found a replacement for her affections? No. The Ros he knew was loyal and trustworthy. She was not so fickle as to settle her attentions on a new man already. But, by all appearances, she was making an effort to do just that. He frowned as her laughter floated back to him.

"I cannot think..." She laughed again. "Oh, there was one...with my feet above my head...I'd never had such fun!"

Flint wanted to charge ahead and yank Ros bodily from the carriage. The bits and pieces of their conversation were outside of enough! If he could hear its entirety, he was sure he would go mad with—realization loomed over him like an angry green specter. He was jealous? Impossible. Pushing the notion aside, he focused on staying close to them.

The pair's laughter continued to torment him, almost more than his ribs. Though that at least offered sweet bliss with the bite of pain. With each passing moment, it grew harder to ignore the fact that though he wanted her with every fiber of his being, she would never be his. Despite that truth, he refused to sit by and watch Lord Cunningham use her as little more than yet another way to inflict pain on him. If he believed for a moment that the cad had any interest in her beyond her connection to him, he would back away and leave them be. But in his heart of hearts, he knew this was another barb thrown at him.

Determined to not miss anything, he risked edging closer in hopes of catching their full conversation.

Ros tipped her parasol so that her face was mostly blocked from his vantage point, though he couldn't help but stare at the gentle curve of one cheek. "Tell me, Lord Cunningham, how are you acquainted with Lord Flintshire?"

"Why, I've only met him in passing a time or two." The man looked positively sallow at the mention of Flint.

It pleased him to know how disquieting his nemesis found her mention of him.

Ros turned to look at Cunningham more fully. "Do not think I shall believe such balderdash. It was quite obvious at the Halpern's ball that you two know each other. I thought we were becoming friends."

At her obvious displeasure, Cunningham cracked a laugh. "You are a no-nonsense sort, are you not?"

"Indeed. I'm far past the age where nonsense is welcome. I am no green girl, and I have no time to entertain such business."

Cunningham sighed. "Very well. Yes, I've known Lord Flintshire since we were boys."

Ros remained silent, merely staring at her companion.

"Though we were never friends, nor do I expect we shall ever be such."

Flint nodded in agreement. There was little chance of the pair ever being chums. Not when Cunningham thrived on other people's pain.

Flint thrived only on his own. Even reveled in the orgasmic bliss that came with the manifestation of his own physical pain.

"No. I dare say that is unlikely." Ros tipped her head away from Cunningham, as though regarding him more closely. "Though I won't deny I'm curious as to why."

He, too, was curious. How would Cunningham explain the nature of their relationship?

"I would lay that at the door of different approaches to life. He and I simply do not see eye to eye on most things." Cunningham shrugged.

Ros hummed as though she might not fully accept his explanation. But Theo and Stone pulled up going the opposite direction, slowing briefly.

"Good afternoon, Lord Cunningham, Mrs. Smith." Theo smiled, and then her head tipped up just a bit higher. Flint's stomach cramped as Theo's grin grew impossibly brighter, and he suddenly knew she was going to out him. "Lord Flintshire."

Utterly exposed, Flint tipped his hat and swung past the two vehicles to make his escape. As he rode down the lane, he could feel Ros's angry stare boring into his back.

Flint knew he needed to talk to Ros about her choice in suitors. But after having been caught trailing her in the park, he was not looking forward to the prospect. Nevertheless, he returned to Ros's townhouse after riding around a bit and waited for her to return. He'd been standing down the street for twenty minutes when Cunningham's equipage pulled up. Flint grit his teeth as the cad climbed down from the landau and then assisted Ros. Watching the other man's hands linger where his own had once touched caused a ferocious burning sensation to spear through his chest. His limbs trembled as though he'd suddenly contracted a palsy, though that was obviously not the case. The need to plant his fist in his rival's face nearly overwhelmed his self-control much as it had when he was young.

In the blink of an eye, Flint was a boy of thirteen again. He'd just emerged from the boy's dorm, having found one of the younger scholarship boys in a bloody heap in a corner. He'd seen Cunningham—for though a boy, he'd borne one of his father's lesser titles as a courtesy even then—and two of his lackeys strolling out of the same hall where he'd found the boy. Enraged by the callousness of the act and the pure viciousness of the abuse, he'd settled the boy in his bed and summoned the school nurse. Then he'd promptly stormed outside and found the trio harassing yet another victim. It was outside of enough.

He'd marched up to Cunningham and spun him around so they stood face to face—or as close to that as they could, considering the older boy had probably a foot on Flint at that time. "Why don't you try picking on someone who can fight back?"

Cunningham looked him over and sneered. "And who might that be? You?"

The lackeys laughed along with Cunningham as Flint trembled with fury. In his mind's eye, the bully who'd taunted his twin brother appeared looming over the broken body that lay at the bottom of the well.

Close to losing the battle with his anger, Flint jutted his chin out. "That's right."

Again, the trio laughed. That was when the rage broke free. With a cry of anger so ragged that he could barely speak for days after the fight, Flint had swung and landed a solid jab to Cunningham's chin. The older boy reeled, stumbling back a few steps. But he recovered quickly and stepped forward. The problem was, he had no idea what had been unleashed. Flint swung again, landing another blow to his face, and sending the taller boy to the ground. Still screaming bloody murder, Flint dropped on top of his opponent and continued to pummel his face until the headmaster snatched him off the struggling form.

Leaving Cunningham bloody and crying in a heap on the ground, Flint stood next to the headmaster who had a firm grip on his arm as he jerked him once and then a second time. "Enough you two!"

Flint straightened up, the fury receding until he could see the damage he had wrought. In the end, they had both been expelled, at least for a short time. Cunningham's father had eventually convinced the school's board of trustees—by way of a *very* generous donation—to allow his son to return. Flint's father had offered no such mitigation. Instead, Flint had been forced to live with the consequences of his actions, resulting in a lonely pursuit of his education with a personal tutor under his father's disappointed, yet watchful eye.

Cunningham's carriage clattered by, pulling him out of his memories.

Drawing on his courage, Flint approached Ros's front door and knocked. Johnson answered, greeted him, and bade him wait a moment. In very short order, he returned to deny Flint entrance. "Tell Mrs. Smith, that I shall not go away until she sees me. I shall happily stand on her front stoop like some besotted suitor."

"Oh, for goodness sakes." Ros appeared from around the corner where she had clearly been listening to her butler send him off. "That will be all Johnson. I shall speak to the man here."

Flint steeled himself as her soft floral scent tickled his nose and reminded him of how delicious she smelled. Suddenly, the need for violence and confrontation slipped away, only to be replaced by a gale-force wind of desire. But she stood feet away, aloof and no longer his. One question pealed through his mind as he struggled with his control once again. *What have I done?*

Chapter Twelve

R os stood at her front door, violating every rule of etiquette she knew, and she was sure a few she had never heard of. Yet it was all for a good reason. Possibly the best one—self-preservation—because she was positive that if she allowed Flint to cross her threshold, she would instantly lose all her resolve, all of the fury that simmered deep inside, and beg him to reconsider their split.

Instead, she turned up the flame on her anger, coaxing it to a rolling boil as she stared at the too-handsome lord on her front steps. The man had had the nerve to send her packing only to slink behind her as she tried to move on. And now, he'd presented himself to...what? Why was he there? Curiosity got the best of her. "Why is it that I find you on my doorstep?"

Flint's dark brows slashed downward as he frowned. "What do you mean why? I should think that would be obvious."

"Unless you've come to beg my forgiveness—which I am not inclined to grant at the moment—I have no idea why you have come." She glared at him. She could only think of one other reason he would be there—and it seemed the most likely, considering what she knew of Flint. He was there to warn her off Lord Cunningham.

Flint resembled his namesake in that he could be quite intractable, so him relenting on their split was highly unlikely. And, all in all, she refused to make this easy on him. If he had something to say, he could bloody-well spit it out.

He sighed and gripped the back of his neck with one hand. "You must stop associating with Lord Cunningham."

She snorted. She knew he would say it, and yet it was still absurd. Had the man gone barmy?

"Ros, I say this in all earnestness. I fear he is using you to attempt to hurt me." His voice sounded wretched and worried, but she refused to take his words at face value.

"I must say, you have quite a high opinion of yourself if you think Lord Cunningham finds you worthy of his attention. Beyond that, how could he use me to hurt you? We are no longer associated. You have no feelings for me, or at least none strong enough that I might be useful in striking out at you. Certainly, any fool, let alone a man of Lord Cunningham's intellect, could determine that."

He growled as his gaze snapped up to the portico's ceiling as though he might find some guidance there. "I promise you, he is aiming at me. I'm sorry to upset you with that notion, but I could not in good conscience allow his pursuit of you to continue."

"Have you gone daft? You have no say in who pursues me or not. You surrendered any right to speak on that topic the moment you walked away from us. Now, if you are finished, I must get dressed to go out." She pushed the door closed but found it stopped abruptly.

A glance downward for patience revealed that Flint's foot blocked the door's progress along with his hand. "You must heed my warning. That man is out for revenge, and he will use any avenue afforded him, including you."

"Have a care for the wood." She glared down at his foot and then up to his hand. Perhaps it was instinct or simply ingrained manners, but he drew his appendages back across the threshold, which allowed her to neatly slam the door in his face.

The nerve of the man, to come to her door and insist she stop seeing a man she barely knew. It was too much. It wasn't nearly enough.

With a sigh, she trudged upstairs. Men were tiresome creatures. Her life had been so much calmer the last few years since her husband's passing. No strife. No one snapping orders at her or making demands. No warm embraces...tender kisses....

She harrumphed and strode into her room. A glance at the clock told her she needed to hurry. She was due at her parents' home for dinner within the hour.

Ros hated fidgeting. Inevitably, when she was with her mother, she wound up fidgeting. Which led to her mother scolding her—as if she were a girl still—for fidgeting. And like the vicious circle it was, she then fidgeted even more. It was a tiresome yet unstoppable loop.

Determined to break the pattern, Ros rose from her chair in the front salon of her parent's home and paced.

"Ros, that is a most unladylike habit. How are you going to attract a man of any quality if you choose to lumber about like a dockside floozy?" Her mother's pinched face and sharp tone brought Ros to a stop.

Had she truly just compared her to a whore? Worse yet, she'd commented as though someone stuck in those circumstances had a choice about it.

"If I were attempting to garner someone's attention, I promise you I would not pace as a means of doing so. There are far more *effective* means for a motivated young woman." She dropped enough innuendo in her comment to stop a horse. Surely, her mother would understand her point.

Her mother gasped. "That is outside of enough, young lady. Such vulgarity." Her mother paused—for dramatic effect, no doubt. "I blame your sister for this. Her hoydenish ways have tainted you."

"I dare say it's more likely that the years spent near a battlefield following my husband is the culprit. You do realize that other than wives, the only women in a military camp are the women who service the men's carnal needs, don't you?"

Her mother turned red, like a ripe tomato, yet persevered nonetheless. "Wherever the behavior came from, you should be doing your best to cease it at once. What would Lord Cunningham think if he saw such a display?"

"I should think he would assume I had something on my mind." Ros stared at her mother.

Drawing a deep breath, she suspected the direction this conversation would veer was not one she preferred. Her mother had pushed Lord Wallthorpe on her sister until she'd married Lord Wolfington in order to escape the former's clutches. It appeared her mother was fixating on Lord Cunningham in a similar fashion, which had the opposite effect of her mother's intention. Had she learned nothing from her dealings with Julia?

"I should think he would find such behavior unbecoming of his Viscountess." Her mother let one brow drift up in punctuation.

Ros snorted. "Well, lucky for him, I do not have my sights set on his person...or his title."

Her mother gave a short, sharp bark of disbelief. "Foolish, foolish girl. I have seen how he looks at you. For some benighted reason, that man has his sights set on you. You would do well to cultivate his attentions. I assumed after you broke with that hideous Lord Flintshire, that you had grown wiser when it came to choosing your next husband."

Stiffening at her mother's obvious glee over her break with Flint, Ros drew a deep calming breath and counted slowly to ten. "When I broke with Lord Flintshire, I did so because he wished it. I still care a great deal for him, though I *am* smart enough not to pursue a man who does not want my attentions. So, please do not take my current state as indicative of my being in need or want of a husband."

"That's ridiculous. Of course, you are in need of a husband. However will you live now that you are no longer able to live off your sister's largess?"

Her mother was going all in, it would seem. "I am well enough off on my own that I am not in need of either funds from my sister or a husband. I live as I do because I am an able-bodied woman with a modicum of intelligence. Were it not for my guidance, my husband would have spent us into the poor-house. *I* am the one who not only stopped him from wasting his monthly pay but took what was left after our meager expenses and multiplied it through smart investments."

Her mother possibly looked more shocked by this revelation than when Ros had informed her that she previously associated with camp prostitutes.

"Well, I never. A daughter of mine engaged in *business*?" Her mother pressed her handkerchief to her lips and then to her forehead as she sank back into her chair and moaned.

Ros's father strode into the room, apparently having heard the commotion. "What is going on in here?"

Fed up with her mother's pressure as well as her theatrics, Ros sailed toward her father. "You chose to marry her; you deal with this. I'm quite finished with her histrionics."

With that, Ros left her parent's home and went in search of her carriage. It was past time she went home and achieved a sliver of peace and quiet. Her day had been one stressful encounter after another. She wasn't sure which was worse, dealing with Flint's ridiculous demands that she stop seeing Lord Cunningham, or her mother's insistence that she cultivate the man's attentions. And the thing of it was, she was damned if she wanted to make either one of them happy. But what was she to do?

Chapter Thirteen

F lint was doggedly trying to move on. Some—mostly his friends, and most certainly their wives—would have said he was in denial. He preferred to think of it as shaping his destiny. In either circumstance, he was not allowing himself to think about Ros. Mostly.

Instead, he was out running a few errands and doing his best to stay focused on his own agenda. He first stopped by his haberdasher and picked up a new brown felt riding hat, then he was to swing by his club for lunch with Stone, Cooper, and Wolf. After that, he was off to his solicitors for his dreaded monthly update.

By the time he was settled in Mr. John G. Brown, Esquire's office, it was mid-afternoon. With the sun weakening and his belly full, he was already feeling drowsy. Of course, Mr. Brown woke him up immediately. "My lord, it seems your...uh...rather particular investment has experienced some difficulties."

Flint tried to imagine what the man was referring to. "Do stop with all the vague euphemisms. Which investment of mine are you referring to?"

The tall thin man peered down at Flint from behind his spectacles. "The one you wished to remain extremely private."

"Ah, I see." Flint looked around. "I believe we are the only ones in the room unless you are hiding someone beneath your desk."

The lawyer looked rather startled at the notion, even bending down to peer under his desk. Once he straightened back up, he looked as dour as ever. "No, my lord, there is no other individual in the room. We are quite alone."

Flint managed to suppress his sigh. "Then, please feel free to discuss the topic openly."

"Very well. It seems the boy's home in Flintshire has a well that has gone dry. In addition, coal supplies are looking bleak this coming winter, and most, if not all, of the boys are in need of new clothing."

Confusion slithered through him as he tried to reconcile his lawyer's words with what he believed to be true. "Do we not send them monies in accordance with their requested budget each quarter?"

Mr. Brown looked distinctly uncomfortable. "We do, my lord. However, the headmaster has indicated that he never received last quarter's funds. This is impossible as I have the receipt for the quarterly allotment right here. It was dispatched at the end of the previous quarter via courier, and received a few days later."

Flint considered the situation. Perhaps he was due to take a break from the city? It would certainly give him time to clear his head and put one strawberry blonde from his mind.

"There is also the matter of the dwindling funds in the particular account you fund the home from. We have not seen the usual frequency of deposits of late, my lord."

Too true. Flint hadn't fought much while he had been busy paying court to Ros. Though he was certainly making up for lost time of late. "Yes, well, I'll take the necessary funds from my personal account when I head to Flintshire to see what has occurred. If you will send me the details of how much is required, I shall ensure all is on the up and up."

Mr. Brown inclined his head. "As you wish, my lord. Might I suggest you have someone accompany you in case something foul is afoot?"

Flint laughed. "I believe I am quite well equipped to protect myself should the need arise. But thank you for your concern, Mr. Brown. Now, on to the rest of the business."

An hour later, Flint stood and stretched the first vestiges of stiffness from his back and shoulders. While important, he did not find these sessions to be overly interesting.

Two hours later, he gratefully exited his solicitor's office and headed toward home. It was a fine summer day, which put him in mind to walk since his home was not far. Clearly, he was not alone in his inclination since the sidewalk was full of people walking to their destinations in lieu of a cab ride.

Anxious to make arrangements to travel home so he could deal with this unexpected problem with his boys' home, he considered what Mr. Brown had been able to tell him. By all accounts, it would seem that either the courier or his headmaster was proving to be dishonest. He had vetted the headmaster's credentials and references when he'd been hired two years earlier. The courier came from a bonded and licensed firm. In either case, it was a truly disappointing turn of events.

Puzzled by the whole thing, he was lost in thought when he was suddenly pushed into a dark alley. The two buildings creating the narrow throughway rose so tall that the summer sun was nearly blotted out. He quickly recognized one of the three men currently surrounding him, the ringleader from the first message he was given.

"This is a rather unfortunate state of affairs, my lord." He sounded truly sorry, which instantly raised Flint's hackles. "It seems you did not take my first message to heart. My employer is rather displeased by this."

Flint snorted. "Well, he should accustom himself to such feelings as I don't suspect I shall be any more apt to heed your warnings this time around."

Flint warily eyed the two hulking giants on either side of him. Up to that point, they'd made no move to lay hands on him, but he suspected that would change shortly. The question was, should he wait until they made their move or make one of his own?

The leader sighed. "We were afraid you might feel that way." He gave a short nod to one of the men.

Flint knew his time was up; he had to make a move or choose to take another beating. The man on his right stepped in and reached for Flint's arm. He jerked away from him and used his elbow to crack the man on his left in the nose. He'd been caught with his hands down, reaching for where he'd expected Flint's arms to be, which left his face vulnerable.

With the man on the right off-balance, Flint shifted toward him and jabbed him in the face. The brute grunted and kept moving toward him.

That was unexpected.

Stepping backward, he let the big man slide right past him, allowing him to place his foot on his arse and give a mighty heave. This sent the man from his right side careening into the man from the left who was still howling about his broken nose.

Flint turned and sprinted toward the alley, but then suddenly, everything went dark.

Lying on his back on the sodden cobblestones of the alley, he blinked as a dull ache rolled through his head. Abruptly, he was heaved to his feet.

"My apologies, my lord. I didn't mean to crack you so hard, but I was aware from our last meeting that you have a penchant for fighting and a rather thick skull." Apparently, he had not been out for all that long since his assailants were still with him.

"Bloody hell. Couldn't your employer simply send round a note?" Flint's head felt like it had been split open.

"Well, since you barely seem to listen to these messages, I rightly suspect you'd simply toss a note in the fire and keep moving."

He was likely spot on, Flint had to concede.

"At any rate, you've not heard the new message," he started and then paused.

Annoyance and a worsening headache made Flint even more impatient than normal. "Do get on with it."

The ringleader laughed. "Very well, then. My employer highly recommends you reconsider his previous offer."

"No, thank you. I shall still decline. Are we quite done here?" Flint straightened up, regaining some of his own power.

"Here now." The man shook his head. "You haven't let me finish."

Flint stood with the two thugs hands firmly gripping his arms, which allowed him no opportunity to move away.

"If you continue to be stubborn about this, then I am to point out that if you do not do as we ask, your lady friend—Mrs. Smith—shall suffer the consequences."

Fury, sharp and bright, shafted through him. With a surge of energy he could not credit, he lunged toward the ring-leader dragging the two very large brutes holding him along the way. "If you should dare to lay a finger on that lady, I shall hunt you and your employer through every gutter, turn over every rock, and search every stinking tavern in London and beyond until I end you. Do not make the mistake of believing I would sit idly by."

The messenger looked rather taken aback by the whiplash of anger Flint had unleashed. Though, he seemed undaunted. "You would do well to heed this warning, my lord. The only way to protect her is to do as my employer wishes."

And with that dire warning, the man turned and dashed down the alley and out onto the streets. The thugs shoved Flint to the ground and followed suit. By the time he'd scrabbled to his feet and made his way to the busy street, the trio had melted into the crowd and disappeared.

Fear and anger thrummed through his veins, making his head pound all the more. They had threatened Ros. Despite his best efforts to separate himself from her, he had failed. His mere association with her had put her in danger, and now, he had no choice but to protect her as best he could. It was quite obvious that leaving her alone was not working from any perspective. It had left her vulnerable to both Cunningham and now these thugs.

Still gripping his head, he staggered into the street, ignoring the shocked looks he received as he made his way home.

An hour later, he sat in his study with two of the Lustful Lords, Linc and Arthur. And despite his throbbing head, he found himself focused and ready to take action. "Gentlemen, I thank you for coming so quickly. It seems I have a situation on my hands that requires your assistance. As you both know, I have long been involved in the dockside fight circles. Somehow, I have garnered the attention of an unsavory sort who has requested in no uncertain terms that I throw my next fight. I, of course, refused this request. As a result, I have received a couple of beatings—little did they know how ineffective that sort of persuasion would be with me."

"Bloody hell!" Linc growled as he sat forward. "Do you know who is behind this?"

"I do not. Not yet, at any rate." Flint paused. "The situation grew more dire as of today's message *cum* beating, which included a threat against Ros."

Both of the men cursed at once.

Flint gave them a moment to settle back down. "David, one of my footmen and occasional sparring partner, is watching her home as we speak. Considering she is as likely to shoot me as listen to me if I tried to speak to her at the moment, I believe having someone watch her is the best way to keep her safe. I am hoping that you two will be willing to assist with that."

"Of course, we are happy to help." Arthur looked at Linc, who nodded in confirmation.

"Thank you. If one of you two could relieve David later on, I would greatly appreciate it. I have a call to make to try and get to the bottom of who is behind this mess."

"Flint, having gotten to know the Fairchild women, I would encourage you to alert Ros to the situation sooner rather than later." Linc shook his head.

"I shall consider your suggestion. I plan to ask Lucifer for information. If that proves fruitful, I hope I am able to resolve this issue without having to alert her to any possible threat."

"I assure you, Emily would be furious if Cooper or I kept something like this from her. I do not suggest you delay," Arthur added his voice.

Flint sighed, he knew they were likely right, but first, he had to convince the woman to speak to him again.

Following through on his plan, Flint followed the hulking form of Frank Lucifer's second-in-command along the gallery overlooking an empty gambling den. He counted himself fortunate that all he earned from a second encounter with this messenger was an aching head that had yet to ease. It, at least, kept his mind off the fact he was walking into an uncomfortable and unpredictable situation.

For the first time in as many years as he could remember, he was not in a position of power. His size and skills were of no use. His wealth was likely to hold little value. His title meant nothing to a man who dealt in information. And since Flint was not in the thick of society, he had little information that could be considered of worth. He was simply a man who needed another man's help.

He felt vulnerable. Impotent in a way he had never experienced before.

His guide opened the double doors to Lucifer's office. It was tea time, the late afternoon slipping into early evening for the civilized world—clearly, that did not apply to his host. With his dark hair tousled and a hastily tied robe that left far more chest exposed than Flint was interested in seeing, Lucifer made the fact that Flint had interrupted him more than evident. "This is an unexpected turn of events. How is it that you have come to visit me at such an unseemly hour?"

Flint snorted. "Most of London has been dressed for hours and is sitting down to tea and sandwiches as we speak. I hardly classify this time of day as unseemly."

Lucifer pulled an unlit stump of a cigar from a metal tube sitting on his desk and rectified that problem. "That may well be true for most of society. After all, they *do* have all those tedious social obligations to attend to. However, those of us living in the underbelly of London have somewhat different social mores. Turning up on someone's doorstep at five in the afternoon is akin to paying a morning call actually in the morning." He drew on the cigar and relaxed back into his chair. "In any event, here you are, and I must say I am keen to hear why."

Having had little interaction with Lucifer, and certainly none so intimate as a conversation, there was an air of familiarity to him that—though faint—Flint found bothersome. He let the silence draw out between them as he tried to put his finger on what had caught his eye. The elusive notion slipped away as good manners and the rather pressing nature of his business took the upper hand. "I am in need of information of a sort I believe you are uniquely qualified to be of assistance with."

Lucifer's brows drew together as he sat quietly across from Flint.

Undaunted, Flint continued. "It seems I have attracted the notice of someone who feels very strongly that I should begin losing my fights. So much so, that they have now accosted me twice on the street, the first time using physical means to attempt to persuade me and, most recently, having made threats against someone important to me. I am inclined to solve the mystery of *who* is behind these threats."

"I see. That all sounds fairly ominous. Why haven't you approached the Metropolitan Police? Certainly, the Raw Lobsters might be of assistance to you in this?"

Flint snorted. "I suspect your going rate would be cheaper than theirs, besides I'd hazard that your network is far stronger."

"How is it you think I—or my network—may be of assistance?"

Fear, insidious and chilling, snaked down his spine. It was a bitter pill to swallow that this man could easily say no to his request, and he would have little recourse. He would have to find another way to end the threat against Ros. "You are an information broker. Frankly, I don't know if I have anything you might value, but I am willing to pay for the name of the person at the root of this problem."

Lucifer remained impassive—inscrutable, even—merely sucking on his cigar. The pop and hiss of the burning tobacco the only sound between them. For long moments, doubt assailed Flint, convincing him the man across the desk would deny him. Turn him away without a by-your-leave, and render him impotent in protecting Ros. It was a truly humbling moment.

Standing, Lucifer stubbed out the cigar carefully, ensuring the likely expensive vice did not heedlessly turn to ash in his absence and returned it to the tube. "I'll look into the matter and be in touch." Then he stepped from behind the desk to leave.

Confused and off balance by the abrupt departure, Flint rose and reached out, stopping Lucifer with a hand on his bicep. Lucifer stared at Flint's restraining touch.

Desperation pushed Flint past any sense of good manners or self-preservation. "When will I hear from you? How much do you want?" He drew back his hand and shoved it through his hair, ignoring the way it shook slightly. "Hell, *what* do you want as payment?"

Lucifer drilled him with a hard stare. "You will hear from me when I have something to tell you, not before. As for what I want? That will depend."

Flinching, he cursed silently. "On what?"

"Any number of things." Lucifer's deadpan statement offered no balm to Flint's worry. "Now, if you don't mind, I have two eager ladies keeping my bed warm until I return."

With that dismissal, Lucifer walked out of his office through a door tucked off to the side. Alone and with little more hope than when he'd entered the place, Flint retreated. He needed to let his solicitor know he would be postponing that trip to the boys' home for a bit. In fact, perhaps he'd better find someone to look into that situation? He needed to focus on finding a way to convince Ros to either take him back or, at least, let him protect her. Again. Failure was not an option he could stomach, but what would he do if she sent him packing? He supposed he'd find out soon enough since Ros was his next stop.

Chapter Fourteen

Ros had thrown caution to the wind. She'd left her parasol at home and ventured out with a bonnet that had little enough brim that she could still catch someone in her peripheral vision. Some might say her behavior was shocking. She would have informed them that she had perpetrated far worse atrocities as the wife of a military man, let alone in her pursuit of Lord Flintshire. Strolling without a parasol was hardly a drop in the midst of a London deluge.

"It is quite a fine day, Mrs. Smith. And I am grateful you agreed to accompany me for such an unconventional outing as a stroll in Hyde Park at such an unfashionable hour." Lord Cunningham grinned as he patted her hand tucked into the crook of his arm.

She resisted the urge to roll her eyes. It had barely been two days since their last visit, but she'd agreed to see him once more. Considering the pressure her mother was applying, she needed to decide if she intended to allow his courtship of her to continue. All things considered, the outlook was not favorable for him. While generally pleasant enough, there was something about him that did not sit well. Considering she could not quite put her finger on the issue, she trusted her instincts enough not to continue the association—or, at least, she once would have.

That was part of the problem.

Between her secretly failed marriage and then her failure to recognize Flint's desire to part ways, she was no longer sure of her own instincts. Which is how she found herself trotting along a sparsely traveled Rotten Row sans parasol and in need of some reply to Lord Cunningham's conversational sally. "Well, it is such a lovely day, how could I have said no?"

She was not a practiced flirt, and the entire exchange felt awkward and unwieldy in a way she had never experienced with Flint. A walk with him would have been full of comfortable silences and shared amusements. Perhaps even a few discrete caresses. Pushing the unwanted thoughts aside, she forced herself to cease the pointless comparison. It was unfair to Lord Cunningham—to any man, really—and a complete waste of her prudent thought processes. She needed those blasted things to fend off Lord Cunningham while not giving him offense. She sighed. She really must find a way to gently send him on his way.

Her companion looked pleased as punch, his glee causing her insides to twist and tangle. She had once seen a cat caught in a hedge, his body snared by tightly woven branches and leaves. He struggled to free himself, first yanking on his back legs, then twisting this way and that, all to no avail. By the time she'd crossed the field so she could free him, he was positively stricken with the notion that he would never be free.

That was how she felt at the moment.

Trapped. Unable to free herself from her entanglement. And afraid that something awful was bound to happen as a result.

That was when she noticed that Cunningham had slowed their pace. Concern nudged her to speak up. "My lord, is everything well?"

He sighed softly. "I have told you to call me Donald, or at the very least, Cunningham. Your hesitation to be more familiar worries me."

He stopped them altogether.

"Tell me you are as fond of me as I am you." Then he leaned in to kiss her, his face alive with hope and anticipation.

Surprised, Ros leaned back and placed a hand on his chest to stay his approach. "My lord, I'm afraid my fondness is more of the friendship variety."

The hope slid from his face, the light in his grey eyes dimming as he stiffened. "Oh. I see."

But she didn't think he did as he had not released her yet. Still pressing away from him, her heart pounded in her chest. For someone who had appeared lean and not very muscular, his hold on her was incredibly strong. Panic surged as blood rushed through her veins, the sound of it drowning out everything around her. For all she would have known, she could have been standing on Bond Street at mid-day. So it was quite a surprise when his lip curled in frustration as he continued to attempt to kiss her, only to have him suddenly release her.

Disoriented and off-balance, she stumbled away from him. As she found her footing, a shout rang out, and she looked up into a wall of black. Black horses and a black carriage were barreling down on her.

A scream strangled in her throat as something slammed into her, knocking her from her feet. As she rolled in the dirt and leaves on Rotten Row, she swore the carriage had hit her, but then she realized that wasn't possible. Because if it had, she would undoubtedly be dead. And though she felt like a twenty-stone weight pressed down on her, she did not think she was injured other than the aches one would expect after taking a tumble.

"Ros! Ros, can you hear me?" An all too familiar—and at the moment welcome—voice cut through her own self-assessment.

Opening her eyes, she found Flint's worried countenance a hair's breadth from her own face. "I suspect the whole of London heard you, my lord."

While his weight did little to ease the aches she had only just acquired, she was reluctant to lose the intimate feel of him pressed against her once more. It had been far too long since they had been in a similar position.

He pressed up on his arms. "I must be crushing you."

"Please, don't get up on my account." She couldn't control the huskiness of her voice nor the desire that had snuck in once she realized that she was both alive and unhurt.

Off to the side, Lord Cunningham cleared his throat. "Mrs. Smith! Are you unhurt?"

Flint got to his feet and then reached down to help her up as well. "Ros, are you well?"

Worry still creased his face, but he was, at least, no longer yelling in her face. "I am as well as one could expect to be under the circumstances. Though I suspect I shall feel the impact of your body striking mine for days to come."

"I am terribly sorry about that, but there was no other way to get you out of the way in time. I saw that blasted carriage barreling down on you and simply reacted. I hope I didn't cause you too much harm." Flint glanced about awkwardly.

Ros swore she heard a tremor in his voice. What was the man doing here? Had he been following her again? "I'm certain you caused less damage than that rampaging vehicle would have." She took a breath—not terribly deep, thanks to her corset—and attempted to still her trembling hands. "I suppose I am quite lucky you were here to save me."

"I was just about to pull you back when Lord Flintshire barreled into you." Cunningham huffed and folded his arms, his petulance rather awe-inspiring in the face of her near death.

Annoyance with the overweening man swelled up from deep within. "While I am sure you were about to do any number of heroic things, it seems Lord Flintshire managed to take action. A fact for which I am eternally grateful."

Flint glared at Cunningham as her brother-in-law and sister drew to a halt beside them. "Good day, Flint, Rosalind," Wolf paused and seemed to force a final greeting out. "Lord Cunningham."

"Lord Wolfington, Lady Wolfington." Cunningham bowed and straightened up.

"Is everything well? Ros, you look as though you've been rolling in the grass." Her sister let one brow lift in punctuation of her statement.

"Such a keen observation, Julia. It seems that I was very nearly run over by a carriage a few moments ago. Lord Flintshire was kind enough to knock me to the ground before disaster could have its way with me." She offered a mischievous smile.

"Oh, my! Are you hurt?" Julia leaned forward in concern.

"Well, I do feel as though my bones have been rubbed together. But otherwise, I am unharmed." Ros reached up to pat her head and realized half her hair was dangling from what had been a perfectly lovely arrangement.

"I should think so. Has anyone sent for a carriage to collect you? Certainly, they do not think you should walk home after such a trying event?" Julia stared pointedly at the men who were still standing about rather helplessly.

"We had only just stood up from the ground. I don't think we had progressed so far as to consider how any of us would make our way home," Flint offered. "I don't suppose we could impose on your generous nature and request a ride for your sister?"

Julia beamed at him. "Why we'd be happy to assist you and Ros."

"Oh, well, my carriage is not far off. I would be happy to aid Mrs. Smith in getting home since I was her escort." Cunningham looked decidedly unhappy at the prospect of letting her leave with her sister, but more importantly, in the company of Flint.

"Pish," Julia replied. "My carriage is right here, and she should not be forced to stand here in such disarray any longer than is required. Besides which she is family. Lord Flintshire, you may squeeze in with us since Lord Cunningham seems to have his own means to get home near at hand."

Grateful for her sister's intervention, Ros practically climbed into the carriage on her own before Flint reacted and offered his assistance. The man smartly followed her into the vehicle, and before Cunningham could offer any strenuous objections, they were on their way.

As they drove along, the men chatting about some card game that occurred recently, it dawned on Ros that she had many questions about what had occurred. First, she realized that Cunningham had been attempting to kiss her despite her wishes otherwise. Had he not pulled her off the path to do just that, they would have been in far greater peril walking on the path, oblivious to what would have been behind them. Secondly, she had never asked Flint the obvious question, what was he doing there? Surely he had given up following her about after their last argument? Also, why was that carriage driving so fast? Had the driver even shouted a warning for her? She did not remember hearing any such injunction.

And finally, how had her sister and her husband appeared so conveniently after her spill?

Her head buzzed with the questions, and with the rather violent tumble she'd taken. Once they returned to her home, she would make a point to ask all of those very excellent questions. In the meantime, she merely wanted to rest and catch her breath.

Upon their arrival, she retired upstairs to put herself to rights. By the time her hands ceased to shake, and her hair was back in a neat coil, she felt more composed. With a determined sense of purpose, she returned downstairs to find her sister and brother-in-law had departed. Flint sat alone, looking somewhat more restored as well.

"I see our erstwhile saviors have gone." She couldn't help but suspect something was afoot. Though, she wouldn't go so far as to think Flint had somehow arranged to have a carriage try to run her down.

"They needed to return home to change for a dinner party." He sat with his hands gripping the edge of the settee as though his hold were the only thing keeping him anchored.

"Perhaps that is for the best. I have some rather direct questions I would appreciate answers to." She paused and pressed on. "How is it that you came to be in Hyde Park today right when I was in need of rescue?"

His jaw clenched and released only to repeat the movement again. She might have missed the minuscule motion had she not been looking at him so intently.

She sighed. "You were following me, despite my previous objections."

Rising to his feet, Flint prowled about the confines of her small salon. After a few moments of his walking back and forth while he muttered to himself and shoved his fingers through his hair, he finally halted in front of her. Then he ground out a reply, however reluctantly. "I did not believe you to be safe under the circumstances. Your safety has always been of prime importance to me."

Frustration bubbled up and over. "I am perfectly capable of taking care of myself. Regardless of what you or my sister think, I am not incapable of a little self-preservation."

"It was not a question of your capability." He dismissed her concern as easily as one swatted a gnat. Looming over her, his gaze had turned a stormy gray that reflected the whirlwind of emotions he struggled to control. Then he grabbed her shoulders and hauled her into his arms. "I've never met a more capable woman. Capable of marshaling everyone about her. Capable of storming past all my defenses."

And then he slammed his lips down on hers. A groan ripped from her throat as she melted into him despite all her concerns. Her excellent questions dissipated on the tides of his passion as he demanded entrance to her mouth. Past logical thought, she opened to him. Welcomed him. If this was all she might have, she would take it and savor the feel of him pressed against her for years to come.

Chapter Fifteen

F lint couldn't believe his luck. His headache had finally abated, despite the tumble they'd taken, and Ros was in his arms—for the moment. But did this mean she was his to take to bed and pleasure? Perhaps it was ungallant of him, but he had always acknowledged that he was not quite a gentleman. And there was no question a gentleman would release her and step away.

In his defense, it had been weeks since he'd touched her. And he recognized that his feelings for her grew stronger every day—only to be enflamed by seeing her put in danger. Add to that, he had yet to mention the threat against her, and he feared that when he did tell her, she would refuse his protection. Refuse him altogether after the abhorrent fashion he'd employed to drive her away. Wanting her with every fiber of his being, he couldn't possibly let her go. Not in this moment. Perhaps not ever.

Despite being in a relatively pain-free state, his cock was hard and eager to sink into her warm depths. It was unusual for him to be so aroused without the benefit of a little pain, but he welcomed the change. Welcomed having her in his arms again. Breaking the kiss as he climbed the stairs, neither spoke. Each seeming to choose to be complicit in their avoidance of any discussion about what was about to happen or ascribing any meaning to whatever it might be.

Inside her bedroom, he saw touches of Ros everywhere—the cheery pink and white wallpaper, her floral scent hanging heavy in the air, making him dizzy with desire. He had yet to put a name to the smell, but it never failed to conjure images of Ros spread open to him. Made him harden with a need only she could satisfy. Even without the added pleasure of physical pain, he found no lack of interest in taking her to bed.

Letting her legs down first, he pressed her closer to his chest, causing her body to slide against his. Her breathing grew labored as their gazes met, and then she licked her lips as though his kiss lingered there. With a groan born of pure need, he captured her mouth again, letting the chance to speak slip away once more. While there were things they should discuss, the need to touch her and reassure himself she was there with him and safe far outstripped the need to speak.

Their tongues twined, a sensuous tangle as the faint taste of mint invaded his senses. The cool fresh taste made him wonder if she had hoped for just such an outcome. He certainly had. The heat of her seared him through the many layers of clothing they still wore, becoming a silent reproach for their overdressed state. Removing his hands from her person, he reached up and unfastened her gown, slowly working the back of it open. Once it was loose enough to tug it off her shoulders and down to her waist, he began working on her corset. All the while, he cursed the many layers dictated by the arbiters of women's fashion. Would that they lived in a simpler time, such as the Romans with their ever practical togas, because then he would have her flesh exposed. His to touch and taste once more.

Instead, he wrestled with the never-ending layers of clothing. He attacked her petticoats and hoops until the whole mass of fabric swooshed to the floor. Still kissing her deeply, reveling in her sweetness, he loosened her corset and peeled it off her, before finally tackling her chemise and pantalets. With naught but her stockings between her and his touch, he shifted his focus to his own clothing.

She tore her lips from his as she helped jerk his coat off. "Hurry. I need you."

Enflamed by such raw honesty, he worked faster to free himself. He tore at his necktie as she opened his trousers. Between the two of them, without her distracting kisses, he was stripped bare in a fraction of the time he'd needed to accomplish the same for her. With his heated skin exposed to the cooler air—after all, there wasn't much that wasn't cooler than a raging inferno—he sank to his knees before her. Part supplication, part worship, and all need, he tugged one of her legs over his shoulder and clamped his hands down on her arse.

The luscious roundness filled his hands as he pulled her wet pussy toward his mouth.

"Flint, wait." She grabbed a handful of his hair and used it to pull his head back from his goal.

The slight sting of pain only served to inflame his desire as he looked up at her. "What do you need, Ros?"

"You. I need you inside me." She hesitated, pulling harder on his hair as he tried to press forward to taste what was so tantalizingly close. "Please," she begged. "I ache."

He looked up at her, could see the tight pucker of her nipples, the way her chest rose and fell with each harsh breath, and the deep flush of desire riding high on her cheeks. She needed him as much as he needed her, and he would never deny her what he could give. Still relishing the sting of his scalp, he released her leg and rose to his feet, breaking her hold on his hair. "On the bed, sweet."

Eagerly, she turned and scrambled onto the mattress, sprawling across it in open invitation. His cock throbbed, almost vibrating with expectation. Crawling between her thighs, he returned her leg to his shoulder, notched his shaft at her entrance, and then sank deep within her in one desperate stroke.

Heat engulfed him, wrapped around his cock, and squeezed as though it could extinguish his desire. Instead, his need grew, doubled, tripled with each slide out and then back into her tight pussy. It seemed he sank deeper with each stroke until his hips met hers, and he could grind against her clit.

"Yes!" She shouted loudly as he worked in and out of her. Her fingers gripped his arms, sinking her nails into his flesh with a sharpness that only added to the conflagration of his lust. The small bites of pain merged with the heat and sweet slide of her body wrapped around him until he felt his balls draw tight.

Bracing on one arm, he reached down and dragged his thumb over her swollen nub. Once. Twice. And then with a third stroke paired with his cock stretching her, filling her, she finally crashed over the edge. With a scream of satisfaction that pushed his own release closer, he pumped inside of her over and over, driving toward his own release. With his thumb still strumming her clit, his own climax slammed into him harder than the runaway carriage would have. He shouted his own pleasure as he withdrew from her heat and pumped his shaft in his hand while spilling on her stomach.

Exhausted, he slumped down on top of her, letting his seed mark them both as he lay there, panting for breath, his sides heaving. All the while, Ros caressed his back and shoulders as she sighed softly in his ear. The gentleness of the moment overwhelmed and welcomed him, all at once. He had to fight hard not to burrow into her, to beg for the succor she offered at a moment when he'd never felt more exposed. Because he knew, in that moment, if he looked her in the eyes, all the emotions he felt for her would be visible, and he wasn't sure he was prepared for such vulnerability. The depth of his feelings was so new, like a raw nerve had been uncovered.

While it was a sweet pain that he welcomed, he needed a little time to become familiar with it, to understand how it would change him. Because there was no question it would. He snorted mentally, hellfire it already had. But what would it mean for them? For their future? What if something happened to him? What if he couldn't be the man she needed? What about his need for pain? Certainly, their interlude was hot, rife with caring and emotion. Would that be enough? Could he give up his pain laced ways? Doubt assailed him until it drove him from her arms and her bed.

"Let me get a rag to clean you up." He gave her his back, hiding his truth as he pulled himself together.

"Flint, don't retreat from me." Ros rose up behind him, reaching out to stroke his back before he stepped away.

He glanced over his shoulder and offered what he hoped was a distracting smile. "Not retreating, merely getting a rag."

She smiled at him, but the apprehension clouded her lovely green gaze as she let him go. He hoped it would be the last time he forced her to do such a thing because he wasn't sure he could survive walking away from her again. Despite that, he had never been so terrified in all his life. Terrified to stay, to feel, to fall in love.

He found a rag and returned to clean Ros off. With a few firm swipes, he removed the evidence of his claiming. If only he could wipe the distinct sense of vulnerability away so easily.

Was it only a few days ago that he'd thought he'd felt exposed?

Asking Lucifer for help had nothing on how raw he felt looking at Ros lying in bed and knowing that for the first time since his twin brother died, he had a weakness.

Chapter Sixteen

I t had been two days since her reconciliation with Flint, and she still hadn't been able to remove the grin from her lips. Happiness was a state of being, not just an emotion—her obstinate hair had curled just right, the sun shone brightly, the birds sang sweetly, and Mrs. Johnson had made sweet rolls that morning. Despite the joy bubbling through her, there was one shadow hanging over her charmed existence. Flint still required pain, yet he had spoken not a word of his desires.

Since the weather was so lovely, she'd decided a jaunt would be an ideal way to deal with her short list of errands. The brisk walk would help her mind work through the question at hand: How did she manage the issue of Flint's need for pain?

As she passed people on the street, she considered what she knew. Flint was a man who preferred to be in control, but he had not been incapable of letting her take the lead. He clearly fought down by the docks as a way to receive the pain he craved in an acceptable manner. And there was a sexual component to the whole mess that she still wasn't quite sure about. Oh, and he was not aware that she had discerned his secret.

Theo had suggested she visit Mistress Lash, who was known for her skills with floggers, whips, and the sort. Ros considered that a conversation with the woman was in order to, at least, help her understand what might make a man crave pain the way Flint did. Such a conversation might lead to other possibilities.

"Mrs. Smith, how are you doing today?" Lord Cunningham stood before her on the street, blocking her way forward.

"My lord, I am well." Her body tensed as she drew up short. An instinctive desire to retreat warred with her awareness that to do so would give the man the upper hand. She pressed on with her walk and her coming errands.

Despite her obvious wish to be on her way, Cunningham stayed her with a hand to her upper arm. A breach in etiquette if ever there was. She stopped on the sidewalk and stared down at his hand on her arm. When her gaze met his, she could not ignore the coldness that settled in his eyes. "Do not be fooled by Flintshire's supposed heroics the other day. I dare say he likely arranged for that *accident* to occur so that he could swoop in and rescue you."

"My lord, I had wished to put that incident in the past. However, if you are insisting on bringing it to the fore, I dare say you had far more motive and opportunity to make such an arrangement. Perhaps I should be considering the same of you?" She let one brow lift in arrogant inquiry.

He sputtered as though grappling for words and then sneered at her. "I see that you are already tainted goods. Only a woman engaged in inappropriate behavior with a man such as Flintshire—one of those, so-called Lustful Lords—would defend him. It was best I discovered the truth before I made more of a fool of myself chasing after you."

And with that comment, he released her arm and stormed past as though they'd never stopped to chat. Put out and annoyed by such churlish behavior, she pressed on with her walk. She refused to let that man ruin her day.

With the sun hanging high in the sky, she had accomplished her errands and returned home. It was possibly a bit early, but she decided to send a note over to the infamous Mistress Lash and see if she might be amenable to an early visitor.

Two hours later, she found herself exiting a cab in front of The Market. The white façade was rather elegant, and that effect continued upon entry into the establishment. With a grand staircase sweeping down from the second floor, the foyer was quite imposing. The butler remained standing with the door open as though she might suddenly understand where she had entered and need to remedy such a mistake. "My lady, how may I be of assistance to you?"

"Good afternoon. I am Mrs. Smith, here to see Mistress Lash." She took off her bonnet and handed it to the flabbergasted man.

He took the headwear as if by reflex, and not through any independent thought. Gathering his composure, he closed the door and nodded. "Of course, madame. I shall be but a moment."

The butler departed, leaving Ros to stand about in the foyer. She appreciated the courtesy of allowing her inside to wait, versus leaving her on the front stoop as was the usual way. Wandering about the foyer, she took in the art on the walls—most of which depicted men and women in some state of undress—as well as the fine fabrics draped around the windows and covering a lovely little bench. Sitting to wait, she tried to curb her nervousness, and—dare she admit—her excitement at having an opportunity to meet such a woman.

She couldn't help but wonder how it would feel to be in control of her life in such a manner? Would she feel empowered by her ability to choose customers and then dole out punishment to them? Or would she be weighed down by the hand life dealt her? One that forced her into such a career?

The butler reappeared. "Follow me, Mrs. Smith. Mistress Lash will join you in the front salon shortly."

Doing as she was bid, Ros followed the servant into a front room she had not seen on her previous foray to The Market. Of course, that shouldn't have been surprising considering she'd been there to seduce Flint. The room was a cheery yellow that had tall windows to take best advantage of the bright sunshine. Settling on a chair that allowed her a clear view of the salon door, she waited for her advisor to arrive.

Perhaps ten minutes later, a black-haired, gray-eyed beauty strode confidently into the salon. With her long willowy neck and statuesque height, even swathed in a soft gray robe that covered her from neck to toes, she was a stunning woman. No wonder men lined up to receive her not so tender ministrations.

Feeling a bit frumpy in her deep green walking dress with her hair pulled up in a sensible twist at the back of her head,

Ros rose to greet her hostess. "Thank you for seeing me, Mistress Lash."

"Oh, please call me Amelia." She beamed a bright smile at Ros. "The necessary moniker grows tiresome at times. Everyone running around Mistress-ing me endlessly." She sat in the chair next to Ros. "I can't imagine how the titled manage such formality all the time. Must be why so many peers are begging for the bite of my whip."

Ros blinked. "Well, I've never been a titled woman, so I can only imagine it must take some getting used to. Though I certainly do appreciate those of my friends who seem a bit more down to earth and not so caught up in their titles."

"Yes, I do believe you chum about with a good sort. Those Lustful Lords have all proven to be solid men," Amelia agreed. "But what is it that I might do for you?"

Ros felt her cheeks grow warm. "Oh, um." The moment had come. She needed to bare her intimate thoughts to a perfect stranger. "Well, as you may imagine, since I am here speaking with you, I have become intimate with Lord Flintshire."

"Oh, he's a randy one I hear. And likes the bite of pain, too. If I could choose, he's the one I'd throw in with." She winked.

Ros couldn't control the nervous laugh that escaped her, even as her cheeks were scorched. "Yes, well, he is certainly amorous. But it is the pain I am trying to understand."

Amelia nodded. "I see. You're not sure how to meet his needs."

"Precisely." Ros waited, hoping she would have something to offer.

"There is not much to it in my mind. It's just that some people find pleasure in the pain. They're made a little different than regular folks." Amelia shrugged.

"But, will he always be that way? What if I can't give him the pain he needs? Do I need to let him seek it out in other ways? Do I need to tolerate the fighting?" Ros could feel her frustration rising.

"I should not expect the desire for pain to go away. Once someone—man or woman—finds a taste for it, I've never seen it wane. So yes, I'd expect that his needs will continue. As for being the one to give him the pain, not everyone is capable of fulfilling that need. I wasn't sure I could dole it out when I began my career, but once I realized I was providing them something they needed, it was easier to get past all the social rules that teach us hurting others is bad. Because in this particular case, it is, in fact, good."

Ros considered her words. Mistress Lash was merely giving her customers—people like Flint—what they needed. Being a practical sort, Ros could see the reasoning. "I understand what you are saying. But, I don't know if I'm able to tolerate the fighting. He certainly can't carry on with that type of behavior forever."

"True. There will come a point when either his body won't be able to take the abuse or his age won't support his activities. It would probably be best if he had another way to channel his needs. I have whipped him a time or two when I have had cancellations. But he removed himself from my new client waiting list a few months ago." One dark eyebrow lifted. "He was to be my next new client."

He had been on her waiting list? And, he had removed himself? "That sounds as though he too thought the fighting wouldn't last forever."

"Indeed, and that something occurred in his life that made him believe seeing me for my services would no longer be a viable option." Amelia looked thoughtful for a moment. "Would I be wrong in assuming that his plans changed shortly after he met you?"

"The timing does suggest that." Ros considered for a moment and then decided to be impulsive. "Would you consider taking on an apprentice?"

"You're not thinking of getting into whoring, are you?" Amelia looked as surprised as she sounded.

Ros let out a belly laugh. The notion was so ridiculous she couldn't imagine men seeking her out. "Don't be ridiculous. Most men see me as plain. I'm no beauty like you or my sister."

Amelia snorted. "Women are so foolish. Of course, you are beautiful. I've seen your sister, and though she has a vibrancy about her, there is a soft, welcoming glow about you. Your beauty is there in your reddish-blonde hair and soft green eyes, but your inner beauty outshines any of your physical attributes. Men would be lined up around the block for a chance to taste such sweetness and purity. Obviously, Lord Flintshire has found you more than worthy of his attention."

A pleasurable warmth seeped through her bones. What a lovely thing to say about another person. "Thank you for such a lovely compliment, Amelia. I was curious what a woman such as yourself would be like, but the reality is not what I had imagined. It is so much better."

"I appreciate your kindness, as well, Mrs. Smith. And yes, for you, I would be willing to take on an apprentice. I can teach you what I know about wielding a whip, and even about how to pleasure a man, control him if that is what he needs." She looked confident and eager to share her knowledge.

"Oh, well. I suspect just understanding how to dole out what he needs as far as pain is sufficient. I would be uncomfortable with any other hands-on tutelage, beyond that."

"I understand, and respect your loyalty and integrity. When would you like to start your lessons? I should think we could start during the day for now, but once you've learned how to control the whip, we shall need to find you live subjects to practice on."

Ros thought about where and how she would both practice and take lessons. "May we hold lessons here during the day? I have some space in my basement where I am able to practice at home. As for the live practicing, we'll cross that bridge when we get to it."

"Agreed. We can use the dungeon here during the day. Shall we start tomorrow?" Amelia grinned, her eagerness contagious.

"Excellent." Ros smiled back. "I should like to compensate you for your time and efforts."

"I couldn't ask for more than half my usual rate since I appreciate the opportunity to share my knowledge. That and the shock Flint shall receive when you tie him up and whip him the first time will be payment enough." Amelia laughed heartily, obviously picturing him helpless and at Ros's mercy.

"I'll not be rude and argue. I appreciate your generosity. How should I dress for the lessons?"

"Learning the whip is hard work. Wear some of those fancy riding trousers your sort like to hide under your riding habits. That'll give you plenty of mobility for the work you'll do."

A moment of doubt assailed Ros. "Do you believe I am capable of learning how to do this?"

"I've only taught a handful of men how to wield the whip. Most men are too inept and too impatient to manage the tools of the trade with any skill. A woman has a natural delicacy of touch and reserves of patience that lend her to being far more adept at such an endeavor. Needless to say, you're not the first woman I've ever offered to teach, but you are one of the few who have taken me up on the offer. I feel certain you will be more than able to physically manage the use of a whip. The question remains, will you be able to mentally make the needed adjustments,"

Ros considered Amelia's words for a moment. She would not fail, she could not. "Very well, then. What time shall I come around tomorrow?"

"Half-past one will do. I'm usually up and about by then." Amelia rose. "I'll see you out."

With the interview over and a far clearer path ahead than Ros had anticipated, she left The Market with a lightness of spirit she hadn't hoped for. "Thank you for everything."

Chapter Seventeen

F lint was on edge. It had been days since he'd asked Lucifer for his help, and no word had come. Add to that, he'd reconciled with Ros though he had failed to mention the threats against her. And he was living in a constant state of fear for her, despite the assistance Linc and Arthur were providing. It was like an exposed nerve.

It was early afternoon, leaving hours until he was expected at Ros' for dinner. Every tick of the clock was like an eternity of time. It was all he could do to restrain himself from decamping to her doorstep to better protect her. But he knew she would refuse his protection, would deny him the satisfaction of seeing to her safety without greater explanation. And he feared driving her away with that explanation. He was rather well and truly fucked.

Beyond all those issues, he still had yet to get to the bottom of the shortage of funds at the boys' home in Flintshire. Hopefully, the private investigator he hired would discover answers quickly. The man would leave in the morning and send word as soon as he learned anything useful. Flint would have preferred to deal with it on his own, but with Ros in danger, that simply was not possible.

His butler entered and waited for acknowledgment after a stiffly delivered, "My lord."

"Yes?" Flint couldn't deny he was eager for a distraction. Any distraction. Even one of a boring, mundane household nature.

His servant sniffed indelicately. "There is a man here to see you. A Mr. Frank Lucifer."

Flint jumped up and swept past his shocked butler. "Lucifer? Come in!"

Having discarded all propriety, Lucifer appeared in the long hallway off the foyer. He looked a bit shocked by Flint's welcome. "Apologies, but I've been on tenterhooks waiting to hear from you."

He shook Lucifer's hand and dragged him into the study and past a still gaping butler. After a moment, the servant departed, his usual aplomb in tatters.

Flint motioned to the couch. "Sit. May I get you a drink?"

Lucifer looked nervous. His face was a bit pale, and if Flint hadn't shaken hands, he might have missed the tremor in Lucifer's.

"Whisky, if you have some," Lucifer answered, his tone a bit gravely.

"Of course." Flint set about pouring their drinks. Once that was seen to, he sat down across from Lucifer and waited. And waited.

Lucifer looked distinctly uncomfortable.

Impatience pushed him to ignore propriety. "Have you found out who is behind the threats?"

Lucifer shook his head. "No. My people are still working on it. We've found a man who may have some information, but he hasn't given up his connection yet. Seems he is more afraid of him than he is of us."

Flint leaned forward, his arms braced on his knees as he stared at Lucifer intently. "Change that."

"Oh, I shall. Very, very soon. But that is not why I am here." Lucifer licked his lips and shifted in his seat uncomfortably.

"Then why?" Deflated, Flint sat back.

"I have something I need to tell you, and I am not sure how you will receive the news." Lucifer set his drink down.

Flint shrugged. "Just tell me. It can't be worse than the fact some Seven Dials boss is out to get me anyway he can."

Lucifer sighed. "You're right. My mother was a prostitute in Windsor, a tavern wench, really." He paused and drew a breath. "She fell in love with a young man who was attending Eton. She lay with him, thought they would be married, and he would take her away from the hard life she'd known. Instead, he got her pregnant—with me—and then deserted her."

"That's a sad tale, but why are you telling me this?" Flint was confused by the conversation and impatient to have answers about the crime boss that had targeted him. Surely, the two stories couldn't be related.

"Because that man is your father." Lucifer sat there silently while his bald statement sank in.

Flint sat there and stared. Trying to figure out how his father could have sired another child, and he not know about it. Then he snorted, considering his parent's relationship, it was not at all surprising that this had occurred. "So, are you saying you are my brother?"

"Well, a half-brother, at any rate." Lucifer looked strained as he waited for a reaction.

Flint's mind raced. "That's why you've been poking around, asking all sorts of questions about me."

"It is." Lucifer took a breath. "I was trying to determine if I wanted to tell you."

"And what precipitated the need to tell me? Are you in need of something?" Flint couldn't help but ask the question he'd learned to ask early in life. After all, he was the son of a duke.

Lucifer flinched. "Actually, your request for help brought me to this. I wanted you to understand why I refuse to ask for payment. Why I am choosing to help you. And why it is important to me to see this issue resolved for you."

For the first time in his life, Flint understood what it was to be nonplussed. His gut churned, and his head spun. He had a brother—a half-brother—but a brother, nonetheless. Lips gone dry, he tried to lick them and speak, but his mouth was as dry as his lips. "B-but you're the son of a Duke. The eldest son, based on the timeline you presented. Surely you wish to know your father, our father? Or you want some recognition of your birth."

Lucifer, his brother—bloody hell that was a strange thought—rolled his eyes and huffed. "Dear God, no. That is part of what had me deliberating on whether to inform you of our connection. I have no designs on your place as heir, and I certainly have no desire to know the man who could so easily discard the woman carrying his child." He paused, as though considering the merits of continuing. "After meeting your friends and then briefly, you. I was curious about you. Having met any number of peers in my line of work, I was surprised by how dissimilar to them you and your friends were."

"I should bloody well hope so! I do not consider myself to be one of those popinjays parading about London," Flint scoffed and then sniffed in affront.

"I agree, so no need to get your dander up." Lucifer grinned.

Flint sighed. "Being the son of a duke, you can imagine I've heard a tall tale or two in my time. Do you have any proof of this relationship between your mother and my father?"

Lucifer nodded. "I suspected you'd ask for something of the sort." He reached into his pocket and extracted a short stack of letters bound with a simple blue ribbon. "My mother kept these."

Flint had to steady his hand as he reached out to take the packet. With a delicate tug, he untied the ribbon and opened the first letter. It was from his grandmother, who at that time would have been the Duchess of Shropshire. Her name was carefully penned at the end of the missive. Returning to the top, he scanned the familiarly elegant scrawl. He could hear her voice in every word of the letter, right down to the superior, self-assured tone. His heart skipped a beat when he got to the end.

...the enclosed funds should be enough to deal with the result of your wantonness. Though this is not to be seen as the acknowledgment of any responsibility on the part of this family or my son. I expect this shall be the last we hear from you.

Bloody hell! He pulled out the next letter. The tone was even more peevish as his grandmother continued to insist that she had done all she could. It was dated within a few weeks of the first letter. The third and final letter was dated two years later. He and his brother, Marcus, would have just been born. This letter came from his father in reply to what he assumed was another plea for help. His father, having just taken over the title of Duke of Shropshire after his father's unexpected death in a carriage accident, denied knowing the girl or having gotten her with child. He coldly stated that any further requests would be treated as blackmail and passed on to the appropriate authorities. Clearly, his threats had achieved the desired results since there were no further letters in the bundle.

He sat there, holding the sheets in his hand and processing the alarming evidence. Why would his grandmother have bothered to send money to the poor girl if she had not believed her story to be true? And though his father made no acknowledgment of the truth of the story, the way he coldly shut the woman down was rather like driving a nail with a sledgehammer. Had there been no truth to the matter, wouldn't he have simply passed the correspondence on to the authorities and not replied? That was the standing guidance he had been given as his father's heir.

"I see the validity in your story both because of these letters," Flint looked at the man who sat across from him, "and because of the striking resemblance between you and my father. My brother and I always carried more of our mother's features than our father's, aside from the dark hair."

Lucifer looked vaguely uncomfortable. "As I've said, I have no interest in meeting the rest of the family."

Flint snorted and ignored the dull ache that often accompanied any reminiscence of his brother. "Have no fear. I'll not be signing you up for family gatherings. As for my brother—our brother—he died when we were boys."

"I recall seeing something about that in my research, though the details around his death were vague at best." Lucifer tipped his head. "Was he very much like you?"

Flint couldn't stop the half-smile that flitted across his lips. "No. He was everything I am not. He was brave and sure, always willing to take on the fight of others...to protect those who were weaker than him. We may have looked alike, but I was by far the weaker of the pair. Max was named for Maximus Meridius, a Roman General who was betrayed and fell into slavery where he became a revered gladiator. He lived up to his namesake time and again, though he only reached the age of ten."

Flint paused and swallowed down the guilt and remorse that always came with the mention of his brother. "He stepped in front of me when an older neighbor boy moved to push me for being smart. Unfortunately, there was an old well-shaft just behind us with a cover that had rotted out. I fell to the side, and he fell backward and through the cover. He snapped his neck when he landed at the bottom." Silence settled for a moment as Flint struggled with his emotions.

"I'm sorry for your loss, he sounds as though he would have grown up to be a good man."

"He would have." Flint nodded. "And I dare say he would have been intrigued by having a half-brother such as yourself."

"Such as me? I'm merely a Seven Dials escapee who found a way to survive by any means necessary." Lucifer scoffed openly. "I doubt your brother would have found me the least bit intriguing. In fact, most find me disgusting, considering I have preyed on the weak and vulnerable my entire life."

Flint considered the man sitting across from him. "Have you? Or have you merely given the appearance of such behavior to disguise the truth?"

Lucifer rose from his seat and straightened his coat. "Do not deceive yourself into believing such nonsense. My soul is as black as my hair, and a gaping hole exists where my heart should beat. I do nothing that does not serve my own purposes. You would do well to remember that...brother."

Flint watched as his newly found sibling flashed a sharp grin that would have sliced a lesser man to ribbons, and then walked out as abruptly as he had appeared. Despite Lucifer's claims, Flint remained convinced he was correct. His newly discovered half-brother was not all he seemed, not by half.

Still a bit dazed by the realization of a brother and the deceit perpetrated by his family, he sat there alone and undisturbed for quite some time. The afternoon shadows had grown longer and longer until darkness had blanketed his study. A scullery maid shuffled in carrying a large bucket of coal.

"No need to lay coals this evening." He was still seated where Lucifer had left him.

The girl gasped, dropped the bucket, and spun around to face where he sat. "My lord," she exclaimed as she dropped into a curtsey that felt as awkward for him as it must have for her.

"Please, no need for that. Take your bucket and go. I'll not require a fire this evening." He made a shooing motion with his hand, though he wasn't sure she could see it in the gloom. Then he heard her shuffling toward the door she'd come in. Thank goodness, she was leaving.

He glanced about the room feeling as though he were just coming awake after a long nap. He took in the darkness, listened to the ticking of the clock, and glanced down at his rumpled clothing. How long had he sat there? "What time is it?"

She stopped, or he assumed she had based on the thump of the bucket hitting the floor. "It was half-past nine when I started on my duties."

He had missed dinner with Ros. "Bloody hell," he muttered and stood.

The girl gasped again and then snatched her bucket and quickly scooted through the door. Following behind her, he strode for the front door and walked out into the night.

A nearby clock struck ten o'clock as he climbed the steps to Ros's front door. He rapped sharply on the wood surface and waited. A few moments later, the door was opened, and Johnson peered out into the night. "How may I help you, my lord?"

"Please tell your mistress that I wish to see her." He stood there, still struggling to understand all that he had learned that afternoon.

"I shall see if she is at home." Johnson shut the door in his face with an imperious snap.

A short time later, the door opened again. "She will see you now."

Johnson stood to the side and let Flint enter, though disapproval was etched into every weathered crease on his face.

Without waiting for direction, Flint walked into the front salon in search of Ros. She sat composed, still dressed in what he assumed she had worn for their scheduled dinner. The very one he had missed.

He drew to a stop halfway across the room, in front of the settee, having taken in her pinched brow and compressed lips. "Ros, my apologies for failing to make our dinner."

"I was concerned about you when you did not arrive. I sent a runner to your house and was informed you were not available." Her brow had not smoothed out. "I could not determine if you were merely busy or if I had done something to anger you. In either case, a simple note would have at least saved me from sitting here uselessly worrying."

Overwhelmed and feeling raw, the truth nearly burst free. But it was all too new, and he had more questions than answers at the moment. Sharing his newfound knowledge was like striking an exposed nerve. And though he would have thought even he wasn't a glutton for that much punishment, it seemed he was. With his emotions swirling around him, he grappled for an explanation. "I had a visitor this afternoon." Flint's legs gave out, and he sank to the seat. "They brought unexpected news."

Ros appeared caught between her anger at his rudeness and her concern for his well-being. "I take it this was not welcome news."

"More that it was rather shocking news. I'm a bit taken aback by it all." He fought his desire to reach out for her, though the need nearly crushed him under its demand. Setting it aside for the moment—truly a herculean task—he drew a deep breath and let it out slowly. "Mr. Frank Lucifer stopped by my home this afternoon. He shared with me a bundle of correspondence between his mother and both my grandmother and father. It appears that he is, in fact, my half-brother."

Ros stood and moved to where he sat on the settee, her ire with him forgotten. "That is shocking news, and it certainly explains his interest in you of late. You appear to be quite shaken by this revelation."

Flint nodded, the pain of his father's misdeeds still fresh. "Indeed. I am shaken to my core, if truth be told. I thought I was alone all this time...since Maximus' death. But I'm not. And had he not come to me, I would never have known. My bastard of a father would never have said a word."

Ros took his hand and squeezed it. "What can I do? How can I help?"

He looked at her, awareness tingling through his body from where their hands were joined. With the emotional pain throbbing through him and her nearness, his cock had already begun to rise to the occasion. But it occurred to him, once again, how sweet this woman was. "How are you so forgiving? So selfless?"

"Do not be fooled by anyone's perceived selflessness. It seems people always want something from those of your class."

Flint's chest grew tight as he angled toward Ros so he could tip her chin up. Their gazes locked as he tumbled into the endless abyss of her emerald green eyes. "But not you. You are different. Always giving, never taking."

"Don't believe that." Ros finally lowered her lashes a moment before looking up to once more lock eyes with him. "Even I want something. I want you. Not your title, nor your money. But without a doubt, I want you, the man."

Flint's cock twitched in his pants as he leaned toward her. "Well, that's quite perfect, since I want you as well."

And then he captured her lips with his and delved deep into her mouth. She tasted of alcohol and something faintly sweet.

As her floral scent enveloped him in a heady fog, he allowed himself to forget the past few hours and all that had been raised. The seeming fact that he had another brother, that his father had so easily tossed a son aside, and the powerful realization that he was coming to depend on Ros in ways he had never wanted nor thought possible washed over him.

Needing to taste and touch her, he loosened the bodice of her dress and eased it off her shoulders as she tipped her head back and exposed her neck to his seeking lips. He trailed kisses down the column of skin, over her collarbones, and along the curve of her shoulder as he continued to move the material out of his way.

With her arms trapped by the fabric, he moved his attentions to the swell of her breasts. The plump flesh pressed up in offering was temptation itself and had him working on her laces next. Exposing as much of her skin as was possible, he pulled at the constricting corset and then the chemise beneath it until her breasts spilled into his hands. Eager to feel her shudder with pleasure, he leaned over her and sucked one pebbled tip into his mouth as he eased her on to the arm of the settee at her back.

She moaned, low and needy, in her throat.

He sucked harder, relishing the feel of her hot skin against his lips and tongue. Loving the sizzle of touching her, of a living flame in his arms. He switched to her other breast and repeated the attention. She arched into him, pressing more of her breast into his mouth as she pulled at his shoulders. His cock was hard and ached like the devil, but when he pulled back and took in her disheveled appearance, the wanton way she lay sprawled over the furniture, guilt swept in. He should tell her everything—about the threat and, most importantly, about how he felt. But, he was still sorting everything out in his own head. What could he possibly say? *I may very well love you? But I'm not sure what love is, so how would I know that I love you?*

And then the decision was taken from him as Ros freed her arms and sat forward to press him back into the settee. It seemed his lady's interests at the moment were of the more carnal sort. Perhaps he could say what he needed without speaking a word.

Chapter Eighteen

Ros looked up from where she was draped over the settee in her front parlor and saw the doubt flash through Flint's eyes. Was he not interested because of the lack of pain? He hadn't had a fight or other physical damage before he came to her...was the emotional turmoil a viable substitution for pain?

Confused but determined, she pushed herself up to a sitting position and freed her arms. Then with not a bit of doubt or hesitation, she pushed him back until his backside hit the cushion and pried open his coat before pushing it off his shoulders. Next came his vest and necktie, leaving only his shirt as the last obstacle. Out of patience with the many layers of clothing, she jerked on the fine lawn shirt, causing it to tear enough to give her the access she desired. A pity she wasn't strong enough to truly rend the material in two. Pleased with the destruction she'd wrought, she leaned forward and pressed kisses to his neck and chest as he settled back against the settee. His hands sank into her hair, hugging her skull as he dislodged some of the many pins keeping her coiffure in place.

Her breath caught in her chest as he pulled her face up to his. Fear stabbed her through the heart. Fear he would reject her once again. Fear that he would end their interlude. Fear that once more in her life, she would not be enough.

But then she dared to meet his gaze, and all she saw there was desire. Gone was the doubt, the hesitation. And then his lips captured hers once more, and the thrill of victory sang through her body. Or was that just the power of Flint's kiss? Unable to focus on deciphering the difference, she chose to give in to the pleasurable sensation and continue on about achieving her goal.

As their tongues tangled and slid together, she thought surely she could devour him if given the chance. The need for him, for his touch, pushed her beyond civilized behavior. With a lust-filled groan, she reached between them and opened his trousers. It was not difficult to find the rigid object of her search since it practically sprang into her ready hands.

Beneath her, Flint grunted, and his hips jerked ever so slightly. They broke their kiss once more, and he hauled her closer so he could suck on her nipple. In that moment, she was grateful she hadn't worn the formal hoop, opting for a more manageable set of crinolines for a private dinner at home. As he once more licked and sucked on her breasts, she worked on shifting her full skirts out of their way. Once she had the material and underskirts pushed aside, she rose up on her knees, tearing his mouth from her chest. "Please, Flint. I need you to fill me."

"I've no letters with me." He grimaced, clearly dismayed by his lack of protection.

She ground her heated core against him, her pussy aching to be filled still. "I addressed that possibility, I inserted a sponge earlier."

Heat and gratitude filled his gaze. Then on a murmured curse, he grabbed his cock and pressed it to her entrance. With his tip pushing into her, she sank down until he was seated deep inside her.

"Bloody hell, you feel good," he said and then hauled her back in for a kiss.

Together, they moved. His hips thrusting up as she descended until they found a rhythm that worked. She drew back from their kiss, the need to breathe overriding her pleasure in tasting him as a bead of sweat gathered and slid down her spine. The fire crackled behind them, adding physical heat to their own erotic flames. With her thighs bracketing his hips as her hands gripped his shoulders, her gown a rumpled mess around her waist, and her hair half sliding down her back, she rode him hard. She slid up and down his shaft, and her breasts bounced while he watched her every move. In all her years as a woman, she'd never felt more decadent and beautiful than in this moment with this man. It was as though he was entranced by her, a thrall wrapped in her feminine power. And she reveled in it.

But then, her orgasm rose up as if out of nowhere and slammed into her. The waves of pleasure crashed around her, caused stars to burst through her as though they might split her wide open and let Flint see all of her. Her heart, her soul, the very essence of her being. And despite the vulnerability of it all, she did not care. She felt no need to protect herself, not from him.

Then, his own reckoning came, and as she floated down from her breath-stealing peak, she watched Flint come apart—his eyes closed, and his breathing labored, his chest heaving like a bellows stoking a flame. He cried out her name, a yell of utter satisfaction and pleasure all melded together. He shook, his body rigid with his release, and then he was as boneless as a newborn babe as he slumped beneath her on the settee with his eyes closed.

A love seat some had taken to calling it, and considering what had just occurred on that piece of furniture, she found it hard to argue the point. A muffled laugh escaped her as she flopped against his shoulder, utterly done in.

He opened one eye and looked at her. "Dare I inquire as to what you have found so amusing during this delicate moment?"

She chuckled. "I was just pondering how apropos the term loveseat was for my little settee, considering our most recent usage of it."

"Mmmmm. Most apropos, I agree. Though not very comfortable for such activity." He grunted a little and shifted beneath her.

"Oh!" She scrambled off his lap. "I must be crushing you."

He huffed. "Not even hardly. But there is a distinct lack of cushioning in your furniture of choice."

Ros started to put her clothes to rights as much as was possible under the circumstances. "Oh, that is quite intentional. Mother and father are only able to stay so long without a comfortable place to sit."

He laughed at her confession and then grabbed her hand before she could get more than her chemise in place. "Leave that be, I'll play your ladies maid in a moment."

"That isn't required. I just wanted to straighten myself up so one of the servants doesn't walk in and see us in such a state." She smiled as he tugged her back into his lap.

He gawked at her a moment. "You choose to consider that risk now, after we spent the better part of an hour making love in this room?"

Her cheeks grew warm. "I was a bit caught up in the moment and didn't consider that when we came together."

He kissed her soundly and then released her. "Perhaps we should be more careful in the future."

Perhaps we should be more careful in the future, though not with regard to my servants. She considered how close they had been to making love without any protection again. Fortunately for them, she had purchased appropriate supplies that day, having learned long before not to rely on anyone but herself. Though normally, Flint was more conscientious about such things as pregnancy than her husband had been. Even tonight, despite his having been distraught when he arrived at her home, he had tried to stop them when he realized he had no French Letters with him. The realization warmed her insides, as she enjoyed the notion that he cared enough about her to have considered her desires in the throes of passion.

Unwilling to examine her reaction too closely, she rose from his lap. "It's late, we should get some rest."

Flint glanced at the clock and then stood up as well. He tucked his softened cock away and reached to straighten his ruined shirt. With a wry grin, he merely tugged his waistcoat on.

Ros reached out and placed a staying hand on his. "I meant for you to come to bed with me. Not for you to go home." She longed to feel him wrapped around her as he had been their first night together at The Market. To feel the intimacy of sleeping beside him.

He hesitated a moment and then nodded. She took his hand as he picked up his coat, and they started up the stairs together. He stopped with one foot on the bottom stair.

"What of your neighbors in the morning? I'll not have your reputation sullied."

She couldn't help but feel her heart squeeze at further evidence of such care from the man she had come to know. "If it will make you feel better, you can get up early and sneak out the back door. But frankly, I don't give one whit for what the biddies next door think of me."

"I care. I'll just hold you for a bit while you fall asleep." His warm deep tone brooked no argument.

She sighed, thwarted by his protective side. "Very well, though I wish you'd stay."

He brought the hand he held up to his lips and placed a sweet kiss on the appendage. "I wish I could."

And so they went upstairs together, at least for a while. Yet she wondered why he seemed to be keeping this distance between them. She doubted his reticence was due to social mores, but she couldn't fathom what might be the source. The man clearly found it a great challenge to trust anyone. She pushed aside her disappointment and pressed on with enjoying what she could of the man she feared had stolen her heart.

The next afternoon Ros arrived at the back doors of The Market and slipped inside while wearing a deep-hooded cloak to protect her from prying eyes. Inside, she was quickly shown to a dungeon-like room where a stuffed pillow that was meant to resemble a man was chained to a wall.

Removing her cloak, she hung it up on a peg and then strode across the room to greet Mistress Lash. The freedom of movement that came with wearing riding pants without the voluminous skirts on top was refreshing. "Do you go about like this all the time?" Her teacher wore similar attire.

She nodded. "I do inside The Market and when I have clients to see, whether here or in their homes. Though some of them like it when I wear nothing but my skivvies to whip them." Mistress Lash flashed a naughty grin that made her eyes dance.

Ros found herself stifling a laugh, though she couldn't hide her surprise at such a notion. But then, here she was about to take lessons on how to whip the man she loved—and heaven help her, she did love him—, so really nothing should shock her at this point. "Well, shall we get started? I'm eager to begin."

"Of course. I have a few first whip options for you to try." She led Ros over to a table. "The first option is a traditional carriage whip, the next is a cat o' nine tails, and the last is a hunting whip. For your first lessons, I want to keep you to shorter implements. Eventually, if you like, I can show you how to use something longer."

Ros looked at the options and considered. She'd never driven a carriage, so that one was as foreign to her as any other. The cat o' nine tails made her shudder. She easily dismissed that choice because of its association with violent criminals and brutal ship captains. Instead, she picked up the hunting whip. More familiar since she had had occasion to carry one, she thought that was a likely first choice. "Let's try this one."

Mistress Lash nodded. "A good first choice, though the cat o' nine tails is quite a bit of fun as well."

"I'll stick with the hunting whip," Ros said firmly.

Her instructor grinned. "Oh, good show! You'll need to remember that resolve when you have your man chained up and waiting for the bite of your whip."

Ros' heart pounded in her chest as she pictured Flint naked and chained up at her mercy. There was something deliciously tempting about being able to have her way with him...whatever way she chose. Setting that thought aside, she focused on her first lesson. They started by discussing proper stance. Her knees should remain flexed and not stiff, her buttocks relaxed. Then her mentor demonstrated her technique on the stuffed dummy. Ros watched and then, when directed, followed suit. Initially, she merely flung the thong in the general direction with an overhand motion, as demonstrated. Eventually, when she showed some consistency in motion, she moved toward her target.

The first time she arced the whip at the stuffed man, she squealed and closed her eyes. Mistress Lash sighed and came over to her. "You must remember, he wants this. No, *needs* this from you. For Lord Flintshire, this will be a deliciously intense experience. I dare say he will be ravenous to have you by the time you are finished with him. Do not be afraid. Fear will only lead to one or both of you being injured."

Ros's cheeks were red from embarrassment as well as exertion, but she nodded. "I understand."

"Good. Now be confident in your motion, and the whip will fall true. If you hesitate or flinch, you will miss your target. Try again."

Ros kept at it for what felt like hours. By the time her instructor called a halt to the session, her arm felt like slightly warm aspic. It was soft and weak with a distinct gelatinous feel that made clear she had used newfound muscles in her body.

"You did well. I would expect your arm will be sore tomorrow." Mistress Lash handed her a jar of salve. "Use this to ease the ache. Be liberal with it tonight and tomorrow. If you are able to practice at home, do so. I shall see you again in three days."

Ros smiled despite her arm's current state. "Thank you for taking the time to teach me. I shall see you then." Ros picked up her chosen whip as she made to exit The Market. In only a couple hours' time she had learned to at least wield the whip well enough to consistently hit her target. Not consistently or with any strength of impact, but she fully intended to continue to practice at home in spite of any pain so she could improve before her next lesson. The quicker she learned how to aim her strikes and control how hard they were the sooner she would be able to give Flint what he needed.

She settled in her carriage for the ride home and allowed the possibilities of what would come to play out in her mind. She considered how she might whip him lightly, just shy of the pain he craved, until he begged for it harder. Once she gave him what he needed, she imagined leaving him tied up as she knelt before him and sucked his cock, bringing him to completion. A shiver of pleasure snaked down her spine with her wild imaginings.

Chapter Nineteen

Flint had stewed for two days. He'd simmered and considered, paced and trained, and even had a sparring match with his footman who served in that capacity when needed. It was a miserable span of time, and on the start of day three, he decided the only way to answer his questions was to confront his father.

With that in mind, he dressed and appeared on his father's doorstep for breakfast. With his mother still abed, it was only the two of them at the table. Once their plates were empty, he decided to begin the discussion. "I had a rather interesting visitor this week."

"Did you?" His father sounded only mildly aware he had spoken, let alone interested in what he had to say as he picked up his morning paper.

"Indeed. Mr. Frank Lucifer himself paid me a call. He had a distressing tale to share." Flint watched his father for any flicker of recognition. The man continued to peruse his neatly ironed news while sipping his tea. "In fact, he came by to let me know that we were brothers."

He let the words fall into the silence of the room and waited. And waited. And waited.

Whether his father was uncaring or simply oblivious, he did not respond. In either case, Flint felt his temper rise at his father's indifference. "I said, he explained that we were half-brothers," he bellowed.

"Do stop yelling. I heard you quite clearly." His father continued reading, then paused and lowered the edge of the paper so he could look over it at Flint. "I thought you knew better than to fall for such an obvious gambit."

"I would have agreed with you except that he had a series of letters penned to his poor mother from Grandmother and yourself. The handwriting was far too familiar to not be yours, and the content was damning." He sat there with his hands pressed to the flat of the tabletop.

His father slowly set the paper down and looked up at him. "And who, exactly, was this woman I supposedly got with child?"

Flint struggled with the familiar feeling of being called on the carpet by his father. It had been many years since his father had done such to him, long since giving up on chastising him about his penchant for fighting. "A tavern wench near Eton. You impregnated her and then abandoned her."

His father snorted. "Doubtful I did any such thing, girls like that lie about these things frequently. If you had been more..." his father trailed off and stared at him coldly.

"More what, Father?" Flint was familiar with this old argument.

"More what a boy should have been. Interested in schooling and tupping and being social, then you would know what those women are like."

"Bloody hell! Are you actually lamenting that I wasn't a spoiled, entitled prick who fucked anything I could when I wasn't too drunk to get a cockstand?" Flint shook with rage.

"It's a moot point, wouldn't you say? I am merely saying you wouldn't be familiar with that type of woman and the lengths they are willing to go to claim a peer, much less a future Duke as the father of their bastard get."

Flint snapped out of his chair, causing the heavy wood seat to flip backward onto the floor. "You got the girl pregnant, and then when she came to you, you turned her away, treating her as little more than a criminal. At least Grandmother had enough care to send the poor girl funds."

"Damn it all, she should know better than to send money. It only encourages them to return for more." His father sighed, sounding like the most put-upon man in all of England.

Flint had known his father was not a warm man, but he'd never imagined him to be so unfeeling. "You are a ruddy bastard, aren't you?"

"He is not. I had him well after legally marrying his father, and I would appreciate you not saying such ridiculous things." The Dowager Duchess of Shropshire swept into the room. "I could hear you two arguing in the far corner of the East Wing. What is the meaning of all this?"

"Your grandson is of the mind that we have cast off a half-brother of his."

"I am not of the mind, I have read the letters penned in your own hands that tells me so." Flint reiterated, his frustration seeping out.

"It seems, Mother, that you sent a girl some funds, I'm shocked."

"Oh, dear, I did? How very unlike me." She sniffed and sat down at the table. A few moments later, a footman appeared bearing her breakfast.

The room remained silent, though tension stretched like a tightrope from one end of the table to the other. With the servant gone, Flint continued. "The man who is my brother is Frank Lucifer, the owner of the infamous gambling hell. Since he wants nothing to do with either of you and nothing but to help me with a situation I find myself in, I can't imagine he has managed to produce such solid forgeries." Flint cursed silently. "And did I mention he is the spitting image of Father?"

That got everyone's attention. His grandmother spoke first. "Is he?"

"Yes. I'm trying to understand why you two might have let him be raised in a brothel in Seven Dials. Could you not have done better by your own flesh and blood?"

His father looked annoyed by the whole conversation. "Even had I believed her story, I couldn't have recognized him as mine. That would have made him my heir, thereby depriving you of your birthright."

"I don't bloody care about being a duke! I've lost one brother, and now you are telling me I would have lost another had he not figured out I was worthy of the knowledge. You are a foul piece of work." And with that, Flint turned on his heel and stormed from the dining room. He'd gotten as far as the foyer when his grandmother caught up with him.

"Flint, my boy, now wait one moment." She stopped him with a frail hand on his sleeve. "I know the girl you speak of. And yes, I believed her as well. She was different than the others that showed up on our doorstep. She had been an innocent. She fairly reeked of it when I turned her away. And when she later wrote to me, I took pity on her. You may not appreciate your father's methods, but he was merely trying to protect you and your brother. Had he acknowledged the child, he would have had a claim on the title. The way the hereditary writ is worded, only the eldest has any rights to the title and all that comes with it. The man could lay claim to everything and leave you penniless."

The fear in her voice broke through his fury. "Had this family taken him in and raised him among us, I seriously doubt that would have been an issue any more than it would have been between Maximus and me. The man may be notorious, but I believe he is a good man at his core."

She smiled sadly. "It was not a risk we could take, nor should you."

"I disagree." Flint stalked out of the house and did not look back. He wasn't sure he would ever be able to return.

Ros squinted against the bright morning sun as she briskly moved along Bond Street. Julia appeared further down the street, emerging from a small crowd. Her sister waved as they drew closer, and Ros returned the gesture despite the deep ache of sore muscles in her shoulder that accompanied the greeting. Her next stop was Madame Le Fleur's shop. She was in need of more breeches since she had begun practicing with her hunting whip nearly every day. But clearly, she would need to say hello to Julia first.

"Ros! What a surprise to see you here." Julia grinned.

"Why a surprise? I have occasion to shop on Bond Street when I have a need."

Julia laughed. "Of course, you do. It's just that I am usually the one who must drag you here." Julia's gaze narrowed speculatively. "What are you here fetching?"

"If you must know, I have an appointment with Madame Le Fleur." Ros knew her sister was correct; she avoided Bond Street with all its hustle and bustle.

"Oh, dress shopping. How exciting! I have nothing pressing. I shall come along and see what wondrous new creation the inestimable Madame Le Fleur is concocting for you." Julia grinned.

Ros cursed silently. This wouldn't do, not at all. "Oh, no. you would likely die of boredom. It's just a quick visit to clarify a few details for some new riding trousers."

Julia's nose wrinkled in obvious confusion. "Riding trousers? But you don't ride frequently enough to need new riding trousers." She stopped and considered. "Have you taken to riding more often since I married Wolf?"

Ros laughed awkwardly. "Oh, would you look at the time. I must run. We shall have to catch up soon, my dear." Then with a quick air kiss toward her sister, she dashed down the street, leaving a bewildered Julia behind. That was much too close a call. She simply wasn't ready to explain her activities to her yet. Soon, perhaps. Maybe. It was hard to say when she might tell her sister that she was learning to wield a whip so she could beat her lover when required. When might there be a good time for that conversation? Over tea? Perhaps a nice dinner? Certainly not breakfast. Ros sighed. Truly, she didn't think there would ever be a *good* time. On further consideration, it seemed too intimate a detail to share with anyone but Flint. And she had her doubts about whether she could even tell *him*.

As she hurried down the walkway, a man stopped in front of her. "A moment, if you please, ma'am."

Ros sidestepped around him. "I'm terribly sorry, but I am late for an appointment."

Barreling on along the way, she marched into the dress shop just as the clock struck eleven in the morning. She had just made it.

"Good morning, Mrs. Smith!" Madame Le Fleur's fake French accent boomed out across the busy dress shop.

Ros refrained from rolling her eyes as she darted toward where the blonde woman stood smiling. "Good morning, Madame. I appreciate you taking the time to meet with me."

"But, of course! What may I design for you today? A new day dress? Perhaps a new evening gown?" The woman was growing more excited by the moment.

Panic surged through Ros as a few of the women nearby turned to listen in on their conversation. Lowering her voice, she leaned in close to the dressmaker. "Might we speak in private? I require something of a more sensitive nature."

Madame's grin grew broad, and a knowing gleam entered her green gaze. "Ooh la la! But, of course."

A few moments later, in the relative privacy of the fitting room, she sat down and offered a shy smile. "I am in need of a few pairs of riding breeches. Sturdy material, but with a comfortable range of motion. It is essential I be able to bend and move about in them."

Madame looked at her strangely for a moment. "Do you wish to hide your lovely figure?"

Ros considered the question for a moment. "No, in fact, I'd like to accentuate it. Particularly my derrière, I believe."

"Oh, so naughty!" Madame smiled wickedly. "What color would you like? Brown or cream? Perhaps a bright red? Some ladies are choosing to wear noticeable colors in case they are accidentally exposed."

A laugh escaped, Ros. "Oh, these will be noticed since I'll not be wearing skirts over them."

Madame's brows shot up nearly to her hairline. "No skirts! Oh, you are a naughty girl."

Her face heated as she suffered the older woman's scrutiny.

"Indeed. I suppose I am becoming a rather naughty girl. Though black will do nicely for color. And perhaps one pair in leather and one in cloth. You have my measurements, do you need anything else?"

Madame waved. "Non. I shall have them ready for a fitting next week."

"Excellent!" Ros stood. "And, of course, I appreciate your discretion as always."

Madame heaved a sigh. "*Oui*, of course."

With her business concluded, Ros departed the shop. She intended to visit the Burlington Arcade to inquire after a custom hunting whip. She had some design changes in mind to better meet her intended use. With that in mind, she started down Bond Street in search of a cab.

She spotted one a little way down the street and headed in that direction when a man stepped in front of her again. However, this time when she moved to step around him, he grabbed her arm and unceremoniously shoved her into an alley. Alarmed at the rough handling she'd received, she straightened up to her full height only to see that her assailant was both tall and broad. A veritable walking wall. Despite his imposing presence, she was not to be cowed. "What is the meaning of this?"

"My apologies, madam. But I did try speaking to you earlier, and you simply walked around me." The man frowned at her.

She remembered him now, from before Madame Le Fleur's. She had stepped around him, and it seemed he was a bit put out by that incident. "Well, my apologies, but I do not know you, and I was in danger of being late for an appointment." She glanced nervously at the sliver of sunlight that indicated the opening of the shadowed alley. Carefully she edged her body toward escape. "What is it you require?"

The man eyed her warily. "Don't you move, now. I need only relay a message to you, but if you try to run, I'll have to stop you."

That pulled her up short. "Very well, get on with this message."

"You need to talk to your man and tell him to throw his next fight." The hulking man was holding a soft cap in his hands and appeared to be twisting it.

"My man?" Ros was confused for a moment. "Do you mean Lord Flintshire?"

"That's him." He nodded.

"Well, I'm afraid I have nothing to do with his nocturnal activities by the docks." Ros wasn't sure why anyone might think she would have any sway over Flint's fighting. If she did, she'd have him stop altogether.

The man looked worried. "You need to tell him. Make him understand."

Still confused, Ros pressed on. "Understand what? I'll certainly tell him, but as I said, it is doubtful he will listen to a word I say on the matter."

Then the man grabbed her upper arms and shook her. "You *must* make him listen. If you don't, they'll hurt you!"

Jostled and a bit disoriented, Ros was having more and more trouble following the man's reasoning. "Stop that at once." She slapped at his hands. "Now, you must get yourself together and be clear. I must make Lord Flintshire throw—though I am not sure I understand what you mean by that—his next fight. If I don't, someone will hurt me?"

"Now you're getting it." The big man grinned.

As the words sank into Ros's understanding, her heart skipped a beat. "But he won't listen to me."

"He must. They'll hurt you, badly if he don't. Maybe kill you." The man let go of her arms and picked up his hat from where he'd dropped it.

Ros gasped and drew back, away from the vaguely threatening man. Then she spun around and ran toward daylight. With every step, she was sure a meaty hand would reach out and haul her back into the shadows, but suddenly, she burst into the bright, sharply incongruent sunlight. Scared and disoriented, she stumbled into a man who steadied her despite her encroachment of his space. With a few mumbled apologies, she tried to pull away, but the man refused to let her go. Panic welled in her chest as she glanced wildly about in search of a friendly face. Then she looked up and found herself staring into Lord Lincolnshire's pale blue eyes. Though her heart still raced, she calmed considerably. "Excuse me, my lord. I—"

"Are you well, Mrs. Smith?" Linc appeared almost as upset as she was. His brow was damp with a sheen of sweat and his face pink as though he'd been exerting himself unduly.

"Yes. No. I—my lord, I was just accosted and threatened!" The shock was ebbing as her temper surged to the fore. "I don't suppose you are aware of—"

"Perhaps we should have this conversation someplace less conspicuous than Bond Street in the middle of the day?"

Linc glanced around at the flow of people that had shifted to glide around them as if they were a boulder in a river.

"Very well, but do not think I shall be dissuaded from my questions," she said sharply.

He nodded crisply. "Never that, ma'am." Then he turned and hailed a cab that had just released its most recent passengers.

Once they were settled in the vehicle, Linc gave the driver directions to her address, which peaked her notice. As the cab clip-clopped down the street, her thoughts reeled, darting from one moment in the alley to another until she'd replayed the incident in her head. When Lord Lincolnshire had still not offered up any explanation, she decided it was time to ask a few questions of the man. "My lord, why is it that you seem so familiar with my address?"

"I don't suppose you'd believe me if I said I had developed a small infatuation with you?" Linc grinned, his eyes sparkling with mirth.

Ros snorted. "Not very likely, my lord. Perhaps you could explain how you happened to be on Bond Street at the mouth of that alley when I stumbled free of the villain who waylaid me?"

"Mrs. Smith, I assure you there is a reasonable explanation for both points of interest. However, I am unfortunately not the person who can answer your true questions. What I shall tell you is that for the last few days, either myself, Lord Dunmere, or Flint have been near you at all times of day. I apologize that you were confronted in the way you were today. I am afraid I lost you in the crowd for a moment when you exited Madame Le Fleur's." Linc looked at her with regret in his normally dancing gaze.

Ros's hands had finally stopped shaking as they pulled up to her home, but her thoughts were still whirling with questions. Clearly, she needed to speak to Flint to find the answers she sought. With a murmured thanks for Lord Lincolnshire's escort, she retreated into her house and watched from the window as he took up a spot near a tree down the lane a bit and across the street.

As she settled in her front parlor with a cup of tea in hand, a sense of safety finally returned. After two sips, she rose and penned a note to Flint asking him to come to her immediately.

She hoped he would not take long to answer her summons. She had many questions for him, starting with who was threatening her and why?

Chapter Twenty

F lint pulled the crumpled missive from Ros out of his pocket for possibly the hundredth time since he'd first read it and torn out of his house and toward her home. It had been mere minutes of driving, but with each clop of hooves, each tick of the clock, and each beat of his heart, he looked at her note to reassure himself that she was alive.

The hack finally drew to a halt in front of her home, and he bolted from the cab as he tossed the required payment up to the driver. Standing on the front stoop, once again waiting impatiently, he tried to stop the whirl of images from spinning through his mind like a horrific zoetrope that refused to cease spinning. His heart raced faster as Johnson opened the front door and simply admitted him into the house. "Mrs. Smith is expecting you."

Without missing a beat, he charged into the front salon and stopped short when he found Ros sitting in her usual seat. She calmly sipped tea in an unrushed manner that belied her urgent summons.

With a surprisingly steady hand, she set her cup and saucer down before focusing her attention on him. "Good afternoon, Flint. I do appreciate your prompt response to my note."

"Are you well? I was under the impression you had been assaulted." Flint loomed over where she sat.

Ros reached up and patted her hair as though confirming the strands remained in place. "I was quite shaken when I returned home after my run-in with a rather unsavory man just off of Bond Street. But, Lord Lincolnshire was extremely helpful in seeing me home and has since remained at his post just outside."

"Bloody hell! Who was he?" Flint leaned closer, fury twisting his gut and flooding his body with adrenaline.

"Oh, do sit down! I've had quite enough of men looming and leering at me for one day," Ros snapped.

He needed to move, to pace; however, he knew she'd not say another word until he did as she asked. So, he sat stiffly on the settee that made an L shape where it met her chair. It was a good thing Johnson had summarily relieved him of his hat because there was little doubt he would have been mangling it as he sat there waiting on tenterhooks. "I'm sitting, please elaborate."

Flint's breath snagged in his chest as he caught the furious gleam in her green eyes, and he knew the next little while would be a most unpleasant experience doled out as Ros saw fit. He had little recourse but to bide his time, now that he was sure she was relatively unharmed.

"It seems I am meant to deliver a message to you. You are to throw your next fight, or I shall be harmed—badly, if not k-killed." She stumbled over the last word, the first chink she'd allowed in her composure.

Fuck! Flint wanted to leap to his feet and rant wildly, but he knew he needed to maintain his calm, or she might lose her own. "Was anything else said?"

"That was the gist of what was said. I was a bit off-kilter with the way I was accosted and dragged into an alley to receive this message, but I made sure I got the important bits."

Flint ground his teeth as he struggled for his control. "And were you injured in the process of the delivery of this message?"

"Other than a bit of shaking at one point, the man did no more than grab my arms and forcibly move me about. So no, I was not gravely injured. Though I can't say, I relish the prospect of being harmed should you choose not to comply with this demand." She blinked rapidly a few times and then drew a deep breath.

He could not find any such calm for himself. While not as bad as he had imagined on the drive over, it was still not good. And suddenly, the need to feel her whole and hearty in his arms overrode all other thoughts. He stood up and pulled her to her feet. "I am so deeply sorry you were dragged into this unfortunate episode. But I assure you, I shall protect you, come what may."

"You will protect me? How? By having your friends continue to trail me around London?" Fear made her eyes huge as she looked up at him.

He pulled her closer to his chest, pressed her against him so he could feel each breath she took. "Don't worry, I promise you'll be safe."

Her lips parted as though she had more to say, but Flint didn't want to discuss the intrusion of his back-alley existence into his not-so-neatly ordered life. So, he captured her lips in a kiss intended to distract even as it fanned the coals of desire into flames. Their tongues twined and clashed as she grew aggressive in the kiss. Soon, the need to breathe outpaced their need to taste and touch. She drew back and looked at him, her gaze sharp. "Do not think you are getting away with anything, Lord Flintshire. I am allowing you to distract me with desire because it meets my need to feel every inch of you against me in this moment. We shall discuss this again."

"As you say, Mrs. Smith." And then he scooped her into his arms and carried her up the stairs to her bedroom.

Inside the room, he set her on her feet and quickly set about stripping her of the many layers of clothing that kept him from touching her skin. Each time his arousal surged around her without the benefit of pain, he marveled anew. Certainly, he still craved the bite of pain that carried so much pleasure, but he was learning that he could perhaps survive without it. That something akin to normalcy might be within his grasp with the right woman. This woman.

As she stood before him naked, her soft green gaze darkened with desire, his cock throbbed with the need to be inside her once more. He toed off his shoes, then stripped off his coat and vest before tossing his shirt aside. Standing in his stocking feet and trousers, he stepped into her body and wrapped his arms around her. With a soft sigh, she melted into him as their lips once more met. The fierce way she stroked his tongue with hers stirred his lust and made his cock grow harder. He growled a bit as he pressed her backward until they fell onto the bed in a tangle of limbs.

Ros's husky laughter filled the space both in the room and in him. It was quickly becoming apparent that he needed her in the most elemental way. But that knowledge brought a dark and unwelcome fear with it. The kind of dependency he was developing might break him if he were to lose her, or worse, drive her away with his more deviant needs. His heart hitched in his chest, but he dug deep into his reserves and pushed the unwanted emotions aside. He would deal with all the things she made him feel later.

The soft press of her breasts against him drove him to roll until she lay beneath him. He angled himself so he could feast on her nipples, each tightly furled with her need. He sucked on one peak and then the other, alternating as her breathing grew choppier and choppier. One of her hands dug into his hair, holding him to her chest, while the other lay flat against his back. Then, he rose up a bit and opened his trousers. With her help, he pushed them down, freeing his length. She quickly grabbed his hard shaft in her hands and stroked him. She slid her fist down to his base and then back up to swirl her thumb over his tip, gathering the bead of pre-cum that had formed. A shudder of raw pleasure skated down his spine as he watched her handle his cock so eagerly. Needing more than her hands could provide, he pulled back and lowered down between her legs. With the glow of the single lamp near the bed for light, he studied her face as he slid inside her body. Their gazes locked, and the common noises of her staff going about their business and the house creaking as it settled all faded away. All he could do was revel in the warmth of her body's grip, the slick wetness of her pussy, and the soft moans she made as he sank deep. With his balls squashed against her, he paused. And then he drew back, sliding almost out of her before he reversed directions and slid deep once more. With each languorous stroke of his cock inside her, the desire between them seemed to grow, to blossom into something else entirely.

But still, something was missing. Unwilling to examine what it was—because he knew and had no idea how to address the issue—he continued to focus on bringing her as much bliss as he could. Beneath him, Ros moaned low and needy. "More."

He sped up, thrusting a bit faster. But it wasn't enough. She drummed her heels on his arse and demanded, "Harder!"

As he lowered down to his forearms to brace himself, he shoved inside her harder and faster with each stroke. And then she dug her nails into his back and raked them down nearly to his buttocks. The pain seared through him like a fire that had found a spot of dry tinder. He burned fierce and hot as she continued to dig her nails into him, and he unleashed his need.

He ploughed into her over and over as she cried out. "Yes! Yes! Flint, more."

And so he gave her everything, thrusting into the tight clasp of her pussy as she finally found her peak. With her nails sunk deep in his skin, she broke apart in his arms, and it was the most beautiful thing he'd ever seen. With one last thrust, he joined her in bliss.

The next day Flint decided to visit the one address where he'd first run into the men who were demanding he throw the fight. Seven Dials in the daylight was not such an ominous place, though it certainly could do with a bit of basic sprucing up. Hopping from the handsome cab, he tossed the man half of the amount due him.

"That's half of what you owe me!" the driver groused.

"Wait for me, and you'll get the rest plus the return fare." Flint waited, impatient to be about his business.

"You're a wily trickster. Fine, but hurry up about it. I ain't got all day."

Having ensured a ride home, Flint turned to walk up the few steps to the vaguely familiar ramshackle building. It looked worse in the daylight than it had the night he was accosted. The peeling paint revealed old, weathered wood, the shutters hung haphazardly next to windows that were so grime crusted it was impossible to see inside the building. With a shrug, he knocked on the front door.

Nothing.

He waited a few moments and knocked again, harder. But still, nothing. So he listened for any stirring inside and was once again denied.

Determined to find someone, something, anything to lead him to the ringleaders, he reached for the handle on the door and found it unlocked. Pushing the door open, he stepped inside. The interior was equally as worn as the outside but had the added bouquet of must and mildew. Looking about, there was evidence of past occupation, but nothing to suggest a current resident. With a sigh, Flint turned to leave, disappointed by the dead end but happy enough to be departing such a depressing place. Stepping out onto the front steps, he found himself face to face with the very man he'd sought out, the villain who had beaten him previously.

The man pulled up short. "'ere now! What are you about?"

Flint huffed. "I believe you sent me a rather demanding message yesterday. I felt it best addressed in person. Tell your boss I shall throw my next fight—tomorrow night—but you and your friends will leave Mrs. Smith alone. I also suggest your lot makes good on this. It will be a singular opportunity."

"I'll let him know." The man glared at Flint. "Now, get the hell off me property."

Flint wasn't particularly shocked to learn that the man owned the listing building, or at least rented it. With a short nod, he pushed past the thug and climbed back into the back of the cab that had miraculously waited.

Chapter Twenty-One

Despite the delightful distraction Flint had been, she'd kept up with her practice sessions with her whip and, in turn, her lessons. She had been diligent in the few weeks she'd been at it, and she was pleased to think she would be able to demonstrate significant progress to Mistress Lash. Her aim had improved considerably, though she was still working on her power. Some of that would come in time, but some of it was about control. Mistress Lash had told her from the beginning that control was key since it allowed her to increase and decrease the pain according to her recipient's needs.

Tucked in The Market's dungeon, Ros showed off her still new skills on a model that consisted of a shirt and pants stuffed with straw.

Mistress Lash nodded. "Strike the upper right shoulder."

Ros licked her lips and focused on her target. With a practiced move of her arm punctuated by a flick of her wrist, she landed the fall of the whip as directed.

"Now the upper left shoulder," her teacher prodded.

Ros repeated her motion with a slight trajectory change and happily landed with accuracy once again.

"Now strike each arse cheek in quick succession, no pause between." Her instructor stood behind her, out of harm's way.

Again, Ros let the whip fly. She struck the straw man as requested before turning with a triumphant grin. "I told you I had improved since our last lesson."

"Indeed, you have. You are an excellent pupil, but do not think you are ready to service your man." One dark brow rose as Mistress Lash spoke.

"I fear my efforts would be wasted. While I am able to strike with accuracy, I do not yet have enough power to meet his needs."

"Be patient, that will come with time, along with the ability to judge what your recipient needs in lieu of what they may ask for." Her instructor paused and appeared to be considering something. "Indeed, I think you are ready to begin practicing on a real person." She then walked over to the bell pull and tugged.

A few moments later, a servant appeared.

"Tell Amanda we require her presence," Mistress Lash directed before dismissing the maid.

Ros's gut clenched. "I'm not sure I am ready for a person yet. What if I misjudge and hurt her."

Mistress Lash offered a small smile. "Fear not, she will be protected. I would not be so foolish as to give you fresh pink skin to mar so early in your tutelage."

Ros couldn't hide her sigh of relief as Amanda appeared. The pretty blonde was dressed in a padded suit of some kind that covered her from neck to ankle where her sturdy leather boots took over. Then she donned a padded hood that would protect her head.

Mistress Lash waived to the wooden cross shaped in an X with rope looped on each upper arm. "Hold on to the loops, please. I'll not have you unable to step away if needed."

Amanda did as requested, spreading her legs as she faced the wooden X and waited.

"Now, you'll repeat the same exercise you did before. Amanda will be able to indicate how strong your strikes are. She's experienced enough to know what would feel good and what would be too much, despite the padding."

Ros assumed her stance and let the first strike fall. Amanda did not move a bit. Continuing on, Ros struck her other shoulder and then moved down to her arse.

"Amanda, how strong were the hits?" Mistress Lash asked.

The girl looked back over one shoulder. "I felt them, though I do not think they would have done more than reddened my skin a bit. I'd have wanted a stronger bite."

Her teacher nodded. "Good. Try again, Ros."

And so Ros spent the remainder of her lesson working on striking a padded Amanda with the appropriate force per Mistress Lash's directions. With each round, she varied her instructions, testing Ros's abilities. By the end, sweat beaded on her forehead, and her arm ached from the exercise.

"That's enough for one day. Keep practicing at home, and work on deciding how hard to strike before you wield the whip." Mistress Lash ended their lesson and dismissed a rosy-cheeked Amanda.

Ros was excited that she'd made progress. Perhaps, she would soon be able to share her new skill with Flint?

Her excitement eased as she considered her next stop on her way home. She had managed to slip out of the rear of the house and leave Arthur sitting across the street as she went about her lesson. Having slipped Flint's guard's watchful eyes, she decided to take advantage and visit Lucifer's.

Which is how Ros found herself standing on the front stoop of the premier information merchant in all of London—and Flint's half-brother. She had thought Julia was crazy for coming there when she needed help, but strangely, she now found herself in similar circumstances. And her perspective had certainly changed between the revelation of his relationship to Flint and her need for information. Drawing upon all her fortitude, she rapped sharply on the entry. A few moments later, the grand wooden door opened to reveal a rather hulking beast of a man.

"What may I do for you, madam?" His query came out rough and not at all welcoming.

Accustomed to the military men that had inhabited her husband's world once, she ignored his voice and focused on answering his question. "I'm here to see Mr. Lucifer."

The man stood silent, making a full assessment of her person. His gaze drifted over her from her head all the way to the tips of her kid boots that peaked out from beneath her skirts. "Do you have an appointment?"

She bit her lip but pressed on gamely. "I'm afraid not. He and I have not met, but we share a common friend."

The man peered at her, squinting against the bright morning sunshine. "And who might this friend be?"

She stiffened her spine, set her shoulders, and nodded. "Tell him that I am a friend of Lord Flintshire."

Upon uttering the name of her lover, the door was opened wider, and the burly man bade her enter. Slipping inside the shadowed foyer, she clutched her reticule and waited. *It worked!* Apparently, being friends with someone who is related to Mr. Lucifer had opened the door for her.

The giant pointed to a chair sitting just on the left side of the foyer, "You may sit there and wait." And then he lumbered up the stairs, disappearing somewhere into the shadows.

Alone in a darkened building that was a notorious gaming hell, she began to question the wisdom of being there. Doubt crept in as the structure creaked. Soft banging noises could be heard from deep in the bowels of the building, and despite the slivers of morning sunshine that snuck in from small gaps in the draperies, it was not enough to banish her imagined specters. Julia had been to this establishment on more than one occasion and had always returned unscathed. And the man was Flint's brother, for heaven's sake. Ros scolded herself for letting her fears take hold. She could do this. She *had* to do this because not knowing what was happening had become intolerable.

While it seemed to take the man forever to return, she knew it could not have been more than a few minutes that she waited. The thumping of his feet on the hardwood floors heralded his return, whereupon he directed her to follow him. Still nervous, but hopeful that her errand was not in vain. She followed the lumbering giant up the stairs and down the long gallery.

As they approached a set of double doors, the butterflies in her stomach churned wildly about, making her regret not having at least had a piece of toast for breakfast. Determined to see this through, she walked gamely through the indicated doors. Having crossed the threshold, she pulled up short upon discovering a rather handsome man who bore more than a passing resemblance to Flint. In fact, she felt certain if he shaved his beard, they might pass as twins. Had no one else noticed their resemblance? Would she have noticed if she hadn't *known* they were related? Clearly, none of the Lustful Lords nor her sister had noticed anything.

The man in question smiled. "Welcome to my establishment, Mrs. Smith. How is it I may help you today?"

Still clutching her purse. She marched forward and claimed a chair that faced his desk. "I have come for information, Mr. Lucifer. I understand that is your stock-in-trade."

"One part of a diversified portfolio, if you will. But, yes, I do often buy and sell information. Is there a particular bit of information you are in search of, or is this merely a general inquiry?"

She grabbed her purse tighter in her hands and pressed on.

"It seems Lord Flintshire has attracted a spot of trouble from some thugs who would like him to throw a fight. I'm here to learn who that might be. Particularly, since I am currently being threatened in association with this desired outcome."

Lucifer nodded. "I see."

The silence stretched between them. Once it grew unbearable, Ros curtailed the moment. "What precisely do you see, Mr. Lucifer?"

"Perhaps this is a question better asked of Lord Flintshire?"

Ros sighed and pinched the bridge of her nose. "I agree. However, his Lordship has chosen not to share that knowledge with me. And as I am the one currently under penalty of death. I believe I have a right to know who's behind that threat."

Lucifer smiled slightly. "That is difficult logic to argue with, madam."

"Yes, well, I wish Lord Flintshire felt that way. Instead, he has gone to great lengths to avoid answering that question." Ros felt her cheeks heat as she remembered just which lengths he'd gone to.

Lucifer folded his hands and leaned forward on his desk. "Well, it's not all precisely his fault. He, too, is unsure who is behind these threats. But, he has asked me to help sort that answer out."

Ros wanted to curse. Why couldn't the man have simply said he didn't know? Obstinate, overprotective men were quite frustrating. She considered the cagey, bearded man across the desk. "And have *you* determined who is behind these threats?"

Lucifer's considering stare made her feel like a butterfly splayed out and pinned to a board for display.

"If I have and I tell you who's behind these threats, what precisely do you plan to do with the information?"

She considered his question. What would she do? What value was there in the knowing? "Well, Mr. Lucifer, I imagine I shall lean on my considerable resources, both people and money, to press for an outcome that I find desirable. Primarily, bringing an end to these threats, and for these people to leave Lord Flintshire alone."

Lucifer smiled at her, as though she were a small child or a doddering old woman to be indulged. "How very enterprising of you. But I do believe you will find the type of men we are dealing with have little compunction when it comes to dealing with a woman—or anyone, for that matter. Were you to confront them, I feel certain things would not go as you expected."

Ros snorted. "Sir, things never go as I expect. But, inevitably, they work out for the best. And, when I've set my mind to something, I have no shortage of determination and ability to achieve whatever goal I've set." She took a breath. "However, I would, in this case, defer to your greater experience in such matters. Might I ask how *you* would deal with the situation?"

Lucifer sat quietly for a long moment, his handsome face a frozen mask. She began to wonder if he would answer her question at all.

"I'm not sure, I imagine it would depend on who was behind the threats and what threats were made." He lifted one shoulder in an almost apology for his non-answer.

"Yes, well, as I said, bodily harm has been threatened. My body, to be specific. I do not know what threats were made against Flint...er, Lord Flintshire; however, I can't imagine they were any less violent than those made against me. I can easily suppose that Lord Flintshire roundly ignored those threats until they were turned in my direction."

"Well, then, I would likely go right to the source—assuming I knew who it was—and figure out what the end goal is. Clearly, there is something they want as a result of controlling the outcome of Lord Flintshire's fights. If I knew what that was, then I could determine the correct course of action." Lucifer seemed confident with that pronouncement.

Ros merely found it resulted in more questions. "Then I must circle back around to my earlier question. Have you determined who is behind this threat?"

Behind her, one of the doors of Lucifer's office snapped shut, causing her to whip around as Flint lurched into the conversation with all the subtlety of an elephant. "An excellent question, Lucifer. Have you discovered *who* is threatening me?"

Flint remained near the door, his furious gaze darting back and forth between her and Lucifer. Ros wasn't sure which of them Flint was angrier with. Perhaps both?

Lucifer was as changeable as the weather, one moment warm and sunny only to turn calm and cool in the blink of an eye. "Do not think that because you and I bear some relation that you may barge into my establishment at will and interrupt my dealings."

Ros bit her lip and worried that her impulsive action had somehow generated some animosity between the men. Their connection was so new. Could this sudden tension damage it? And then she found herself looking back and forth between them. How could someone not have noticed their likeness? It was like seeing a slightly furrier version of the man she knew. They were strikingly similar.

"Some relation? Was it not you who just the other day informed me we were brothers?" Flint let one brow lift imperiously. "And I shall barge into any room I please when I learn that Ros is alone there with a man other than myself or her father."

Lucifer laughed, a full hearty belly laugh. "I suppose I should have expected such brutish behavior from you when I had Gordie send word of her arrival."

Annoyed by all the male posturing, Ros huffed. "My God, Flint. Your thinking is positively antiquated for a man who tumbled from my bed only this morning."

Flint turned scarlet, and Lucifer laughed again. "Oh, I like you, Mrs. Smith! And here I thought Wolfington had cornered the market on mouthy pieces of baggage."

Flint growled at Lucifer. "Do not speak to her in such a manner. Brother or not, I shall lay you flat."

Lucifer gained control of his mirth and sat down. "Oh, do calm down. I meant no offense. I find Mrs. Smith as utterly delightful as Lady Wolfington. Now, the two of you sit."

Ros took a seat and muttered, "Not surprising, you would find my sister delightful."

"Do not forget I included you in that lot as well." Lucifer winked.

Flint glared as he moved his chair next to Ros's and sat down. Her brain railed against such chauvinism as she continued to absorb his lack of trust.

With a sigh, she attempted to refocus the men on the question at hand. "Mr. Lucifer, do you know who is doing this?"

He sat back and sighed unhappily. "No. I'm having the devil of a time sorting out who is behind it all. The man or woman—mind you, I've known more than one woman who'd slip a stiletto between your ribs as soon as look at you—behind this has gone to great lengths to keep themselves unknown. But, I'll discover them in the end."

"I'm not sure it matters in the end," Flint said. He looked uncomfortable for a moment, but then pressed on. "I've made arrangements to throw my next fight. I figure when I win that will draw the bastards out."

Ros blanched, every drop of blood rushing from her head to her toes. "And what of me?"

"The Lustful Lords shall keep you safe, just as we did for Julia and Wolf. You'll not be at risk."

Lucifer seemed equally displeased with Flint's scheme. "That seems a dangerous way to learn who is behind all this. We still don't know why they want you to lose the fight."

"It's too late, the plan is in motion." Flint stood. "I'd hoped you had sorted out who was behind it, but I cannot continue to put these ruffians off. Send word if you uncover anything." He held out his hand to Ros.

She couldn't help but glare balefully at him, but she still took his hand and rose. "Thank you for your time, Mr. Lucifer."

"Always a pleasure, Mrs. Smith." Lucifer stood up as Flint escorted her from the office.

Once they were settled in Flint's conveyance, she turned to him. "Why didn't you simply tell me what was going on?"

Flint sighed. "It seemed like a great deal to ask of you—to trust me—after we had only just reconciled."

"Perhaps, but should it not have been my choice?"

"You are quite correct, as usual. However, I had truly hoped to avoid telling you at all." Flint's face looked shuttered as he fell silent.

Ros, once more, found herself being shut out of his thoughts. How could she convince him to trust her with his need for pain if he couldn't trust her with what was happening in his life? As they returned to her home in silence, her thoughts raged like a storm. Would he ever trust her? And without trust, what of love?

Chapter Twenty-Two

Flint stood across the circle of bodies from the man he was supposed to lose to. Whoever was behind it all had, at least, had the foresight to pick a *winner* who was large enough to possibly hold such a distinction. Glancing around the crowd, he recognized a few familiar faces. One of those belonged to Lucifer, another, the man he'd made the agreement with. He also saw a few of the poorly disguised Lustful Lords, though he knew Stone and Cooper, along with their wives and Julia, were protecting Ros. Of course, it was all under the guise of a diverting evening with friends.

Determined to make everything look good until the very last moment, he prepared himself to take a beating. In some respects, he anticipated the pain with relish. It had been too long since his last dosing of physical pain, and the truth was the need pounding through him caused a great deal of worry. He'd been considering making this his last fight, and with that prospect in mind, the alarming level of need for pain that pulsed through him had him doubting his ability to quit.

Pushing aside his worries, he focused on the fight to come. The betting was heavy in his favor, as was the norm, with the exception of a few bets placed on his opponent. He saw Lucifer's man, Gordie, place a stiff bet on him to win. Ten thousand pounds was a hefty wager, but Flint wasn't worried. He'd yet to meet an opponent who could outlast him.

The issue for most fighters was that they endured the pain in pursuit of the win. For him, the pain was the win, so taking it for long periods tended to energize him rather than to sap his stamina.

The last of the bets were placed, once a finely turned out servant pressed through the rough crowd to lay a final wager. Flint had not seen who the money was placed on because he was focused on trying to remember where he'd seen such livery. The ostentatious gold trim on the dark blue stood out amongst the dockside rabble like a flame in the darkness. He was surprised the footman had been able to make his way through to place the bet at all, but then again, he cut a rather tall and broad figure. Perhaps the dockside rabble had decided the potential payoff wasn't worth trying to take the toff down.

The chancellor of the fight called them to the middle. "Last one standing wins, that's the only rule."

And then the fight was on.

Flint circled the ring once, watching his opponent. He took in the way he moved, how he balanced his weight, how the man observed him. All of it would matter in the end. They circled again. Finally, tired of the dancing, Flint made his move. He swept into the middle, feinted left, and landed a left jab to the man's face. Then he retreated to the edge of the ring.

"Eh. Don't punch and run, little man." The shaggy-haired fighter taunted as he eased into the open ring.

Flint grinned and waited to see what Shaggy would do next. He wasn't disappointed when he charged Flint. With a deft step, Flint slid out of harm's way. They circled each other a bit more, and then he stepped back into the center of the ring and beckoned Shaggy to join him.

With a low growl, the muscle-packed dockhand lumbered into the ring and set up opposite Flint. Then, he whipped out his fist and slammed it into Flint's face.

Pain splintered through his cheekbone and around his head. As though he'd passed out and someone had waved smelling salts under his nose, his whole body came alive. His muscles bunched and relaxed, ready for action. But, for now, he needed to keep his own successful blows to a minimum. This was meant to be a well-choreographed play.

Time slowly slipped past as Flint took punch after punch. His left eye had swollen shut, his ribs were most certainly bruised, and his kidneys ached from the beating they'd already taken. And that was just what was happening above the waist. Shaggy had not hesitated to throw knees into his thighs, kick at his knees, and even stomped on his foot at one point. It was more pain than he'd received in quite a while.

All around him, the crowd was grumbling at his apparent loss. But by the time another round of punches had landed on his lower back, he was ready to turn the tables. As he landed his first punishing blow and Shaggy stumbled backward, the crowd fell quiet. A few of Shaggy's supporters still cheered him on, but Flint knew it would be to no avail.

He landed a few more punches to Shaggy's face and then turned his attention to his midsection. As he took the upper-hand in the fight, his opponent went from surprised to shocked and, eventually, resigned. By the end, it was clear to everyone who would win the fight, even before he landed a solid uppercut to the chin that put Shaggy down and out.

As the big man hit the cobblestones, all hell broke loose. The thugs peeled away from the crowd and surged toward Flint. He'd never dropped his stance, prepared for just such an event. But before they could reach him, Lucifer's men swept in and delivered a second trouncing for the crowd to witness. Those who were not involved in the brawl had melted into the shadows to wait for either the end of the fighting or the Bobby's to arrive.

Linc and Dunmere made their way through the pack and pulled him out of the fighting. "We've got a cab waiting."

Flint sighed, he knew it was best to leave, but that didn't squash the desire to discover who was behind everything. Lucifer stopped them as they made their way past. "My men will nab one or two of the key men, and we'll get to the bottom of who's behind this. I'll send word as soon as I know something."

"I want to be there when you question them. Let me check on Ros and let her know I am well, then I shall meet you wherever you are headed." Flint was torn between a desire to discover the truth and the need to ensure Ros remained unharmed. He knew the Lustful Lords that were with her would protect her, yet deep down, he *needed* to see her. *Needed* to know she was safe.

With a sharp nod, Lucifer agreed. "Tell the driver to go to the warehouse on Charing Lane. He'll know the place."

He was surprised—though he shouldn't have been, why wouldn't Lucifer have cab drivers in his network? They often were privy to conversations that would otherwise be thought of as private. Without any further contemplation of the matter, Flint was shuffled into the cab and was wending his way through foggy London and toward the woman he loved.

His heart stuttered.

Of course, he loved her. How could he not? She was fierce and kind, with a sweet streak that might cause a man to overdose. But he wasn't the kind of man she deserved. He came with more baggage than a royal visiting party. A woman like Ros deserved a man who could protect her, care for her, be whole for her. Not just some half-feeling beast who needed pain to truly feel alive.

But the thought of giving her up, of pushing her away again, was so repugnant that the contents of his stomach curdled. He had to try to be the kind of man she needed because he knew, without a doubt, he couldn't survive without her in his life. The reality of his decision settled over him slowly as the carriage swayed gently. London slipped by him as surely as the images of his life rolled through his mind. The violence. The fighting. It must all come to an end. If he was going to make a go of it with Ros, to be the kind of man she needed, he would have to learn to live without the pain. Without the fighting.

He shifted on the bench seat, and his ribs cried out in protest. Of course, as fanciful as his thoughts had become, it could have been in protest of his decision to quit the underground fight rings as much as his moving about on the seat.

The carriage slowed and then drew to a halt. With a groan of delicious pain, he climbed from the cab. This might be the last time he felt so alive, so complete. But then he thought of holding Ros, and he pushed the thought aside. Loving her would be enough. It had to be since he couldn't reasonably expect to have both.

He looked up at the rough features of the driver. "I'll just be a few moments. Then you are to take me to the warehouse on Charing Lane."

"Very well, sir." The man nodded and settled in to wait.

Flint took the steps to Ros's home slowly, but the door opened just as he summited the top, and Ros catapulted into his arms in a flurry of perfume and silk. "Flint! I was so worried."

He clenched his teeth as she clung to him, making absolutely everything on him hurt. But, it was a pain to be welcomed and savored—something to be remembered in the future. "I can't stay long. Lucifer's men were there and have scooped up some of the lead men. He expects to get to the bottom of things soon."

Ros pulled back, worry creasing her brow. "You need to see a doctor. I am certain that you are in pain."

He grinned. "Nothing I can't manage. I merely wanted to assure myself that you were safe and still in the company of friends."

Stone loomed in the doorway. "Surely, you didn't think we would desert our posts?"

Flint felt foolish that he'd worried. "Never that, yet I still needed to see her." He found her glittering green gaze in the partial light from the open door and the porch lamps. "Needed to see you."

Then he captured her lips with his and drank in her essence. Drank in all the goodness and beauty she represented in his world. She opened to him, welcomed him as she always did with love and kindness far beyond what he deserved.

Finally, he drew back and set her away from him. If he was going to leave, he needed to do so immediately, or the temptation to stay and hold her would be too great.

"You will come back to me when your business is done." Ros directed—she did not ask.

And he had no intention of doing otherwise. "I shall always return to you. I have no choice in the matter."

By the time Flint arrived at the warehouse, the gray light of dawn was creeping across the sky. Inside, the shadows were chased away by lamps held aloft by a couple of Lucifer's men. The twin pools of light revealed two men who swayed as they stood bloodied and beaten. It was probably a miracle that they stood at all.

"Now that we've all arrived." Lucifer darted a sardonic look at Flint. "Shall we begin?"

The taller of the two men looked up, and Flint recognized him as the thug he'd met in front of the ramshackle building in Seven Dials. The one who likely threatened Ros, based on her description. "Nothing to say. Besides, how much more can you hurt us?"

Lucifer snorted. "You've only begun to feel pain, my friend. Unless you choose to talk, of course. Now, who are you working for?"

"We don't know nothing," pleaded the slimmer, shorter man.

"Nonsense." Lucifer waved his hand in the air. "We simply haven't properly motivated you as of yet. Gordie, please help them recover their memories."

The behemoth of a man stepped into the light. The slim man's eyes widened as if he'd seen a monster. The head thug merely looked resigned. Gordie shrugged and, considering how abused they already appeared, looked at the bigger man. Taking one of his hands between his own, the giant snapped the thug's finger like it was a dry twig. The thug groaned, cursed softly, but refused to cry out.

The slim man looked panicked, as though he might dash behind his bigger protector.

Lucifer sighed. "It seems you may need to do more than break a finger."

Gordie grunted, and then in a lightning-fast move that Flint could barely credit a man his size with making, he jammed his foot into the side of the thug's knee, causing his leg to crumple beneath him as he cried out in pain.

"Who do you work for?" Lucifer demanded as he loomed over the man.

"Mr. Bodwell!" The man cried out as he clutched his now damaged leg.

Flint huffed and stepped forward. "Who the bloody hell is that?"

The whimpering man's gaze darted to his companion and then down to his own leg where his hands held his knee. The slim man stiffened and glanced around the circle of men warily.

A sneaking suspicion tickled the back of Flint's brain as he watched the way the two men reacted. The thinner man never once bent to check on the familiar thug. He also looked more scared despite being significantly less abused than his companion. Something about the dynamic bothered Flint.

Lucifer must have picked up on the strangeness as well. "And who is Mr. Bodwell? Where might I find him?"

Again, the injured man's gaze darted to his friend.

"I'd hazard a guess that he is Mr. Bodwell." Flint pointed at the other man.

The slim man's eyes widened. "I don't know why you'd think I was him."

Lucifer and Flint both looked askance at the man, but it was Lucifer who spoke. "Don't you, Mr. Bodwell? Let me see if I might help clarify things for you. First of all, as someone who runs his own business that has an unsavory side to it, I can spot one of my own. Second, using that same background, there is no circumstance under which I would have hired you as muscle. And finally, your man here all but fingered you with the nervous way he looked your way as though seeking guidance."

The slim man shed the last vestiges of his assumed personae and straightened up to his full height. Still slim, he no longer appeared as diminutive as he had only a moment ago. "Fair enough. I'm Mr. Bodwell, but I'm merely a hired service. I'm not the one who has it in for Lord Muckety-muck, here."

Flint rolled his eyes.

Lucifer chuckled. "I didn't suspect you were. However, you *can* tell us who hired you."

"I've been paid well for my discretion, and if it were to get out that I didn't keep my trap shut, it could damage my reputation," the man said. "Certainly, a man such as yourself can understand, Mr. Lucifer."

Flint snorted in his head. *As if he has a choice in the matter.*

"I'd worry less about your reputation and more about your physical ability to continue breathing." Lucifer countered his concerns in the mildest tone, as though they were discussing the merits of tea versus coffee.

"Ah, you see. The problem is, I am more afraid of the man I work for than I am of you." Mr. Bodwell shrugged his shoulders as though the issue was beyond his control.

Lucifer sighed gustily, pulled out his gun, and shot the man's thigh, causing his leg to give out a bit. "Now, I was generous, and I merely shot the meat of your thigh. An injury that is easy enough to recover from, assuming you manage to avoid infection. My next shot will not be so kind. I'm thinking either a knee or a hand, but I haven't made up my mind which it will be just yet. While I am mulling over that decision, perhaps you'd like to reconsider yours?"

Flint watched the discussion play out with little concern for Mr. Bodwell. He'd played a risky game, and while the rewards may have been worth it had he won, there were no guarantees of winning.

Mr. Bodwell sniveled as he pressed his hands to either side of the wound in his leg. "He'll kill me."

"And what leads you to believe I won't?" Lucifer asked softly.

"That one right there wouldn't get wrapped up in anything so sordid." Bodwell glanced at Flint but quickly focused back on Lucifer.

Flint decided to end any question that might linger around his willingness to see harm done. He pulled his own weapon out and shot the thug who'd threatened him in the arm. "To be clear, you and your thugs threatened what's mine. In fact, you damn near ran her over in the park. Don't think I'd be bothered in the slightest by my brother killing you."

That bit of news caused Bodwell's brows to rise as his gaze darted between the two men. Uncertainty remained etched on his face.

Lucifer lifted his weapon and aimed at the man's other leg. "I suggest you reconsider your stance."

Bodwell closed his eyes and turned his face away, as though he couldn't look.

The thug on the ground that Flint had shot surged upward toward Flint, a knife in his hand. Without a moment's hesitation, Lucifer pulled to his left and fired, killing the man.

When Bodwell opened his eyes and saw his man dead, he paled. "Lord Cunningham hired me. Told me it would only be a few threats. We didn't have nothing to do with whatever happened in the park."

"Why did Cunningham want the fights thrown?" Flint growled.

Bodwell blinked. "Why does any man gamble? Either for the thrill or desperation. In his case, it was the latter. He barely had the blunt to pay my fee."

Flint looked at Lucifer, who nodded. "I've heard rumblings of unpaid creditors, but I did not have any definitive information until now."

Cunningham. Flint had suspected, no—known—it would be him. But, finally having it confirmed brought a sense of relief he could not explain. Finally, he could take action and not have any doubt.

The question was, how would he go about dismantling the man? He was already in dire straits it sounded, so it shouldn't be hard to push him over the edge.

Chapter Twenty-Three

R os sat in the small garden behind her house, reading a book grateful for a respite from her ever-watchful guard, Lord Lincolnshire. Linc was a perfectly affable man, but he took his guard-duty very seriously when he spelled her sister and Wolf, who had become her primary over-seers. She suspected that he felt particularly guilty since he'd lost her that day on Bond Street. The shady corner of her garden—courtesy of her trellis covered in climbing roses—offered a perfect spot to enjoy the warm day without sitting in the sun. All around her was an array of pinks and purples. With the delphiniums, cottage pinks, and peach leaf bellflower all in bloom, only the pink peonies could outshine them.

It had been a week since Flint's fight, and he was healing nicely from his injuries. She had stopped in to visit him along with Julia and Wolf, Theo and Stone, Emily and Coop-er, and even Lucifer on a couple of occasions. With such a gaggle of friends, she dared anyone to besmirch her reputa-tion. Of course, having Lucifer among the group would raise a few eyebrows since it was still a relative secret that they were brothers.

"Ros!" Flint's voice carried across the small garden, draw-ing her attention from her book, or more accurately, her thoughts.

"Aren't you looking hale and hearty?" She smiled and stood up to greet him as he approached.

"Indeed, I am happy to be freed from my prison with the doctor's blessing." He opened his arms and drew her against him.

"Well, that is good news. When we all came by the other day, I thought you were on the verge of attempting an escape, regardless of your health. Not that I do not sympathize."

"I was growing desperate to see you. I told Linc he could go for now." His blue eyes darkened until they were nearly black.

Her heart fluttered, and her pulse raced as she absorbed his words. She had been beside herself with worry when she was not by his side, fretting over his care, and wondering if he was getting enough sleep. She had known how deeply she cared for him, that was easy enough to reason out. But, she hadn't realized how deeply she was affected by that caring. Knowing he was unwell but out of her reach had nearly pushed her to her breaking point. Focusing on her whip practice had helped keep her occupied if a trifle sore. "I was no less pleased to see you. In fact, I am even happier to have you here now, all to myself."

He was leaning in to kiss her when he stopped at her words. "Are you? And what do you have a mind to do with me, now that you have me?"

Never let you go, whispered through her mind, but she bit back the bold words.

Instead, she pressed up on her toes and sought his mouth. Their tongues tangled as his familiar taste invaded her senses. The man forever tasted of mint and whiskey. It was a masculine, earthy taste that made her head spin and her knees weak. But with his strong arms wrapped around her, she knew she was safe from collapse, come what may. So, she clung to him and enjoyed the press of his muscular form against her softness.

Eventually, he drew back from their kiss and studied her flushed face and kiss swollen lips. She felt beautiful as he stared at her as though he could find the secrets of the universe in her face.

"Rosalind, you humble me at every turn. You came into my dark and dreary life and brought light and happiness with you. You shine so brightly my shadows have been chased away." He steadied her and then lowered to one knee and produced a ring that glittered in the afternoon sun. "I love you, and I cannot imagine my life without you in it every day. Would you do me the great honor of becoming my wife?"

She stared at him and then at the ring. The canary yellow diamond dazzled the eye, but for all that she loved him, for all that she wanted this with every fiber of her being, she hesitated because she knew there were still secrets between them. He had not owned his need for pain, had not trusted her with that deepest, darkest truth. But then, she realized she had not trusted him with her own recently discovered secret. She enjoyed the power that came with controlling the whip. The notion of having him under her direction excited her, made her needy in a way she would never have imagined. So, bearing that in mind, she let her love pour out. "Yes. Yes, I shall marry you!"

Flint rose up, slipped the ring on her finger, and swept her into his arms. Once again, they kissed, there in the shade of the climbing roses where they were hidden from prying eyes.

As their tongues twined, need for him swelled up from within. Her hands—almost as though she had no control over them—peeled off his coat and dropped it on the grass. Next, she worked his vest free, impatiently tugging at his lawn shirt as it posed yet one more obstacle in her path. He let his lips coast down her neck and over her collar bones as he worked her laces loose behind her. Her skin burned where he touched her, sending shivers of need through her body. Determined, she flicked open his trousers and worked them down until his shaft sprang free. Pleased to find him without any additional encumbrance, she turned them and pressed him onto the cushion on the stone bench.

His cock strained up from his trousers while desire pulsed through her limbs. Soaked between her thighs, she hauled up her skirts and straddled him as he tugged her bodice down and freed her breasts. The coolness of the shade brushed across her sensitive nipples, causing them to pucker into tight peaks. "Please, Flint. I need you."

And she did. But still, as she sank down on him and savored the way he stretched her open, something was off. He bent forward and sucked one tip into his mouth, tugging firmly on her nipple. Her back bowed, pressing her flesh closer to his mouth as he filled her up.

Rising up, she could feel him slide nearly out of her, and then she sank back down on him. Again, and again, she rose up and slipped back down until his hips thrust up to meet her each time. As they came together, their bodies as one, there was still a separateness. A disconnectedness that haunted her, dampened her pleasure as well as his. As she came, her climax an undeniable surge from deep within, she pulled him over with her. Together, they moaned and kissed, but the power she was accustomed to feeling with him was gone. She slipped off his softening cock and fished into her sleeve for a handkerchief she kept there. Turning away from him, she cleaned herself up as he righted his own clothes. By the time they were once again dressed, she knew she needed to speak up. If he would not share his secret with her, she would simply tell him she already knew.

Determined to fix things, she turned to him. "Flint, if there is anything—"

"There you two are!" Julia's voice cut through the moment.

Ros squeezed her eyes shut for a moment and cursed her sister's poor timing—or perhaps marginally poor timing. A few moments earlier and Julia would have seen far more than either she or Flint would have liked. Ros turned, her face still flushed, to find not just Julia, but Wolf as well. "Yes, here we are."

Flint nodded stiffly at first and then seemed to relax. Perhaps he suspected what she had been about to say? How could he? She sighed and resigned herself to dealing with the issue at hand later.

"We were about to go for a drive in the park and wanted to see if you would like to join us. Johnson told us Flint was with you in the garden." Julia glowed with the confidence of a woman securely in love.

Ros wanted that glow as well, but until she and Flint had an honest conversation, she doubted she would feel such a thing. "Yes, he was just proposing." She held out her hand and grinned, doing her best to summon the excitement of a newly engaged bride—one who has yet to understand the challenges of marital bliss.

Julia squealed and hugged first Ros and then Flint. The men slapped each other's backs, and Wolf congratulated Flint as Julia crowed over the beautiful ring he had given her. The whole exchange passed by like a fog. She could see it happening, but she couldn't touch it. Couldn't make it feel real. What was she going to do if he wouldn't tell her about his need for pain? Was she faced with yet another sham of a marriage? If she couldn't get past his silence on the subject, it seemed something would forever be off. Only she could change that. But, how did one offer to whip their husband?

It had been two days since she'd become engaged to Flint, and with all the well-wishers, she had yet to have a moment alone with him. The one time she'd cornered him at her parents, he had dodged the conversation entirely by kissing her senseless. She'd wanted to be angry with him, but his kisses did wonderful things to her while also addling her thoughts. On her way to The Market for another lesson, she stopped by Flint's home only to discover he had left mere moments before. She suspected subterfuge, but how could she accuse her fiancé of avoiding her? Yet, she knew perfectly well that he was.

It seemed a benefit of her new skills would be a way to ensure she maintained a balance with Flint. The man was prone to overbearing behavior—all of the Lustful Lords seemed to suffer from such issues, as far as she could tell. And having the opportunity to be in control of their interactions, of unleashing her dominant side appealed greatly. Parity could be found, she felt certain, but first, she had to figure out how to get him to acknowledge his needs. She worried her lip for a moment considering her options and found she was at a loss. Perhaps, she could ask Mistress Lash for guidance?

Clearing her mind of the chaotic thoughts, she adjusted the grip of the whip in her hand and let the weight center her. Closing her eyes, she could hear the excited breathing of her "client" as he waited. Then she drew in a deep breath, calmed her annoyance, and opened her eyes. She let the whip fly. The man whose back she was using for practice moaned delightedly. "Yes!"

Ros was masked and had not entered the room until the man was tied up and blindfolded. Mistress Lash had convinced him to leave his pants on since she was training a new Mistress. Though she found the experience of whipping someone to be unsettling in its intimate nature, she knew she needed to practice on someone before she approached Flint. Once Mistress Lash was convinced she had progressed well enough to handle a supplicant, she would allow her to work alone with Flint. The man cried out again, begging for more, harder.

When Ros was done, she and Mistress Lash would slip away as one of the house girls stepped in to take care of his remaining needs. Focused on her task at hand, she let the whip fly once more, this time, aiming for his upper right shoulder. Evenly she distributed the licks until his back shone a bright red punctuated by the slightly raised welts. She called things to a halt when the man began rubbing his genitals against the wall as he begged for release. Mistress Lash nodded approvingly.

Ros stepped into an empty room across the hall from the dungeon and pulled her mask off for a moment. Mistress Lash stepped in and smiled. "Well done! I've trained others using Douglas, but none have read his responses so well before. I would have to say I think you are ready."

Ros sighed. She might be ready, but she wasn't sure her fiancé was.

"You do not seem pleased about this." One of Mistress Lash's dark brows lifted in question.

Ros started to pace. "I am very pleased. It's just that if Flint does not tell me about his issue, how might I raise it without invading his privacy?"

"It's his privacy, that's the bloody problem. The man has needs, and he will not be able to hide them for long. If you do not wish to bring it up, then bide your time. He will eventually recognize he has a problem without the pain, and then he will be forced to tell you."

Ros pressed her lips together. "I shall give him some time. But if he does not speak up soon, I shall have to find some way to force the issue. He's far too stubborn for his own good."

If she'd learned nothing else about him, it was that the man could be as obstinate as a mule.

Chapter Twenty-Four

August 1862

F lint and Wolf stood in the grand hall of Wickerstone Abbey on the Yorkshire moors. Most of the guests of the Earl of Wickerstone were there to kick off the grouse hunting season. Flint was hunting an entirely different animal. But at the moment, he awaited the arrival of his fiancé and her sister. The house guests were all gathering for dinner and table games to kick off the festivities.

It had only been a few weeks since he'd proposed to Ros, but already, the burden of giving up his proclivity for pain was weighing heavily. Although, some of the stress could be attributed to his hunt for Cunningham. Everyone who was anyone had decamped from London and was in the process of making their way from one house party to another as the social season drew to a close. Of course, rumor had it Cunningham was planning to make the rounds, so Flint went in search of the man behind all the threats. He dashed first to the race meeting at Goodwood, then to the Henley Regatta, and finally to the Isle of Wight for Cowes Week.

At each must-attend social event, he would catch a glimpse of his quarry, usually across a great crowd. But, by the time he would arrive where he'd spied Cunningham, the man had moved along. Even more alarming, the rumors that had begun to surface in London were now circulating at the various events. The gist was that the man was in hock up to his eyeballs and in desperate need of funds, all of which Flint knew to be true. And yet, the man had proven elusive in the last weeks of the social season. Finally, Flint was forced to pursue an invitation to Wickerstone as a guest of Cooper.

Cunningham was certain to make an appearance since the Earl of Wickerstone was the key to his entrée into the upper echelons of society. Wickerstone was an arbiter of good taste and held one of the older earldoms dating back to 1585 when one of his relatives won Queen Elizabeth I's favor. Flint suspected piracy—or the more acceptable version, priva-teering—was the catalyst for such bounty. But, Wickerstone never discussed the actual act that won the title, merely the length of its existence.

Not normally one to enjoy such socially oriented activities, Flint had found it something of a challenge to convince everyone he wished to attend the house party. Fortunately, when Cooper questioned the earnestness of the request, Flint had been successful in convincing his friend he wanted to attend by virtue of his honesty. Cooper needed to be aware of what the likely outcome of the party would be.

When Ros descended the stairs dressed in a beautiful teal gown that displayed a dazzling amount of cleavage, with her red-gold hair glowing brightly in the gaslight, he wondered why he'd never liked such events. Beside her, her sister Julia wore a lovely bronze gown that highlighted her fiery red hair. Together, they were a stunning pair. With the ladies in tow, he and Wolf made their way into the main salons where the thirty or so guests were gathering. Cooper and Emily stood chatting with Lord Wickerstone, as well as Lord Cunningham.

Flint barely suppressed his glee.

"Good evening, Wickerstone." He nodded to their host.

Cooper went on to make the requisite introductions, ever a convoluted affair, which Flint could barely stand through, let alone follow. The labyrinthine logic of who should be introduced to whom was beyond his meager social skills. Cunningham had paled at Flint's presence, a gratifying start to his agenda for the evening. Determined to sink his hooks into the man early, Flint smiled and hoped it did not look as predatory as it felt. "Lord Cunningham, I do hope you will stay around for cards later. I hear you play a skilled hand of vignt-et-un."

"I've lost hundreds of pounds to him. He is indeed skilled," Wickerstone said and then chuckled.

"Ah Wickerstone, I merely had a run of luck a time or two. I'm not sure I can claim skill at cards." Cunningham demurred and moved to melt away.

"Well, I'd certainly enjoy a demonstration of such luck." Flint pressed the man, giving him no room to escape. "I hear it is something to behold."

Cunningham glanced around the group of men, his face a mask of composure, though his eyes had the look of someone who was being hunted. Flint took great satisfaction in the way his eyes dilated as his gaze darted around the room. The man tensed at every clink of glass and tinkle of silverware.

"I'm afraid I merely came to do a spot of hunting. I'm taking a respite from gambling for the moment." Cunningham seemed to grope for a way of explaining such an odd statement. Everyone knew gambling was as much a part of a house party as hunting. "A spiritual cleansing if you will."

"Is that so? I swore I heard someone mention your most recent trouncing at Cowes Week. It was quite a hefty sum if I recall. Who was that?" Wickerstone said as he looked about the party as though the person who'd passed along that tidbit would miraculously appear.

Flint's quarry paled and laughed awkwardly. "I'm sure you have me mistaken for someone else, my lord."

Wickerstone drew himself up. "Are you calling me a liar, sir?"

"No! Of course not!" Cunningham was close to full panic. "I merely suggested you confused me with someone else."

Wickerstone looked peeved with the placating dandy. "In any event, it is commonly known that at Wickerstone Abbey, everyone plays cards in the evening, and we do so for stakes. No one sits out."

Cunningham swallowed.

Flint relished how neatly the man had been cornered, and with so little effort on his part. Wickerstone and his well-known addiction to gambling did all of the dirty work.

With no other option but to acquiesce, Cunningham bowed to their host. "Of course, Lord Wickerstone." He turned to Flint. "I shall see you at the tables, my lord."

"Excellent." Flint nodded and let the man escape. He then looked to Wickerstone. "I certainly hope he follows through on that. I would hate to think someone was so rude as to enjoy such fine hospitality as you offer, only to slip away in the night without fulfilling their obligation as a guest."

"Cunningham is many things, but a coward is not one of them. He will be at the tables as promised." Wickerstone nodded and then sauntered off.

Flint was not convinced. But then, neither were any of the Lustful Lords in attendance. Cooper and Stone looked as doubtful as Flint felt, and Wolf merely glowered at the room in general.

Before long, the dinner chimes rang, and everyone moved into the dining room. Cunningham sat across the table and down three seats from where Flint was seated. All throughout the meal, the man talked to his dinner partners, though he barely ate. Instead, he used his fork to push the food around his plate as he smiled and nodded or offered some comment.

After what seemed to be an interminable period, the ladies rose from the table, signaling that dinner had come to an end. The men remained behind to smoke and talk politics, though a few begged their pardon so they could go upstairs and refresh themselves. Cunningham was among that number, causing Flint and his friends to also beg off.

In the hallway, the group quickly clumped together. Flint gave voice to his concerns. "He's going to bolt, I'm certain of it. He doesn't have the blunt to play at the tables."

"I agree," Stone said. "Cooper, go up and check his room. I shall head out front. The two of you should take a look around the stables."

They all murmured their agreement and split off in their various directions.

Flint and Wolf each took an aisle of the stables. Straw muffled the stomp of hooves as Flint made his way along the row.

Each stall appeared to have an occupant until he reached the last two stalls. Meeting up with Wolf at the end of the stable, his friend confirmed that all stalls appeared to be filled. They glanced around, looking for signs of anything out of the ordinary. Seeing nothing, they were about to turn and leave when the creak of leather drew them out of the stable and behind the structure.

As they stepped outside, the trees cast heavy shadows making it difficult to see anything. But then, the snort of a horse drew their attention to the deepest part of the shadows. The tension was shattered when a voice yelled out, "Go! Go! Go!" As the traveling coach lumbered to a roll, Flint realized it was carrying Cunningham away. Refusing to let him escape, he sprang into action. Grabbing onto the coach as it drew past him, Flint was able to swing himself up onto the back of the vehicle. He edged around the outside of the cabin as Wolf sprinted by on the back of a horse and leapt onto the closest horse in the harness. The carriage slowed as they came around the side of the house, allowing Flint to pull open the door of the cabin. Inside, he found Cunningham opening the other door and crouching to leap out. Flint lunged across the small space and dragged the man back inside. "I don't think so, my lord."

"Stop! Cease! Unhand me, you brigand!" Cunningham yelled.

"Oh, shut up," Flint growled and then punched the man in the face.

Once the vehicle stopped, Flint dragged an unconscious Cunningham from inside it, letting him land on his back in the dirt.

"What is the meaning of all this?" Wickerstone demanded as he strode up to the scene flanked by torchbearers. Behind him, most of the guests followed, eager for any hint of excitement.

Flint pointed down at Cunningham. "It seems you had a guest who decided to depart early."

Wickerstone sneered. "While such behavior is in poor form, and certainly speaks little of the man's honor, it is not a crime."

Wolf circled around from the rear of the carriage, holding two large silver candelabra. "Lord Wickerstone, I feel safe in assuming these do not belong to Lord Cunningham as I recently saw them perched in the hallway upstairs."

Wickerstone looked outraged as he sputtered, and the gathered guests gasped. Then the whispers swept through the crowd from front to back. Flint knew then that Cunningham was ruined. However, he decided to make sure the job was thorough. "In addition to being a shoddy guest and a thief, he also had Mrs. Smith accosted on a London street as well as myself on separate occasions. The man is penniless and apparently will do anything to hide that fact."

The murmur of the crowd swelled before settling again when their host finally spoke up. "Fetch the constabulary, and let us bring everyone inside. It seems we have quite a bit to sort out."

Chapter Twenty-Five

September 1862

Ros sat in her parlor nervously, waiting for her first guest to arrive. The weather outside was turning decidedly cool, which meant most of London was still off galivanting around the countryside from house party to house party. Lord Cunningham's ruin was being carried along the way, multiplying its reach with each house party that ended so another might begin. Content with letting London's upper crust complete that which Flint had set in motion nearly a month ago, it was time to turn her focus to more important matters. Hence, the gathering that was soon to take place.

The doorknocker's tap-tap-tap echoed through the house, setting her nerves on edge.

A moment later, Julia sailed into the room, looking fresh with her rosy cheeks and a smart tweed walking dress. "Hello, Ros. Have you been out today? It is just amazing outside. I love the crispness of the air as it pushes the summer stench away."

Just behind her came Theo and Emily looking equally as lovely and excited. "Good day, Ros!" They chorused together.

"I'm so glad you all were able to come."

After a few moments of hugs and kisses all around, they were just sitting when the last two guests arrived. In swept Marie and Madame de Pompadour, both sporting fall-colored day dresses in rich copper and a stunning hunter green that made Ros wish she had chosen something more seasonal than her soft blue day dress. "Welcome, Marie, Madame. Thank you both for joining us."

"Of course! I wouldn't miss such a gathering." Marie smiled and greeted everyone else.

Once they were all settled, Madame cut straight to the chase. "So, how may we be of further assistance to you, Rosalind?"

Taking a deep breath, Ros explained her worry. "As you know, Madame, I have been visiting The Market regularly, though I dare say the rest of you are quite in the dark as to what has transpired. I needed a little time to adjust to the idea, but soon after our last discussion, I embraced your collective recommendation and sought out Mistress Lash for lessons. I have been taking lessons from her for some time now and have become quite proficient in the art of wielding a whip."

Theo clapped her hands together excitedly. "Oh, that is capital! And how have your lessons aided your particular situation?"

Ros tilted her head while her mouth made a small moue. "That is why I have once again called you all together. Flint is unaware of my newly honed skills, and I must find a way to raise the issue as he has continued to stubbornly refuse to discuss his needs with me. In fact, he has gone so far as to insist on having ordinary sex with me."

There were gasps all around as the weight of what she said landed amongst the group.

"Oh no, that is not acceptable at all." Madame shook her head and tsked. "That man is far too noble for his own good."

"My thoughts exactly," Ros chimed in. "So I am seeking your excellent collective council once more. How do I tell him I am prepared to meet his needs,...all of them?"

Julia let one red brow lift. "Simply tell him just that. If I had merely spoken to Wolf of my fears and concerns, I expect we could have tackled our issues far earlier and with much less angst along the way."

Marie smiled serenely, "Oh, I fear our secretly noble Lord Flintshire would not listen to reason so easily. He has clearly already made up his mind to hide his needs from Rosalind. No, I fear she is going to have to rouse him to some heightened emotional state. Fear, anger, jealousy..."

"Jealousy is the one," Theo said. "Flint is capable of managing his fear and anger; he's done so for years. But jealousy—that is an emotion he is not yet comfortable with."

Emily nodded. "Without a doubt, it is the one that would push him over the edge. But how would you rouse such an emotion in him?"

Theo popped to her feet and commenced pacing as Ros was learning she was wont to do. "You must appear to have a clandestine meeting with a man at The Market. The notion shall drive Flint to distraction. But who would he not be likely to kill over such a possibility?"

"Lucifer should do the trick!" Emily offered, her voice raising an octave.

"Oh, I'm not sure about that option. His half-brother..." Ros worried her lower lip. The idea had merit, but would Lucifer co-operate? And if he did, would he do so in the way she needed?

"What?" Theo all but shouted as she froze and faced Ros.

Ros's face heated. Bloody hell! It seems Flint had still been keeping that tidbit under wraps. "Oh, um. Nothing important."

"I disagree, dear sister," Julia said. "Do share with everyone." She eyed her sister, making Ros shift uncomfortably in her seat.

"I fear Lucifer may not be a good choice as it seems that he was interested in Flint because they are half-brothers. Flint found out just before everything with Cunningham came to a head. I must ask that you ladies keep this information to yourselves until he chooses to reveal it to his friends. I very much regret my slip of the tongue." Ros tried to push her panic down.

"Oh my!" Theo sank into her seat, stunned.

The others were all just as surprised with the exception of her sister. Ros turned to her, "You seem particularly unsurprised by this news."

"Indeed. Wolf is aware of the development and has shared with me, considering all the information I had divulged about Flint when I was seeking a solution to the problem with my son-in-law, Wallthorpe. It relieved me to know there was not a more nefarious motivation behind Mr. Lucifer's interest." Julia smiled at her sister. "I've become quite fond of Lord Flintshire."

Ros smiled. "As have I. Perhaps my slip is not so bad as I had thought if he has shared with Wolf. But that still leaves me questioning Lucifer as a possible lover."

"Do you know of another man who would be willing to risk their good health to aid you in this? One who Flint might not beat to death in the moment and one he would believe? Certainly, none of the Lustful Lords would be so bold as to dabble with a woman one of the others had claimed. And with so many of them married off, it simply isn't believable," Madame pointed out. "But Lucifer would be someone he has enough doubts about, that he would believe it if he saw you in a questionable moment. And yet, with their new-found relation, I do not believe he would kill him without *some* discussion. He is the only man who might suffice *and* live to tell the tale."

"I imagine if I explain the situation to him, he might aid me in this endeavor. But, once Flint discovers us, how do I turn that to his need for pain? How do I make him see me as his lover, a wife, and someone who is able to deliver the pain he needs?"

"When he snatches you from Lucifer's arms, I promise it shan't be difficult to get him to listen to you. Should I prove to be wrong on that front, we shall have a set of footmen wrestle him to the dungeon where you shall simply show him that you are more than capable of giving him what he needs," Madame de Pompadour said rather confidently.

Ros considered her options. She could simply sit down and try to discuss the topic with him, as Julia suggested, or she could go with the plan hatched by the rest of her council. "I fear you may be right, Marie, but I should like to attempt the conversation with him one last time."

Julia nodded. "I believe he will listen to reason. But, should he not, at least, you will have tried the most straightforward path first. If he leaves you no other choice, I shall support your little subterfuge in the name of love."

Julia's support bolstered Ros's confidence in her plan. She would speak with him that night and see if he might listen to reason.

"Excellent. Be sure to send around a note once the issue is either settled or the determination is made that action is required. I shall stand at the ready." Madame rose gracefully. "With that, I shall bid you all adieu."

Mrs. Johnson wheeled in the tea cart just a Madame departed, prompting the rest of Ros's guests to grin conspiratorially as they waited for the privacy to resume their chatter.

Ros sat in her front parlor, watching Flint flip through the book he'd brought along with him that evening. They had taken to behaving much like an old married couple as they sat quietly in her parlor, she with her knitting needles, and he with some book or stack of correspondence to review. Eventually, they would retire upstairs together where Flint would make staid, unfulfilling love to her.

It was enough to drive a woman mad.

"Flint?" Ros kept working her needles as she waited for him to respond.

He looked up from his book. "Yes, Ros?"

She set her needles aside. "I wish to raise a delicate issue that is of some concern for me."

He, too, set his distraction aside. "What is upsetting you?"

His obvious concern spurred her on. Surely, this time he would be open to the discussion. "Well, it has come to my attention that something has changed between us..." she hesitated, her nerves besting her for a moment, "...in the bedroom."

"Oh?" His brows rose—both of them.

Her cheeks heated as she dredged up the words. "You see, I am quite certain that you have needs that are going unmet as things currently stand."

He looked surprised. "I have no idea what you mean! I am quite content with how things are between us when we make love. I have no needs—as you put it—that require being met. I love being with you. Being inside you. You are enough to make me happy for the remainder of my days."

Ros sighed. She knew this was a distinct possibility. It was time to use plain speech. "Flint, I know why you sought out those dockside fights. Without the pain that fighting brought you, your level of arousal has been less. Making love as we have is not enough to satisfy your preferences since you've ceased fighting. I want you to know I am prepared to meet all of your needs." She hesitated, giving him a moment to absorb what she had said. "I have been taking lessons—"

"Cease this conversation at once." Two patches of red appeared high on his cheeks. "As I said, I have no needs that are not being met. I do not know what link you have imagined between my fighting ways and our intimate moments, but you are wrong." Flint looked uncomfortable and bordered on being angry.

Ros got up and crossed to where he sat on the settee. "But I know how to give you what you desire. I've taken lessons so that I may safely deliver the pain you need—"

"Rosalind, do you love me?" he asked, his tone gruff.

"Of course, Flint. You know how I feel about you. But I need you to trust me with all of you. The light and the dark within you because I have the same elements within me. And I need you to love me anyway." Fear that he would push her away coursed through her veins as she watched the wary man.

"Then please, leave this concern you have behind. I do love you, and I have no need for anything beyond the normal bounds of what we share. The fighting is over, I promise you I shall not put you in such danger ever again."

She sighed, but pressed on, desperate for him to hear her message. "I've learned to wield a whip, and I enjoy it immensely. I want to give you—"

"Enough!" Flint stood. His body thrummed with tension as he stared down at her. "I believe I should go. I don't know what has gotten into you, but this is too much."

And then he fled her home as though a pack of hell hounds nipped at his heels, leaving his book behind. Ros sat alone, contending with an overwhelming sense of defeat. How could their conversation have gone so badly? Tears slipped down her face as she grappled with what she knew needed to happen next. She must show him that she was capable of meeting his needs. It was the only answer because she refused to give him up.

A week slipped by, during which Flint assiduously avoided her. She allowed the behavior to stand since it played into her plans. The time apart would serve to strengthen the desire that bubbled between them so that when the time came, he would be unable to deny the truth. And with each passing day, she knew she would literally have to tie the man up and show him that she could provide what he needed. With time to consider her friends' loosely plotted plan, she could see a few necessary changes were required. Her first stop was to discuss her altered plan with Madame de Pompadour so that she could prepare to take the appropriate action. Then, she needed to meet with Lucifer to strike a sort of devil's bargain. She just hoped it wouldn't cost her the very thing she hoped to win. Fortunately, she would soon know how it all turned out.

Chapter Twenty-Six

Flint, Linc, and Arthur sat in Flint's billiards room. Linc was in the process of soundly trouncing Arthur at the game.

"Bloody hell! That's another three points," Arthur complained loudly.

Flint sat morosely, sipping a whiskey, mostly ignoring the pair. He had spent the last six days coming to terms with the truth of Ros's words. She was correct. He could not continue to deny the part of him that needed pain to enhance his arousal. Without it, he was only half a man. Half a lover.

But how could he thrust that burden on to one as gentle as Ros? Or worse, ask her to stand by as someone else gave him what he needed? Certainly, she was the one who raised the issue, but could that mean she was prepared for what he required? How could she truly understand what it was she would have to do to fill his needs? Yet, he knew at the very depths of his soul that he needed her as much as he needed pain. He needed her love, her laughter, her companionship as he grew old. Under no circumstances could he imagine his life without her in it. Once again, he was back to the only answer he could come up with. He would have to learn to live without the pain because living as half a man was better than living without all of Ros.

And so the vicious circle continued until Arthur intruded on his mental solitude.

"Flint, would you please get off your arse and give this man the trouncing he deserves?"

Flint ignored his friend's plea, still mired in his mental gyrations.

Linc grinned. "Leave him be, Arthur. He's muddling through whatever obstacle he imagines lies between him and Ros."

"I wouldn't call it imagined." Flint raised his glass to his lips and drank.

Arthur stopped and peered at him. "No, I wouldn't say it was imagined either. Regardless of it taking physical form or not, an obstacle is an obstacle. Until you talk it out with someone, it may always seem immovable."

Flint grunted. There was no chance he would willingly discuss his sexual predilections with anyone else. He barely understood his own needs; how could he explain it sufficiently for anyone else to comprehend?

"Where the bloody hell are you hiding, Flint?" A newly familiar voice boomed down the hall and into the open door of the billiards room. Flint didn't bother to respond, since the clomp of feet indicated he was already headed in the correct direction. A moment later, he was proved right when his newest visitor appeared.

"Lucifer!" Linc greeted Flint's half-brother jovially.

"Hello. You all seem to be having a jolly time." Lucifer hesitated as he spotted Flint sitting in the corner. "There you are, brother-mine."

Flint looked up for a moment before waving toward his friends. "The joviality is all over there. You'd do well to keep to that side of the room."

Lucifer ignored his guidance and sat down next to him. "Oh, I don't think you would want me to do that. I come bearing news for you."

"News? I can't imagine what news I might wish to hear."

"How about this news? Your very own Ros is even now entering The Market for a night of sin and debauchery." Lucifer used such a grave tone that Flint found it impossible to laugh at his poorly chosen jest.

"I am not amused. Not that any such jocularity would have its desired effect tonight." Flint took another swallow from his glass and savored the burn of the liquor.

"Who suggested I was making light of such a serious subject? I come to you in earnest. Ros is at The Market, and

I cannot imagine any good shall come of it. We should go and... and... save her from herself." Lucifer looked worried.

More than worried, truthfully.

Flint stirred from his emotional morass. "What the devil do you mean, Ros is at The Market?"

Lucifer cursed soundly. "Have you listened to a bloody word I've said? Ros is at The Market. I strongly suggest you attend to her immediately before she gets herself into trouble."

Shaking off his confusion and the fog he'd allowed to shroud his last few days, Flint stood as he set his drink down and strode toward the door of the game room with Lucifer close on his heels. "How did you come by this knowledge of her whereabouts?"

Lucifer shrugged as they pounded down the stairs and out the front door. "I have eyes and ears everywhere."

Flint grunted as he hailed a cab. He was grateful that Lucifer had come to him with the news, but it still seemed strange that he would have been informed. Though, he supposed that since his brother trafficked in information, it made sense that someone would sell him this bit about Ros. Yet something about the idea that Ros was at The Market seemed strange. Certainly, she had been there once to see him, but how would she have gained entrance a second time? Julia wouldn't give her sister an entry coin. Would she? Everything about this seemed off, and he couldn't help but wonder what the hell was going on.

A quarter of an hour later, Flint strode through the main salon of The Market in search of a particular redhead. Everywhere he looked, he found blondes and brunettes of varying shades, but no one with red hair. Trailed by Lucifer, he circled the main floor of the establishment, moving through the front salon, the card room, and the foyer, which seemed busier than London Bridge at mid-day.

Frustrated, Flint turned toward the grand staircase of the house. Lucifer caught up with him. "Where are you going?"

Confused by the question, since he thought it was perfectly obvious, he stopped. "I'm going upstairs to look for Ros, where else would I be going?"

Lucifer sputtered. "You can't just go upstairs and start opening doors looking for a woman."

Flint hesitated. "Well, no, I was thinking to look at the Hall of Mirrors."

"Oh," Lucifer hesitated. "I suppose that does make sense, although you could more quickly eliminate the public spaces on the lower floor."

He looked at his brother. Was he steering him in a particular direction? No, surely not. But now, he was curious, so he turned and headed down the stairs he had intended to ascend. Heading down, he stepped into the long wide hall the provided access to the two public rooms where a fair amount of sexual activity was permitted. One side held a room designed much like the upstairs salon, but it was dotted with little nooks that offered a minimal amount of privacy for those who only wanted a semblance of such.

The other side was the dungeon. That was where many of the member sadists and masochists came together. Flint was all too familiar with the typical inhabitants of that room since he sometimes had found himself bound to the wall or a cross for the express purpose of receiving the pain he required. It was not a choice he made often because he found such a public display of his more deviant needs disquieting. Fighting in the back alleys of London's wharf did not carry the same stigma of deviance that being chained to a wall and whipped did, though he found the latter far more satisfying.

Of course, once he found Ros, none of it would matter. He would whisk her from The Market and then discover what had driven her to visit it when he was not there. And she knew he would not be there since he had ceased visiting while they had been engaged. The question of why pounded through his head as he wended his way through the salon side of the lower floor. After ten minutes of peering at one couple after another in varying degrees of intimacy, he was both aroused and more concerned that he had yet to find Ros. Doubt seized his heart. Was she upstairs in a private room? No. Not his Ros. Whatever had brought her to The Market, there would be a worthy explanation. He was sure of it.

"Flint!" Lucifer called to him. "In here."

Flint stopped in the wide hallway and stared at where Lucifer had disappeared into the dungeon. Surely, she was not in there! She couldn't possibly be in the dungeon. The Ros he knew and loved would never be found in such a place. Would she?

Chapter Twenty-Seven

S weat trickled down her spine, tickling its way over every knob and dip until it found the crevice where her cheeks met. Her arm wasn't tired yet; after all, she'd only been lashing the man currently chained to the wall for ten minutes. After hours of practice, she had more resilience than that.

No, the sweat was a product of her nerves.

Waiting for Flint to appear in the dungeon of The Market was excruciating. All-day she'd waffled between going through with her plan and calling it off. Doubts had assailed her. What if he was angry that she'd hidden her lessons from him? What if he was jealous of the man she was currently whipping? What if he was appalled that she'd learned such a skill? What if he simply rejected her offer? Would any man truly want his fiancé—let alone his wife—to do such a thing to him?

Her gut churned, but she remained focused on the man who needed her for the moment. With his pants still on at her request, he stood waiting in anticipation for the next fall of her lash. When she let loose with the leather and struck flesh, he moaned—loudly.

Caroline, his house companion for the night, stood at the ready. As soon as he'd had enough to get him worked up, she would swoop in and take care of his sexual needs. Ros was simply filling in for Mistress Lash. The dungeon was abnormally quiet, allowing Ros to hear the rattle of the man's chains, the creak of her leather pants, and the snap of the whip as it landed on his back. Normally, there would be a chorus of moans as men and women were pleasurably tortured. But tonight, in order to assure everyone's safety, Flint would find her here with as few witnesses as required.

"Oh, God, Mistress. Don't stop!" The man cried after she'd paused for a few moments.

Prompted to return to her previously steady rhythm, she lifted the lash once more. And again. Soon, she pushed all her worries from her mind and concentrated on the fall of her lash.

"Flint!" Lucifer's voice broke through her trance-like state. "In here."

The moment of truth had arrived, but she focused on her arm movement. The last thing she wanted to do was hurt the man who had trusted her because she was distracted.

Thud. Thud. Thud.

"Lucifer, I told you she can't possibly be in here." Flint strode into the room.

Ros knew her mask obscured her face, but she'd left her hair to tumble in a cascade of curls over her shoulders. There was no possible way for Flint to mistake her for Mistress Lash or any other woman.

"What the bloody hell?" Confusion colored Flint's normally confident tones.

"Uuunnhh!" The man chained to the wall cried as his knees gave out.

Caroline raised her hand. "Enough. He's had enough."

Ros pulled in her whip, coiling it in her hand. Caroline and a footman released the man and helped him walk from the room. But before he passed her by, he insisted on stopping. "Thank you, Mistress R. Thank you."

His effusiveness made Ros uncomfortable, mostly because she'd only learned how to whip someone so she could help Flint. She was not cut from the same cloth as Mistress Lash. "You're quite welcome," she mumbled as his companions led him from the room.

Confusion still reigned supreme for Flint. "Ros?"

With the relative privacy of just the four of them—Flint, Lucifer, a footman, and herself—she decided to remove her mask. She wanted Flint to have no room for denial. "Yes, it's me."

Flint sucked in a sharp breath. "I don't understand."

"Oh, I think you do. Just stop and take a moment to consider what you've seen." Ros stood there, holding her mask in one hand and her whip in the other.

Flint glanced around the space, his gaze hardening. "How long has this been going on? Why don't I know this about you?"

"I've been working with Mistress Lash for a few months now. She agreed to train me at my request. Tonight was the second time I have whipped one of the guests of The Market. Up to then, I have used stuffed shirts and some of the ladies of the house who appreciate such activities." She drew a breath. "As for why you don't know this about me, well, in large part, it is because you have hidden this side of yourself from me. Was I to invite you over for tea and then announce mid-sip that I have taken up the hobby of whipping people for pleasure?"

Lucifer chuckled as a strangled sound escaped from Flint. "I- I- I suppose you are correct. That would be awkward."

"Indeed. Almost as awkward as the evening I did, in fact, try to discuss your needs with you, and you shut me out. You refused to hear what I had to say. You left me no choice but to *show* you the truth."

Flint remained nonplussed. "But I do not want this from you. For you. Have you done this all because of me?"

Ros's heart pounded in her chest, seeming to cause her ribs to ache with each beat. "Of course, I did this for you. I love you. And I refuse to allow you to have any needs fulfilled by someone else. If you need pain to become aroused, then I shall be the one to deliver it."

"No. I cannot ask that of you. Cannot expect someone gentle and kind to deliver pain in pursuit of pleasure. *It* is wrong. *I* am wrong." Flint stepped backward, pulling away from where she stood. The divide between them seemed to yawn and grow wider.

"It would be wrong for you to deny this part of yourself. It would be wrong for you to seek out someone else to provide you the pain you need. *You* are *not* wrong."

Pain and panic surged through his dark eyes. "A woman of quality, a wife, should never be asked to debase herself in such a way. To fulfill such dark needs. I cannot..."

Ros's gut twisted. She'd hoped it would not come to this, but clearly, she had no other choice. She turned her gaze to Lucifer, who had stood quietly by. "He leaves me no choice."

With that remark, Lucifer and the footman each grabbed one of Flint's arms. Like a desperate animal, Flint roared as he thrashed about trying to dislodge the pair. The footman lost his grip and stumbled backward until he landed on his backside. With his left arm free, Flint swung at Lucifer, who ducked in the nick of time.

Coming up behind Flint, Lucifer bent his brother's arm back and up. Bent over by the move, Flint could do nothing to free himself without risking a break to his arm. "Come on, little brother, stop fighting the pretty lady."

"No. I can't do this to her. Please, don't allow this to happen." Flint sounded pained as Lucifer nudged him toward the manacles that hung from the wall.

Pulling the metal bands down, the footman quickly slipped them over Flint's wrists. Then Lucifer moved over by the pulley system to draw his brother's arms up.

Ros had dreaded this possibility, but she believed she could show him how things could be between them. It seemed strange to her that she had come to accept his need for pain, yet Flint had not. He obviously still struggled with his own needs.

"Lucifer, could you please cut his coat and shirt off? This will be more effective if I have access to his skin."

"Don't Lucifer. If you have any hope of us being brothers, you must stop this madness," Flint pleaded.

Lucifer grunted and leaned in close to Flint. Ros could not hear what he said from across the room as he cut the clothing from Flint's back. But as Lucifer drew away, Flint lunged toward him cursing wildly.

Ros felt her face drain of blood, her doubts rising on a fierce tide. Was she doing the right thing? What if he hated Lucifer for this? What if he hated *her* for this? For making him face his own desires?

Lucifer walked toward her as the footman stepped out of the dungeon. "We shall remain just outside the door. When he's had enough, let us know, and we shall help you get him to a room." Lucifer turned to leave.

"Wait." Apprehension made her limbs heavy as she continued to struggle internally. "What did you say to him to make him so angry?"

Lucifer smiled with a debonair, positively seductive upturn of his lips. "I told him that if a woman as sensual and arousing as you wanted to whip me, I'd happily strip naked and submit. So if he didn't want you, didn't want to take what he needed from you. I would be more than happy to step in and oblige you here and in bed."

Ros inhaled sharply.

"He threatened to geld me if I laid one finger on you, so I have to assume the man is head over heels in love with you, even if he is living in denial about his need for pain. Once you help him see the truth, all will be right between you. Do not doubt that your course is true."

Her heartbeat slowed, and her doubts receded. Love would see them through this trial.

As the door of the dungeon closed, Ros gathered her courage and her determination. She would see this through. She loved Flint too much not to fight for him, even if he was the one she had to best.

Chapter Twenty-Eight

F lint struggled against the iron manacles around his wrists. He knew it was pointless, but he couldn't stop trying. He had to prevent Ros from doing something she would regret. Prevent her from doing something that would fundamentally change who she was. He refused to be responsible for that. Couldn't live with that on his conscience; there wasn't room for both his twin brother and Ros to live there.

So, he yanked on the chains that had him stretched out, though both his feet were firmly planted on the floor. Behind him, he heard Lucifer speaking to Ros, and it made him crazy to think the man might be low enough to offer himself up to her. Flint knew Ros would never take him up on it, but it still rankled. It still made him want to rage at the thought.

Ros couldn't be permitted to do this. His future wife should not be tainted by his dark needs. His deepest shame. It wasn't right. Loathing surged to the fore. Loathing for himself and for the fact he did not have enough self-control to cease needing the pain.

It was laughable, really. He was known for his self-control. For the cool façade he seemed to always possess, even in the face of the greatest provocation. And yet, despite all of that, he could not stop the need from curling up his spine and wrapping around his heart. He couldn't stop his darkness from contaminating the one true and pure thing in his life—Ros.

Despair opened beneath him like a gaping maw waiting to swallow him whole. Had he not been chained to the wall, he might have dove in headfirst, but instead, he stood there dangling above it. Waiting. Waiting.

The dungeon door closed with a dull, unremarkable thud.

Leather creaked behind him as he stared at the stone wall in front of him.

"There are a few things you should know before we begin." Ros's voice cut through the silence. "First, I love you. This all begins and ends with that. Second, this may have started out because I wanted to do this for you, but somewhere along the way, I found that I enjoy wielding the whip. I don't want to do this with anyone else, but you should know I also never want to cease doing it. This is now as much for me as it is for you. And finally, if you need pain to feel whole, to become aroused, or for any other reason, *I* am the one you will come to. I shall not tolerate you seeking out anyone else."

Flint's body trembled with the need to take action, to stop her. Yet he remained at her mercy. "Ros—"

"Silence. You will not speak unless you are asking for more or less, harder or softer, or for me to stop. If you need this all to end, then say pineapple. Otherwise, I shall continue until I am sure your needs have been met. Are we clear?"

A shiver raced down his spine. To his great dismay, it was a shiver of need laced with desire. Ros had trotted out her field marshal voice, and it did things to him. Made him want her, want to tame her, to dominate her, and make her submit to him. But first, he would have to submit to her. Submit to his own needs.

Fear and anxiety surged. Good or bad, everything would be different after this.

The fall of the whip sketched across the stone floor, and goosebumps broke out over his skin. Anxiety shifted to anticipation, and fear morphed into hope.

The crack of the whip broke the silence a split second before the bite of the lash came down over his right shoulder. Fire licked up and down his body, searing everything in its wake. A second crack and bite of pain on his left shoulder. The fire settled into a muted heat that coiled low in his belly.

Another lick of pain, the hum of pleasure in his ears drowned out the crack of the whip. His upper back sizzled, and the coil of heat slid lower to settle in his balls. Two more lashes landed, and his body vibrated with pleasure and heat. Behind him, Ros paused in applying the whip. The scuff of her shoe on stone alerted him to her proximity. Then he felt the gentle caress of her fingertips as she traced down one stripe on his back, causing a tingle to ripple across his skin.

She leaned into him until her breath whispered past his ear. "You may fight me all you wish, Flint. But, I shall break your resistance." She reached down and stroked his hardening cock. "Already, your body is responding to me. To this."

It seemed to take forever for her to return to where she'd been standing. And then nothing. No movement. No sound. Not even a breath.

Was he too stubborn? Had she given up on him?

And then the crack of leather and the bite of pain came once again. Relief soared through him. The pure joy of knowing she was near.

His cock swelled as he relaxed and ceased to fight the inevitable.

"More," his voice cracked as he asked for what he knew he needed.

He heard her inhale sharply, and then the lash came fast and furious. She unleashed a hailstorm of blows across his back and shoulders that brought him to an intense state of arousal. His breath caught in his chest as bliss pummeled him. For a moment, panic set in as he realized he was a hair's breadth from releasing in his trousers. But then the barrage eased up, slowing to a rhythmic cadence that lulled him into that place he always sought when he needed pain.

The walls around him fell away, and he seemed to float.

It may have been mere moments, or he could have been there for an hour. He wasn't sure. Honestly wouldn't have cared, except he wanted to feel Ros's arms around him. Wanted to know she was near.

When male hands—he assumed they were male since they were not delicate enough to be Ros's—eased him down from the shackles and stretched each of his arms over broad shoulders, a low moan escaped. Ros, he wanted Ros.

The stretch of his skin reignited the fire across his back, but only in the best way.

By the time he was eased onto his stomach on a bed, he was finding some level of coherence. Lifting up, he sought Ros out, but she was not where he could see her.

Then a hand was placed on his upper back, and he was pushed back down. "Lie still."

He reached back for her. "Come here, Ros."

"Do as you're told. You may hold me when I'm certain your back is cared for."

He lay there, feeling chilled as she rubbed a salve on his skin. Then she helped him sit up and drew a soft linen shirt over his head. He pushed his arms through the holes and then looped them around her waist before she could escape him once again. With his head pressed against her breasts, he felt as much as heard her chuckle. "Impatient man."

"Bloody right. I've waited far too long to have you in my arms again."

With a strength born of need and an incredible amount of gratitude, he hauled her into the bed alongside of him. He lay back, easing his weight down. His back ached, but it was the pleasurable ache that drove his desire higher. And he'd received that pleasure at the hands of the woman he loved. He looked over at her, let his gaze snare hers, and studied the bright green depths.

As hard as he peered, he could see no darkness. No taint, as he had feared.

"You'll not find what you are looking for. I'm whole and happy, the very same woman I was an hour earlier," Ros protested his search for some hideous blackening of her soul. And that is what he had been seeking. He needed to know, to believe what she'd said, that by meeting his needs, she was not damaging herself in some hidden manner. He cared too much, not to be certain.

"You are sure that you won't come to despise me? Despise what it is that I need from you?" Fear and doubt danced around the burgeoning hope that fought to banish them.

"How could I despise the very thing in you that answers to my own dark needs? It would be like hating myself, and I gave up on such useless emotions years ago. I love you, Flint. You. Exactly as you are."

As he heard the clarity of her conviction in her words, hope and love shined bright, chasing all other emotions away. No shadows were left, and it felt wonderful.

"I love you, too, you brash wonderful woman." And then he captured her mouth with his, delved past her lips to explore deeper.

She inhaled and met his tongue stroke for stroke, both of them twining and twisting as each tried to take control. The burn of his back melded with the joy from within as they kissed. Time stood still as their limbs became intertwined—their hearts beating as one.

Chapter Twenty-Nine

S he had done it! She had finally whipped Flint, and he had responded. Even now, Flint was kissing her. Loving her. And all of her worry over the past weeks had disappeared like so much jetsam. Her shoulders felt lighter. Her heart fuller.

Sitting up, she drew back from the kiss and began unhooking the front of her corset. Picking up on her intentions, Flint's wandering hands joined hers and made short work of the task. That left her boots and trousers as the next obstacle.

Needing to be naked so she could feel him skin to skin, she clambered off the bed and tugged her boots free of her feet. Next, she yanked her trousers down and took her drawers with them. With just her chemise remaining, she drew near the bed. Flint lay there with his trousers open and his cock standing at the ready as his half-lidded gaze swept over her. Goose flesh rippled over her sensitized skin as her nipples pebbled even tighter. Around her, the luxurious room shrouded in shades of blue faded away as she reached for his pants. Carefully drawing them down his legs, she drew the moment out, letting the tension stretch and grow between them.

"Ros." Flint reached toward her but couldn't make contact. "You're killing me."

"You're stronger than that." She chuckled. "I dealt you far more pain earlier than waiting a little longer for my touch could provide."

He shook his head and sat up with a grunt. "You've no idea what it costs me to be near you and not touch you."

Then he grabbed her chemise and tugged her until she fell on top of him. As her weight landed, he rolled her beneath him, giving her no time to regain the upper hand.

"Flint, your back!"

"Is fine. A few welts are a small price to pay for the pleasure you've already delivered. Now, it's my turn to make you feel good." His voice grew husky with desire as he spoke, and then he kissed her.

As their tongues tangled once again, she reveled in the weight of him pressing her into the mattress, adored the heady sandalwood scent mixed with something uniquely masculine that was Flint. Lost in the moment, she slipped her hands up his sides and around to his back. When she stroked the soft linen over his back, he moaned and ground his cock against her aching pussy. Even with the linen pressed between them, the zing of pleasure shot from between her legs to each of her limbs. The promise of more had her meeting his kiss stroke for stroke, slide for slide.

Easing away from her lips, he dropped kisses along her jaw and then down her throat. As he neared the juncture of her neck and shoulder, he sank his teeth into her skin, sending shivers of delight along her spine. This was what had been missing from their lovemaking, this undeniable connection that made her feel beautiful, desired, and sexy.

While he moved lower, he tugged the neckline of her chemise below her breasts, granting himself access. As his lips captured one beaded tip, his fingers sought out the other. And in a synchronized move that had her arching up off the bed, he pulled and sucked. A full body spasm wracked her as Flint commanded her pleasure. Remaining where he was, he switched breasts and repeated what he'd done. Ros cried out, "Oh, God. Please, more!"

He looked up at her from where he crouched and grinned. "Oh, love, I've just gotten started."

Then he shifted even lower and spread her thighs wide. Making room for his shoulders, he pressed his palms to her inner thighs and pushed them out and then up. Lying spread open to him, she knew she would let him do anything to her in that moment, give him anything he wanted. He already owned her heart and soul; her body was merely part and parcel to the package.

He hesitated as he stared down at her, then slowly reached down to draw a finger through her wetness. "The question I have is, what leeway will you grant me to your body?"

Confused, she was pulled from her blissed-out haze to find Flint staring at her intently. "What leeway? There is nothing I would deny you."

Using two fingers, he plunged into her pussy, filling her suddenly and stealing her breath. With a ruthless sensuality she could not recall him possessing before, he worked his fingers in and out of her while he stroked her clit with his other hand. Swept away by the intense pleasure he elicited, she gasped and rode the wave until he stopped moving.

"Don't stop!" The words were more moaned than spoken, but she felt sure he understood.

"Look at me, Ros." The command in his voice drew her focus once again. "You'll tell me if I hurt you in any way."

A moment of doubt had her breathing in sharply, but this was Flint. He'd never hurt her. "I trust you."

"That's not what I asked. You'll tell me if I cause you any pain. It's not your preference, and I don't want to do that to you."

She nodded. "I'll tell you."

"Very good. Now, take a deep breath." Then he drew his soaked fingers from her channel and carried them lower down.

When he pressed against her tight rear entrance, she hesitated. But then he leaned over and drove his tongue inside her as he pushed a finger past the tight pucker. Concentrating on her breathing, she tried to relax and let his tongue distract her from his finger. Then he pumped his finger in and out of her backside a few times. Just as she'd grown accustomed to the foreignness of his intrusion, he added a second finger. Feeling terribly full, she wiggled against him.

"Easy, love. This is all I'll give you this time." And then he sucked on her clit as he fucked her arse with his fingers.

Intense, deep pleasure pounded through her like a stampede of horses. She cried out, bucking against his fingers and mouth as she tried to throw herself off the edge of ecstasy. But he refused to let her wrest control, and he carried on with his ministrations, leaving her dangling at the cusp. And then his tongue swept over her clit as his fingers sank inside of her arse, and her entire world shredded into bliss. She screamed his name as she broke apart, sure that he would be there to catch her when she fell.

Long moments of nothing—no sound, no light, no touch—surrounded her until she slowly returned to a coherent state. She hadn't passed out, but it had been a close thing.

"There she is." Flint smiled as he cradled her against his chest.

She looked up at him and shook her head to clear it further. "Bloody hell, Flint. You should warn a girl."

He laughed as he returned to kissing her, drawing her back into their passionate haze. But, she couldn't help but think that if that was what an oral orgasm was like post whipping, she wasn't certain she would survive when he fucked her.

Chapter Thirty

Flint sucked on one of her nipples again, loving how responsive Ros was. Her body arched into him, demanded more. And more he would give her. She had given him so much, the satisfaction he offered her in return felt paltry. With his cock aching to be inside her, he shook as he stirred the coals of her desire. Finally, she cupped his face in her palms as she plucked him off her breast. "I need you inside me. Stop dawdling."

His heart felt like it might burst from his chest. "What have I done to deserve a woman such as you?"

She bit her lip and smiled at him. "You silly man. You were brave, loyal, and idiotically protective. But mostly, you loved me."

With that, he stopped wasting time and shifted on top of her again. But once more, she halted him.

"Not like this." And then she scrambled from beneath him and got on all fours. "From behind, please."

Flint grinned—at this rate, he might never stop. "As the lady wishes."

Then he lined up with her entrance and sank inside of her in a single thrust. Seated to the hilt, he caught his breath as her heat and wetness enveloped him. And as he leaned over her, the skin on his back pulled, sending little sizzles of pain out from the welts she'd gifted him. The pain and pleasure melded into a storm of sensation that had him pumping in and out of her.

In an effort to draw things out, he tried to recall the last play he attended scene by scene in all its tedious glory. But between the soft moans, the soft backside cushioning each thrust, and the way she pushed back to meet him, he quickly realized he would not last. So, he reached down and found her clit as he shuttled in and out of her tight pussy. With a few well-timed strokes of his finger, he felt her spasm just as he lost his own control. Together they came with a scream he was certain could be heard as far as Westminster. He continued to push into her until she collapsed beneath him, then he followed her down, landing on the bed beside her.

Lying there, with Ros cradled in his arms, he knew there was no denying the truth that resonated deep within him. If he was honest, it had resonated since that first night she had marched into The Market, seized control, and tended his wounds before blowing his mind in bed. That was the moment he first glimpsed the woman that had taken command in the dungeon and delivered what he needed in amazing fashion.

His back throbbed in time with his heart, but it was more like a pulse of pleasure that lasted and lasted. With a sigh of contentment, he gathered her closer. "I'm never letting you go."

Ros laughed. "I fear you will have to at some point if you plan to ever groom yourself or bathe again."

"Not at all. I shall drag you into my bath every day and force my valet to groom me while I hold you in my arms." He squeezed her tight.

A soft sigh escaped Ros, lifting his heart. Rolling her onto her back, he pushed the loose strands of her hair back before holding her face in his hands. He locked on to her soft green gaze. "I tried to set you free, protect you from my dark needs. When that failed, I tried to hide those needs. And still, you refused to let me hide. Refused to let me short change you in any way. Ros, you have become the center of my world. My everything." He leaned in and kissed her. Long. Slow. Deep. When he finally drew back, he smiled because he couldn't contain the urge. "I love you."

A tear slipped down her cheek as she smiled up at him. "I fell in love with you the moment you walked into my parlor and offered to be my temporary beau." Then the softness melted away as the fierce Mistress from the dungeon appeared. "And if you ever try to hide from me again, know that I shall hunt you down and re-stake my claim."

Then she yawned, utterly ruining the effect.

"Sleep, my love, and know I shall be right here when you wake." Flint rained kisses over her cheeks and nose before he settled into the bed next to her, and together, they began to drift off to sleep.

"Oh, Flint. Before I forget, about your brother."

Flint grunted. "I shall deal with him in my own time."

Ros pushed up on one elbow. "He helped me because he cares about you. Do not hold that against him."

"Go to sleep, Ros. I'll sort out how to address what happened with Lucifer later." He leaned over and kissed her once more. "Now, sleep."

Three days had passed, and all was right in her world. Ros had won the heart of the man she loved, and they were currently ensconced in his morning room having breakfast together. Despite all of that domestic bliss, there was a small knot in her stomach. She needed him to forgive his brother. With that in mind, she had taken action—once again, without Flint's knowledge. He really was as stubborn as a mule.

Flint was busy eating his eggs when his butler appeared in the sunny yellow room bearing a silver salver with a letter. "My lord, this just arrived by courier."

"Thank you." Flint set down his fork and picked up the correspondence before breaking the seal. He read the missive, his brows drawing together.

"What is it?" Ros asked as she sipped her coffee.

"A letter from my investigator. It appears that the courier who carried the funds has been arrested for theft. I was not the only delivery from whom he stole funds; however, mine was the first that he was brazen enough to take the entire delivery." Flint grunted.

"Who were you sending funds to?" Ros couldn't help but inquire.

Flint hesitated, but then set the letter down and picked his fork back up. "I sponsor a boys' home in Flintshire."

Caught off guard, Ros stared at him. "Do you really?"

"Indeed." Flint tried to continue about his breakfast as if he'd just imparted the news that it would rain that day.

"Flint, why have you not shared this with me? That is a wonderful thing." Ros swore her heart swelled with even more love for him.

He shrugged. "Well, I had to do something with all the money I won fighting. It seemed a worthy cause."

Ros grinned. "Do not pretend indifference with me, Lord Flintshire. I see you for who you are."

That was when Flint's butler reappeared. Before he could announce their visitor, Lucifer breezed in just behind him.

"Good morning!"

The butler proceeded with his duties, though he sounded most aggrieved. "Mr. Lucifer, to see you, my lord."

"Yes, I can see that." Flint once again set his fork down, though this time with a clatter that made Ros flinch. "And to what do I owe this...visit."

"I am merely answering your lady's summons. Again." Lucifer sat down across from them and stretched his legs out. Upon noticing the carafe of hot coffee sitting on the table, he pointed at the silver pot. "Oh, do you mind?"

Before either of them could reply, Lucifer leaned forward, took a cup, and poured for himself. With a healthy inhale, he sniffed the pungent brew. "That is a lovely way to start the day when one has been dragged from their bed so benightedly early."

Flint sighed.

Ros huffed and slapped her napkin onto her half-full plate of food before standing. "Flint, your brother merely did what I asked of him. You will have to forgive and forget."

"He offered to sleep with you *after* he helped you manacle me to the wall. He should be begging my forgiveness." Flint looked outraged.

Lucifer sipped his coffee and watched their byplay with rapt attention.

"I am well aware of what he said to you. Did you for one moment consider he was prodding you to help you past your reluctance?"

"Oh, good show, old girl!" Lucifer cheered her on.

"Do shut up, Lucifer. It might help if you apologized for being so cheeky." Ros glared at him.

Looking chagrinned, Lucifer set his coffee down. "If it at all matters, I had no intention of touching her. She's right, I was merely trying to help you see how important she is to you."

Appearing somewhat mollified, Flint picked his fork back up and took a bite. After chewing and swallowing, he looked at Lucifer. "I'll grant you that, but I begged you not to shackle me, and you did it anyway."

Ros sank into her seat, falling silent as the two finally were picking their way through things.

"Flint, I'd never have done that had I not believed it was the best thing for you. You needed to be made to accept your darkness. To embrace it, and only Ros could do that for you."

Flint set his fork down again, this time much gentler. He looked at Ros, then at Lucifer, and then back to her. "You may be correct, but you're my brother. That should always come first."

"And it did, which is why I shackled you. Why I agreed to help Ros at all. And if it needed to be done again, I would do it to ensure you were happy." Lucifer huffed and shifted in his seat as though the very conversation made him itch.

"I want to be angry, but I understand." Flint tugged at his shirt collar as though it had grown tight. "Thank you."

Lucifer rose. "Excellent. I shall see you later, then."

Flint looked over at Ros, "I should expect so since we'll need you for the wedding."

"What wedding?" Ros and Lucifer asked in unison.

"Our wedding." He looked at Ros. "You will marry me."

She eyed him with annoyance. "Perhaps, when we have set a date and invited all of our friends."

"Oh! Did I forget to tell you?" Flint looked around, patted his waistcoat, and then pulled out a piece of paper. "I have the special dispensation right here." He hesitated a moment. "I don't wish to wait another day to call you wife."

Ros's heart pounded in her chest as she stared at Flint. And then the joy within her bubbled up and broke free. "I don't wish to wait either. But what of all our friends? My sister?"

Flint grinned. "Everyone will arrive in a few hours. Except for the ladies, they will be here shortly."

And then Flint rose and swept her into a long kiss. At some point, she swore she heard the door close, but for all she cared in that moment, Lucifer could have remained standing there.

After all their ups and downs and all the doubts, she knew that this was forever. The trust that wove them together made their relationship unshakeable. She had finally found what she had been looking for. Had fought for and won the man she loved. The man she would always love.

The End

His Hand-Me-Down Countess
Lustful Lords, Book 1

His brother's untimely death leaves him with an Earldom and a fiancée. Too bad he wants neither of them...

Theodora Lawton has no need of a husband. As an independent woman, she wants to own property, make investments and be the master of her destiny. Unfortunately, her father signed her life away in a marriage contract to the future Earl of Stonemere. But then the cad upped and died, leaving her fate in the hands of his brother, one of the renowned Lustful Lords.

Achilles Denton, the Earl of Stonemere, is far more prepared to be a soldier than a peer. Deeply scarred by his last tour of duty, he knows he will never be a proper, upstanding pillar of the empire. Balanced on the edge of madness, he finds respite by keeping a tight rein on his life, both in and out of the bedroom. His brother's death has left him with responsibilities he never wanted and isn't prepared to handle in the respectable manner expected of a peer.

Further complicating his new life is an unwanted fiancée who comes with his equally unwanted title. Saddled with a hand-me-down countess, he soon discovers the woman is a force unto herself. As he grapples with the burden of his new responsibilities, he discovers someone wants him dead. The question is, can he stay alive long enough to figure out who's trying to kill him while he tries to tame his headstrong wife?

His Hellion Countess
Lustful Lords, Book 2

A duty bound earl and a jewel thief might find forever if he can steal her heart...

Robert Cooper, the Earl of Brougham must marry in order to fulfill his duty to the title. He's decided on a rather mild mannered, biddable woman who most considered firmly on the shelf. But, her family is on solid financial ground and has no scandals attached to their name.

Lady Emily Winterburn, sister of the Earl of Dunmere, is not what she seems. With a heart as big as her wild streak she finds herself prepared to protect her brother from his bad choices, even if it means committing highway robbery. But marrying their way out of trouble is simply out of the question. What woman in her right mind would shackle herself to a man, let alone one of the notorious Lustful Lords?

Cooper's carefully laid plans are ruined once he must decide between courting his unwilling bride-to-be and taming the wild woman who tried to rob him—until he discovers they are one and the same. And when love sinks its relentless talons into his heart? He'll do anything to possess the wanton who fires his blood and touches his soul.

His Scandalous Viscountess
Lustful Lords, Book 3

Once upon a time, a boy and a girl fell in love...but prestige, power, and a shameful secret drove them apart.

Julia fled abroad after the death of her husband, Lord Wallthorpe. She has finally returned to England, but little has changed.

Except for her.

As a dowager marchioness, Julia lives and loves where she pleases. And the obnoxious son of her dead husband does not please. But what can an independent woman do? Why, create a scandal, of course!

Viscount Wolfington is no stranger to the wagging tongues of the ton. Between being a Lustful Lord and the scandal of his birth, he learned long ago that society had little use for him. So when he walks into The Market and finds the woman who once stole his heart being auctioned for a night of debauchery, he jumps at another chance to hold her—even for just a single night.

As Julia and Wolf unravel their pasts, will villainy win again, or will love finally conquer all?

His Not-So-Sweet Marchioness
Lustful Lords, Book 4

He's shrouded in shame, fighting with his demons in the shadows. Until she sets her sights on him...

Mrs. Rosalind Smith once followed her heart and love to the battlefield and left a widow. Spending the remainder of her life alone is enough... until she meets a man who's need for pain sparks an answering flame deep within her soul.

Matthew Derby, the Marquess of Flintshire is a fighter, it is all he's known since childhood. Throwing his fists is the only way to keep his need for pain at bay, and a certain gentle woman off his mind. She deserves a better man than him—Lord or not. Though when faced with the prospect of losing Ros, Flint realizes he has found something to fight for...something to live for.

To Ros' dismay, everyone around her believes her demeanor too sweet for someone like Flint. When his world begins to unravel and his dockside violence bleeds into the drawing room, a shocking family secret won't be the key to all the answers. Questions remain, can he solve the mystery, tame his dark needs, and still win Ros' heart?

His Reluctant Marchioness
Lustful Lords, Book 5

*A notorious woman must rely on the devil himself for help.
Too bad she learned long ago never to trust anyone...*

Frank Lucifer is having one hell of a week. His gambling hell is short staffed after firing his floor manager, and his half-brother has offered him a title—one he doesn't need or want. Then the woman he's obsessed with dismisses him from her bed, and the problem is he doesn't know who the hell she is.

Mistress Lash has her hands full. Her apprentice is missing under sinister circumstances, and Scotland Yard refuses to lift a finger. A liaison with Frank Lucifer—however attractive she finds him—is something she no longer has time for. Besides, someone should take the arrogant rake down a peg or two.

She sets out to find her apprentice on her own, but everywhere she turns, up pops Lucifer. He's following her, and she's growing suspicious about why that is. When he suggests they join forces, she reluctantly agrees. After all, one should keep their friends close and their enemies closer... she's just not sure which he is. Yet.

Working together to find her missing apprentice, she worries about her ability to protect both her heart and her own secrets from the perceptive man. And as events play out, she must decide if Lucifer is the villain she is searching for... or just the devil who haunts her scorching hot dreams?

Other Books by Sorcha

The Market Series
Discover the series that started it all...

In this sizzling series The Market becomes the setting for Londoners of all walks of life to discover pleasure, lust, and even love. But can they do what is required to claim the ones they've fallen for?

Love Revealed (The Market, Book 1)

Love Redeemed (The Market, Book 2)

Love Reclaimed (The Market, Book 3)

The Market Series Books 1-3 (Boxed Set)

Love Requited (The Market, A Short Story)

One Night With A Cowboy

The One Night With A Cowboy series is a set of short stories linked by cowboys and Soul Mates Dating Service, a dating service with an uncanny ability to match up soul mates. These sizzling little treats are perfect for a quick hot read.

Claiming His Cowgirl (Book 1)

Taking Her Chance (Book 2)

A Cowboy's Christmas Wish (Book 3)

Roping His Cowboy (Book 4)

One Night With A Cowboy Books 1-4 (Boxed Set)

Stealing His Cowgirl's Heart (Book 5)

www.ingramcontent.com/pod-product-compliance
Lightning Source LLC
Chambersburg PA
CBHW061255210726

48293CB00003B/967